Round Up

Round Up

REBECCA CONNOLLY
SOPHIA SUMMERS
HEATHER B. MOORE

Mirror Press

Copyright © 2021 by Rebecca Connolly

Paperback edition

All rights reserved

No part of this book may be reproduced in any form whatsoever without prior written permission of the publisher, except in the case of brief passages embodied in critical reviews and articles. This is a work of fiction. The characters, names, incidents, places, and dialog are products of the author's imagination and are not to be construed as real.

Interior design by Cora Johnson

Edited by Joanne Lui, Lorie Humpherys, and Laramee Fox

Cover design by Rachael Anderson

Cover image credit: Period Images

Published by Mirror Press, LLC

ISBN: 978-1-952611-13-1

Lost Creek Rodeo Series

Round Up

Chute Boss

Rough Stock

Full Rigged

Half Hitch

Ace High

CHAPTER 1

THERE WAS NOTHING WORSE than a cold rain down your neck.

Ryan Prosper growled in irritation as he tugged on the post he was out in this mess to fix, water dripping from the brim of his hat as he hefted it back into place. He shook his head as he held it there, looking down at the ground.

The post wouldn't stay for long, not with the ground being as soggy as it was, and not with the hole being widened with its collapse. Whoever had redone the fencing last summer had royally screwed up, there was no mistaking that.

"Didn't drive it deep enough, idiots," he grumbled, leaving the post for a minute to head around the back of his truck. "Now I'm gonna have to shim the whole thing into place until we can get more rails and redo it. Just perfect."

It was ridiculous, and this was not one of the things he had missed about ranch life when he'd been away. The productivity of the place, absolutely. The sense of accomplishment and purpose, without a doubt. The day-to-day care of animals, land, products—all of that he had certainly missed.

Fencing repairs, not so much.

But as the new ranch manager of Broken Hearts Ranch, such things now fell to him or one of his ranch hands.

They only had half a dozen ranch hands right now, given it was barely March. More would come in with the planting, and next week, their usual gang would return to work the horses, but there weren't many people he could call upon to do this sort of thing for him. Any of the ranch hands who lived on site would have, but he was already out. Might as well just get it done.

Returning to the post, he jammed several thick slivers of wood alongside it, pounding them in farther still with a heavy mallet from his tool belt. He'd have given anything for a post driver to make everything more secure, but he hadn't been that smart when he'd driven out here to check things out.

He was just supposed to take a look at things and see what the damage was after the storm last night, but he couldn't leave a fence post down like that. The cattle could get out or cut their hooves on the barbed wires, critters could get into the pasture that he didn't want in there, and it would make the place look more run down than he already felt it was.

Broken Hearts Ranch. More like Broken Everything Ranch.

He stepped back and looked at his handiwork, not pleased. His father would have whooped his hide for doing a job halfway, but it was good enough for beans, as the man would also have said. Besides, he'd have a guy come out later in the day or tomorrow to fix it properly, and likely examine the fence as a whole.

"Good enough," Ryan told himself again, turning for his truck, feeling damp and chilled. He tossed his tools into the passenger seat in the cab, then slid in, slamming the door hard. Leaning his forearms on the steering wheel, he took a moment to exhale heavily.

What was he doing here?

It was a stupid question, honestly, but he kept coming back to it. Months of rehabilitation to get back his strength and prove his agility, and he was back to working the ranch he grew up on. It wasn't a bad gig, but it wasn't what he'd wanted.

None of it was.

But he couldn't compete at pro-level anymore, unless he wished to be a chute boss or a clown. So he'd withdrawn from the Professional Rodeo Cowboys Association.

A man could get his bell rung until he sang like a canary and come back to bronc riding with a doctor's note. But you lose a kidney in a hooking incident with a particularly aggressive bull, and you were toast. Thank you for your time, cowboy, now hit the road.

His doctors had been a little kinder than that, but the sentiment had been the same.

Years of training and experience, waiting and hoping, busting his tail and taking names, all gone just like that.

No one would see Ryan Prosper's name on the rodeo docket again.

Ever.

He should be grateful he'd only lost a kidney, he'd been told. He'd been close to losing all sorts of things, if not his life, the doctors said. But he had his strength now, the remaining functional organs, and his life, and he'd gotten used to having them all back. It wasn't that he was ungrateful to have those things.

He had just lost the passion of his life, and no amount of rehabilitation, physical therapy, or bribery could get it back for him.

If it hadn't been for Kellie, he'd have been worse off.

His sister had been as torn up about his rodeo news as he had been, given she was his biggest fan and number one supporter. His first circuit in college, she'd had Team Ryan shirts made up for the family, every one of whom had turned out for the show. Rodeo was in his blood, and having that taken away was a brutal loss.

The very next day, she'd come to him with a job offer, paperwork and all.

Broken Hearts Ranch was hers, but it was getting too big to run alone, she'd insisted.

All because of her little side project.

The side project that had become bigger than the ranch itself, come to think of it. He was probably getting his wages out of the admission fees.

He'd balked when he'd first heard what she wanted to do with the ranch once she'd taken it over. A women's retreat on a ranch? He'd even teased her about ladies sipping wine on the sofas while the cows roamed free, which had earned him a solid bruise on his arm.

He knew better now. He could see the good she was doing, and he was proud of it.

Women who'd had their lives completely upended, mostly by no fault of their own, came to their ranch to find themselves and start again. They worked on the land, they made the jams, they fed the animals, and did any other tasks they were willing to take on. Kellie had created a very particular list of options, and no one had to do more than they felt capable. Some of the ladies he'd seen come through here, just in the short time he'd been back, had a work ethic that could school him, which had shut up any and all snarky comments he could make.

Kellie was rebuilding lives on her side of things. The least he could do was rebuild the ranch itself.

Nodding to himself, as this pep talk always seemed to make him do, he shifted the truck into gear and turned around, heading back for the homestead. The gravel took care of the water on the main roads, but the side roads would be miserable. He'd need to have boards laid out in bad places, or there would be hell to pay.

Rain in Texas wasn't unusual, but it sure was a pain in the behind.

He pulled into the circle drive of the homestead, heading over to the grass to keep out of the way, as usual. He couldn't keep track of arrivals and departures, and his regularly filthy truck would not be a welcoming sight for anyone.

Why they had to pretend to be fancier than they were on this ranch, he'd never know. Dirt was dirt, and mud was mud, and high-maintenance guests would have a wakeup call being here. Maybe they should have tried a retreat down in the Bahamas or some such if they couldn't handle the look of his truck.

Scowling at the insult nobody had given him, Ryan shut the truck off and got out, moving around the side of the house to the kitchen door rather than the main entrance.

Muddy boots weren't allowed in the front.

Whatever.

He stepped inside and removed his hat, tossing it into the antique chair in the corner, as he always did. "Kells?" he called out, rubbing his hands together. "Kellie?" When there was no answer, he whistled.

As he predicted, two grey-colored dogs with black freckled fur came trotting toward him, tongues lolling.

He grinned and squatted down. "Hey, Casper. 'Sup, Frankie? Did you boys miss me? Huh?"

They sniffed and licked his face, their cold noses nudging at his hands.

"Nah, I don't have any treats," he told them reluctantly, revealing his empty hands. "Not this time. Sorry."

Casper whined low, then turned and wandered off, his tail brushing Ryan in the face as he did so.

Ryan watched the dog leave, then turned to Frankie, who still stared at him, panting happily. "What's his deal, huh?" He scratched Frankie's head, paying particular attention to his left ear. "What's his deal?"

"His deal," his sister's voice answered, "is that you've spoiled him, so now he expects treats all the time."

He grinned up at her as she entered the kitchen, her hair in a loose ponytail over a black-and-white flannel shirt, trusty jeans tucked into her favorite sweater-like slipper boots. "Someone has to spoil them. You won't let them into the main part of the house anymore."

Kellie rolled her eyes and moved to the coffee machine on the counter. "They'll get over it. They go everywhere in your house, even when they're full of ticks. They're only inside now because of the storm."

Ryan frowned at Frankie, still scratching his head. "I'm gonna get custody of you, okay? She doesn't treat you right."

"Oh, good grief," his sister groaned, pulling down two coffee mugs from the shelf. "Coffee, Ryan?"

"Please." He straightened, patting Frankie's head once more. "You lose power?"

She shook her head as she poured their drinks. "No, thank goodness. Thought we might for a minute there, but we were good. You?"

"Nope." He moved to the side of the doormat, wiping the bottom of his boots carefully. "Fence post went down in the west pasture, though. I don't know what you paid them last summer to do that, but you should get a refund. Wasn't down near far enough, and we'll have to replace it, if not the entire line."

Kellie sighed, nodding. "Okay. Thanks for doing that."

She came over to him, setting his mug on the island near him. "Black, right?"

"Always." He flashed her a quick grin. "Like my heart."

She raised a brow at him. "And your humor." She shook her head, moving to the fridge, no doubt wanting her vanilla creamer.

Gross.

"Hey, Kells?" Ryan said quietly, turning his cup just a little on the counter and sliding his hand through the handle, letting the heat warm him. "You don't have to thank me every time I do something. It's my job now."

She paused with her hand on the handle to the fridge, giving him a confused look. "I know that. I hired you."

He sipped his coffee slowly, the beverage still burning his mouth. "Yeah, I remember. But doing my job doesn't require thanks, you know? I'm just doing what I'm supposed to."

Kellie frowned and came over to stand opposite him, pouring the creamer into her coffee while staring at him. "I know that, too. Doesn't mean I can't appreciate that you were up early and driving out to check stuff after the storm."

"I don't want to feel like I'm doing you a favor," he confessed, looking down into the dark liquid in his cup. "Like I'm your brother helping out on the family farm."

She set her coffee down and covered his free hand with both of hers. "Ryan."

He glanced up at her, embarrassed by this entire conversation, though it needed to happen. She'd put on her big sister voice, and he had never been able to resist that. "What?"

Her bright blue eyes could have bored into him. "Stop."

Huh? That wasn't what he'd expected from his therapist of a sister, especially when she'd put the voice on and everything. "Excuse me?"

"Excuse yourself," she said simply, still serious. "I did not hire you out of pity. I know the timing might lead you in that direction, but for me, it was like being hit with the lightning of inspiration. I needed better hands here, you needed something to do, and it was the easiest decision I have ever made. Trust me when I say that there is no one else I would want running the ranch. You've got the experience to fit the job, you actually care about the place, and you aren't going to pull punches on me. That's what I need, okay?"

Sometimes, he forgot what a tough cookie his sister was, and how direct she could be. He threw her a lopsided grin. "So I need to pull up my chaps and get to work?"

"Pretty much, yeah." She returned his grin and slid her hands from his. "And if I want to thank you for getting up at the crack of dawn to do your job, I'm gonna thank you, okay? I'd do the same to any of my employees."

"Whoa, whoa, whoa," Ryan protested, embarrassment gone now. "Employees? I'm your *partner*, remember?"

Kellie picked up her coffee and blew on it gently, shrugging a shoulder. "If you say so, Ry-Ry."

He scowled at the childhood nickname. "That's going to get old real fast."

Rolling her eyes again, she put the creamer back in the fridge and moved around the island to a bar stool. "I promise not to use it when we're meeting with investors and Ms. Harland."

Ryan shuddered for effect. "Please don't make me meet with Ms. Harland. I'll beg."

"She is wonderful!" Kellie protested, slapping a hand on the counter. "Ryan, we couldn't do this without her! The ranch wasn't providing enough on its own, and last year was the first time I've ran a profit since taking over. She's an angel for financing this, and all she asks for is a case of jam and to sponsor our horses."

"She hates me," Ryan pointed out without any shame whatsoever. "She makes that hum of disapproval every time she sees me."

"Oh, grow up." Kellie snickered and took a drink of her coffee, her eyes turning mischievous. "You know it's only because of that circuit in '14, right? You bested their grandson in the finals, completing the Original Six sweep. She couldn't stand that, and her husband was cranky for weeks."

Ryan scowled at the memory, sinking onto a bar stool himself. Hank Harland had been the biggest name in the rodeo business for ages, and his wife might have been a bigger name. When he'd died a few years back, Ms. Ginny had taken over the businesses. If there was a rodeo around, their business had a stamp on it.

It wasn't Ryan's fault their grandson couldn't stay on a bronc.

"The Original Six," he murmured slowly, spinning his mug in thought. "I haven't seen most of them in a while."

"Probably not since your injury," Kellie echoed. "Think any of them will come down this year?"

Ryan shook his head. "I don't know. The season starts in a few weeks, and I haven't seen the docket. You?"

"Nope. Might be good to see them, though."

"Maybe."

They sat in silence with their coffee for a few minutes, lost in thought.

The Original Six had been a name given to him and five other guys that had formed the first rodeo team at their university, a small agricultural school not far from Lost Creek, less than an hour away. Not only had they started it, but that first year, they had taken regionals, starting the tradition of star rodeo teams there. Lost Creek was now the home of that team, and the event was always a fun exhibition for current and former riders to take part in.

Ryan had done it every year.
Up until last year, anyway.
And this one, now that his career was over.
Would they come down? Did he want them to?
"I don't know," he said again, with a long swig of coffee. "But I could find out."

Chapter 2

"Thank you for calling Memories by Melanie. This is Talia, how may I help you?"

"Oh, I'm sorry, I think I have the wrong number."

"No problem, have a nice day."

Talia pushed the call button on the side of her headset and stared at her computer screen with the same blankness with which she'd answered the phone. It was the fourth wrong number call she'd had today, which didn't bother her all that much.

Less conversation.

Quicker return to quiet.

Less work to do.

Her job wasn't horrible; she simply didn't enjoy it. It wasn't such a crime to feel that way. Most people probably did, unless they had managed to find their dream jobs in this world. It was a good enough job, and it paid her bills.

That had been enough once.

The hours were fantastic, not that it mattered anymore. She could take time off pretty much whenever she needed, which had helped in the past. It was a small photography business, meaning she wasn't a cog in a machine, but it didn't stop her from feeling like a robot now.

It was the only thing she felt like now.

One foot in front of the other, one call after another, one tick of the clock at a time. One by one by one, and eventually, the day ended and she could go home. Where time stopped, and she was only ever cold. Eventually, she would sleep, and then she would wake up. Toss, turn, roll over, sleep again. She might even go to her bed, if she felt like it, but the couch was good. Her alarm would go off, and she would shower, eat, and take the train to the office.

Day after day.

She was even working the weekends now, which her boss did not like, but she needed time to pass without tears, without emptiness, and without feeling sick.

She needed purpose, even if it wasn't fulfilling. All she needed was something to fill her time and her days.

Which this did.

"Talia."

She blinked at the sound of her name and glanced up. Her boss, Melanie, stood there, hands on her hips, brow wrinkled in concern. "Hi. You need something?"

Melanie pursed her lips, shaking her head. "No, I'm fine. Talia . . . it's five-thirty."

Talia blinked again. "Is it?" She looked at the clock on the wall across from her, the time registering but having no effect on her. "Oh."

"You should have left hours ago." There was no accusation in the statement, which was a change from what it would have been last year. Where once there would have been concerns about overtime, now it was simply a concern.

And an unspoken question that no one had ever asked aloud.

Talia hated that question. Everyone had it. Everyone.

And she didn't have an answer. When would she be okay? She didn't know. When would she be better? She didn't know. When would she get over it?

Never.

How did anyone get over the loss of a child?

"I guess I'll go now," Talia murmured, turning back to her computer and clicking out of the windows there, logging into the timeclock and punching out.

"That wasn't what I meant," her boss insisted in an awkward tone, though it was clear she did mean it.

Everybody meant it.

Talia forced a smile and shook her head. "I lost track of the time, that's all. See you tomorrow." She started to walk away, fiddling in her bag as though for her keys.

It was all part of the act.

"Talia."

She stopped, the reluctance in that tone making her go cold.

Don't say it. Don't say it.

"Do you need to take some time off?"

Talia closed her eyes, exhaling slowly. Was it always this difficult for childless parents to go back to work after the loss? Or was she just a special case?

She glanced over her shoulder, not turning. "I'm fine."

"Take some time off, Talia," Melanie said firmly, leaving absolutely no room for questioning. "I've already worked it into the schedule—you'll get paid time off."

Talia swallowed, slowly losing feeling in her legs. "I don't have that many hours banked."

"We've arranged it," Melanie replied. "You have all that you need."

That wasn't possible, and that wasn't accurate.

What she *needed* was Austin.

What she was getting was basically a suspension to get her act together.

"How long?" Talia asked quietly, trying to ignore how dry her throat was becoming.

"Three weeks. More if you need it."

Talia exhaled a sarcastic laugh. "You can't hold my job for three weeks, Melanie. Not at this time of year."

"I've worked it out. If you come back in here tomorrow, I'll fire you, and I don't want to do that."

And yet, the threat was there.

Talia bit back a sigh and nodded. "Okay. Thanks, I guess." She nodded and walked out of the office, heading for the back of the building and the employee entrance.

She didn't mean to sound like she had an attitude problem, and honestly, her boss was probably right. She needed time off, needed to get her head on straight, needed to find a way through her life without her boy, but she didn't know how to do anything except go through the motions.

What was she supposed to do? Find a guidebook on grieving the most incredible seven-year-old and memorize the thing?

Pulling her phone out of her back pocket, she tapped out a quick text. *I need pancakes and a hug. Someone in town?*

She hadn't even tucked the phone back into her pocket before she had a response.

Grizz: Yes. Where?

Talia struggled to swallow, emotion rising as she stared at the straightforward message from her cousin. Grizz McCarthy was an all-star pro-baseball player here in Chicago, and despite his fame, fortune, and popularity, he always had time for her.

They'd all grown up together, a mass of McCarthy-spawned cousins racing around backyards and parks, if not all of Chicago. Grizz was one of four boys. They had four other

McCarthy uncles with varying numbers of kids, and Talia's mom had been the only McCarthy girl, meaning Talia had been the only kid at family gatherings without the matching last name. Not one of her cousins had ever made her feel like she was anything less than a part of the group, which was a feat, considering she was the baby of the family.

She was starting to type out a reply to Grizz when another response popped up.

Clint: Same. Turnsberry Waffle House?

Now she was completely baffled, and she gaped at the screen as she walked the sidewalk in the early evening light. Clint was in town, too?

Clint was Grizz's younger brother, and a pro-hockey player based out of St. Louis. It was easy enough to assume Grizz would be in town in March, but Clint . . .

She'd texted them both out of habit, the three of them being the caboose of their cousins and therefore closest, but she hadn't expected . . .

Eyes swimming in tears, Talia sniffed and texted back. *Perfect. See you soon.* She dropped her phone into her bag and stuffed her hands into her coat pockets, the city feeling just as cold now as it had in January. At least it wasn't snowing.

She hated the snow.

She shook the dark thought out of her mind, turning to head into the train station, swiping her card on the turnstile and pushing through. Fortunately, she could take the same line to get to the restaurant as she'd take to get home, and it would only be two stops early. Her car would still be at her home station, but it was easy enough to catch a cab or something.

Or she could walk.

Walking was good for her. Walking cleared her head. Walking was action.

Walking made her feel.

It had also helped her lose fifteen pounds in the last few months, but there were a lot of factors there.

Her timing was perfect, catching a train just a minute or so before it left the station, and she slid into an unoccupied seat. In the next moment, her headphones were in, and her audiobook was playing, safely giving the signal to any around her that she had no desire to talk to anyone. She didn't even need to listen to the book, but it gave her mind something to focus on that was safer than music.

She'd gone through this book five times in a row now, and she still wasn't sure what the plot was.

Either it was a terrible book, or she was a terrible listener.

Maybe both.

Leaning her head against the window and shutting her eyes, Talia exhaled heavily, the sound probably registering as a sigh to anyone around her. She'd done the research on this one day at three a.m., and she could safely say that exhaling without the emotion of relief, fatigue, sadness, or something of the sort was not a sigh.

Considering she felt nothing, she had not sighed.

Technically.

It was the strangest thing, going through the motions of life without feeling anything much. Life went on, but she wasn't actively participating in it. Somehow, her heart still beat, her lungs still worked, and her brain sent signals all over her, all without her feeling any of it.

She'd had days and weeks of feeling every heartbeat, every contraction of her lungs, every impulse of every nerve, every sensation on every inch of skin. She'd felt everything with a hypersensitivity that had been agony, and the gravity of the earth had doubled.

None of that happened now, and when it left, so had the ability to feel anything.

The tears at seeing her cousins text so quickly had been the first burst of emotion in a week. Which was better than last week, so at least she was improving.

Her mom would like that.

Talia had begun to drift off to light sleep when the PA system announced, "Next stop, Bathurst. Next stop, Bathurst."

Blinking, Talia sat up and pushed to her feet, slinging her bag over her shoulder as she moved out into the aisle and made her way down to the doors, the motion of the train swaying her into a couple of empty seats.

She didn't need to hold onto anything as the train slowed, then jerked to a stop, the motion of it all second nature to her after years of daily commutes on the train. There was always a small thrill of pride in being able to do so, some strange victory in not needing assistance to maintain her balance.

There was some irony in that, but she didn't have the energy to address it.

The Bathurst train station was small, like most of the stations in the suburbs along this line, and she passed through it easily, moving out to the street and opting to walk to the restaurant. It was only a few blocks, and she knew the way well.

It had been a favorite location of the cousins for years, which was probably why Clint had suggested it. They had never gone anywhere else for breakfast food, and certainly not for pancakes, which they unanimously agreed were best at Turnberry's. It was still the greatest small, family-owned, diner-inspired place ever, cheap on the menu but generous in portions, and most of them could afford nicer places, but they didn't care.

There would only be Turnberry's.

Talia rubbed her arms, feeling the cold almost as much now as she had downtown, and quickened her step. She paused at a crosswalk, looking up and down the street, then hustled across, glancing up at the restaurant at the next corner.

For all the joyful memories she had of the place, the sight of it didn't fill her with any of them. She simply wanted to be inside where it was warmer, eat some of the best comfort food she could think of, and hug her favorite cousins. She couldn't even say if any of that would make her feel better, but she did know one thing.

She did not want to be alone at home with a microwave dinner again.

She was pretty sure she was out of those, anyway.

A couple exited the building, their arms linked in a cute familiarity, and met her eyes with the warm smiles usually exchanged by people who appreciated the same place. The elderly gentleman turned to hold the door for her, tipping the brim of his tweed flat cap as she neared him.

"Thanks," she murmured, managing a weak smile as she went past.

He returned her smile easily. "Have a good night, ma'am."

Part of her wanted to watch him and his wife walk away, wondering if they would keep their arms linked or shift to holding hands, if they would talk quietly or enjoy the silence, if they would be cuddly or formal.

But the rest of her just wanted to ignore it all, avoid human interaction, and pretend nothing remotely adorable had happened.

Talia kept her eyes straight ahead, locking on the chipper teenager standing at the hostess podium, smiling too broadly. "Welcome to Turnberry's! How many?"

It was all she could do to retort a question asking how many it looked like, but she swallowed back the spite and smiled blandly. "I think my party is already here."

"Great!" came the response. "Have a look around, and if they aren't, I'm happy to seat you!"

"Thanks." Talia walked past, relaxing her face into her usual lack of emotion and looking for the familiar sight of two imposing, masculine, dark-haired men with bright blue eyes.

If she looked for people staring, she could probably find them.

Moving around the tempting display of desserts and baked goods, she entered the dining area on one side of the restaurant, glancing around the half-full room. She felt her lungs give way when she caught sight of the table in the back, where the very two men she was looking for sat, deep in conversation.

She swallowed hard, adjusting her purse and moving toward them. Grizz saw her first, as he was facing her, and his quick grin flashed amongst the dark scruff on the lower half of his face. Considering he was usually fully bearded while in season, seeing him like this was a change.

"There she is!" he called, though without much volume, and pushed back his chair to rise.

Clint, sitting across from him, did the same, grinning in the same crinkly-eyed way, fully clean shaven.

"Hey," she murmured, going to Clint first and slipping her arms around him.

He nearly crushed her with the ferocity of his hug. "Hi, hon. It's really good to see you."

She smiled with some difficulty, oddly near tears as she patted his back. "You, too. What are you doing in town?"

Grizz chuckled at the question. "What do you think? He's off right now, so he jetted up to wedding plan with Bree. Or listen to her plan, anyway—I don't think he's doing anything."

Clint released her, giving his brother a scowl. "How much planning did you do for yours, huh?"

"Come here, kiddo," Grizz grunted with outstretched arms, addressing Talia only and completely ignoring his little brother.

Talia moved into his arms easily, touched by how gently yet securely he held her. He was a decently big guy, for a baseball player, and one of the most bear-like men on the planet, hence his nickname, but he had also been one of the tenderest of her cousins.

A rare thing in a McCarthy man.

"You okay?" he murmured, his hands running up and down her back. "You look exhausted."

She nodded against him, but her momentary hesitation beforehand would not go unnoticed. "Rough day," she evaded, stepping away and trying for a smile. "And I'm starving."

Her cousin's serious expression told her he didn't buy a word, but he gestured for her to join them, and she slid over to a chair beside his, dropping his bag to the floor. She sat and smiled at Clint. "So how are the plans? Still set on September?"

He nodded, exhaling slowly. "Yep, with our fingers crossed. Both Bree and I are hoping there will be a gap between my hockey season and the baseball season. We've got two baseball players with prime invitations, right? And four more, if we're lucky."

Talia nodded, recalling Grizz's involvement with a group called the Belltown Six Pack, his best friends from college and arguably some of the most famous baseball players around. Clint's fiancée, Bree Stone, was the sister of one, so the pair of them would have a special understanding of the situation.

"I keep telling them," Grizz broke in, "that it doesn't matter, Ryker and I will make it as long as they don't put the wedding on a game night, the others if they can, but they really want to make it complicated for themselves by thinking of us."

"We're nice like that," Clint shot back with the perfect little brother comeback. He shifted his eyes to Talia, and the light in them told her the direction his thoughts had gone. "Do you really want to talk about my wedding, cuz? Or are you just talking to talk?"

She hated when he did that, but it did negate the need for small talk, which she appreciated.

She shrugged, her eyes moving to the glass of water in front of her. "I'm stuck," she admitted, the words scraping against her throat.

Grizz immediately put a hand to her back and rubbed gently. "Anybody would be, sweetheart. It's only been five months."

"Then why does everyone expect life to be normal? Or me to be normal?" Her voice broke on the question, and she shook her head, looking away and putting her elbow on the table, a palm going to her head. "I still can't breathe in my house."

Grizz's hand moved to the base of her neck, and he squeezed gently. "Oh, Talia . . ."

Clint's hand shot across the table, taking her free one. "Austin was everything to you, and he was a great kid. That's going to be impossible to get over for anyone. It's okay."

Talia shook her head, swallowing a sob. "I feel nothing. I'm just going through life like a robot because I have nothing else to do." She sniffed and turned her watery eyes to her cousins, relieved now to not be fine. "Do you know what Aunt Tami told Mom? She said it was a perfect time for me to think about my own life in a new way. That I have plenty of time now and nothing tying me down or holding me back, like I had before. That I was free."

Grizz hissed, his pressure on her neck tightening a little. "She's never had tact. But she also had a lot to say when you got pregnant, remember?"

"Oh yeah." Talia nodded firmly, bitterness rising. "She couldn't look at me the whole first trimester. We all know I was a stupid seventeen-year-old, but I stepped up, didn't I?"

"You did," Clint agreed. He smiled and rubbed his thumb over her hand. "You were an amazing mom to Austin, and you know that. You did everything right."

"And in one way," Grizz said slowly, "Tami has a point."

Talia jerked away from his touch, glaring at him in betrayal. "What?"

He held up his hands in surrender, eyeing her the way one might a wild animal. "Hear me out, okay?"

Given Grizz's track record with being on the money where she was concerned, Talia nodded, willing to listen, but also ready to bolt if he was wrong now.

He lowered his hands and gave her a searching look. "You ought to think about yourself now. Do something for yourself. Make adjustments to your life."

Talia stared at him, letting that sink in, and hating that it was sinking in. "Moving on," she murmured. "I should move on."

"Yes and no," Clint answered quickly. "More like . . . More like move forward. You're stuck, right?"

She nodded. "Yeah. In time, in life . . . I have nothing."

Grizz dropped an arm around her shoulder and tugged her against him. "We need to figure out how to get you unstuck, and get you moving forward. Austin never let you sit still when he was here, and I highly doubt he'd want you stuck now."

Her thoughts flashed to her boy, her funny, energetic, smiling with missing teeth boy, complete with a cowlick at the back of his sandy brown hair. She could see his toothy grin, hear his infectious laugh, remember the exact location of the last scratch he'd shown her, envision their last outing to the park before the snow would come.

"Come on, Mom! Don't be a slowpoke!"

And her heart seemed to crush like an empty soda can within her.

"He would hate it," she admitted as tears rolled down her cheeks. She looked up at Grizz again, her jaw quivering. "I miss my baby, Grizz."

He enveloped her in a tight hug, and she could feel him swallow hard. "I know you do, sweetheart. I know. We miss him, too. You go on and miss him. That's what a good mom would do. We'll find a way to help you out, I promise."

For the first time in weeks, Talia let herself fully cry, burying her face into her cousin and ignoring how her tears flowed.

CHAPTER 3

"Watch it, watch it . . . There we go, nicely done. Close it off, Caleb."

Caleb shut the gate quickly, then turned to grin up at Ryan. "Not bad, boss. Not bad at all."

Ryan nodded at the ranch's longest-standing employee, then smiled at the woman on horseback riding up to him. "You hear that, Amy? Caleb here says you're not bad. We're gonna miss you around here, make no mistake."

She laughed, her copper braid slung over one shoulder. "I had some good teachers. Can't believe you let me do this, honestly, but it is so much better than picking up rocks."

"Anything is better than picking up rocks," Caleb agreed, thumbing his hat back a little. "My kid loves it, though, so whatever the ladies don't get when they sign up for it, he's more than happy to."

"It's important," Ryan pointed out, leaning on the horn of his saddle a little. "Though I swear, rocks actually grow on our land. We clear them every year, and every year there are more."

Amy didn't seem to be listening anymore, looking out

over the land. "I'm going to miss it here, you know? Going back to Ohio will be strange."

Ryan sobered at that, nodding to himself. He didn't know what had brought Amy to Broken Hearts, nor did he ever know the particulars of why the guests came, but at the end of their thirty days, or whenever they went back, it probably would be strange to return to the life they had left. Especially when, hopefully, they had changed so much in the time they were here.

He rarely asked his sister about the details of the guests, and was never allowed to know the personal situations of each, but every now and then, one or two would pique his concern enough to inquire about. Having them help out on the ranch was part of Kellie's model for the place, giving them a schedule, structure, and purpose, and the value of hard work in improving recovery and mental health. Most of the time, their chores were fairly basic though useful, but every now and then, they had ambitious guests who wanted to learn and do more.

Amy had been one of those.

"Well," he ventured slowly, "if you're ever out in Texas looking for a job, I think we could make room here. What do you think, Caleb?"

Caleb nodded with perfect timing. "Absolutely. My wife would love having you back; Jenny said you guys get on great."

"We did," Amy agreed, flashing a bright smile. "And thanks for that, but I don't think my husband would want to move out here. He's pretty miserable without me, so I think I better play fair for a while."

"What's he do for work?" Ryan asked, his picture of Amy shifting slightly based on what she'd said. A happy, healthy relationship with her husband? What would have brought her here, then?

She raised a brow. "He's a CPA. Tax season is coming, so he really wants me home."

"We pay taxes in Texas," Caleb pointed out.

Amy laughed at that. "I'll be sure to tell him. Better get back to the house, though. Early flight tomorrow, and I'm not even close to packed." She nodded at them both, and turned her horse with a decent hand, galloping away in a way that made Ryan proud, given she'd never been on a horse a month ago.

"I don't say this often," Caleb grunted as he watched her go, scrunching his face up in thought, "but I'd wish the stay was longer than thirty days if it meant she'd hang around longer."

Ryan gave his friend a look. "They have real lives, remember? It's not an internship here."

"I know that. You're the one who asked about her husband."

"Don't go there," he groaned, dismounting from his horse and moving over to the gate to see the cattle they'd separated just now. "She's gotta be forty, and I didn't see her that way. Besides, I'm well aware of the rules."

Caleb chuckled darkly and turned to look over the cattle as well. "Everyone is aware of the rules. Kellie makes sure of that."

Ryan would give him that, but he also saw his sister's point all too clearly. A retreat for women on a working ranch in Texas could bring a whole slew of problems if there weren't restrictions, especially given the flirtatious nature of a lot of young men he knew in the area. Lost Creek itself had adopted the ranch, so they knew the rules, too, though they didn't technically extend to the town. But having a rodeo in town meant lots of visitors.

Visitors could mean trouble.

He was grateful he hadn't been around for the process of figuring out logistics for the ranch's new model. He got a headache now if he thought about them for too long, and they'd been in place for a few years now.

"Holt's bringing some horses back over today," Ryan told his companion, his attention moving from the cows to thoughts of the rodeo again. "The west barn and stables should be all right."

Caleb nodded once. "We need to do much with them? Rehab or breaking or anything?"

Ryan shook his head, resting his arms on the rails of the gate. "Nah. I guess they're for the Lost Creek rodeo, so we're just boarding 'em."

"Did you cut him a deal?"

The jab made Ryan chuckle, and he looked at the burly man with a grin. "Nope, you know better than that."

"Trust me," came the quick response. "I'm not gonna forget the ridiculous amount your relative charged when we needed a break."

"It wasn't that bad," Ryan protested, still smiling, though feeling it a bit of his duty to defend his cousin.

"Just don't tell him I call him Scrooge behind his back, okay?"

Ryan snorted a soft laugh at that. There was no question that his cousin was a tough customer, and Prosperity Ranch was all the better for it. "At least he pays. Knox would ditch us first."

"True enough."

The men fell silent, watching the cows move about their new location. They'd sort out a few for auction, and the rest would roam free for a while, but Ryan, for one, really wasn't in much of a hurry to get any of it done.

He had a lot on his mind.

He'd finally tracked down the entries for the rodeo in Lost Creek in a few weeks, and three of his former teammates were coming in. He'd not decided yet if he would watch any of the events.

He hadn't been to a rodeo since his injury. He'd watched some highlights after the fact, but he hadn't made himself go in person. Kellie had wanted him to, but he hadn't done it.

If his teammates were coming in, he should probably make an effort to see them, if not support them in their events.

It would sting to do it, but he'd have to get over it sooner or later.

Get over it.

What a ridiculous phrase. Instantly minimizing and shamefully patronizing, and he could safely admit that he had been shaming himself for his reluctance for ages.

Didn't change anything, but bullying himself was getting old.

"Did you see the lineup for Lost Creek?" Caleb asked, as if reading his thoughts.

Ryan nodded once. "Yep."

"Couple of your old buddies coming in. Gonna see 'em?"

"Not sure," Ryan admitted, narrowing his eyes as he pretended to examine individual cattle. "We lost touch after I got hurt."

Caleb made a noncommittal sound beside him. "Tom Hauser says they're struggling to get full numbers for the events. An early rodeo isn't as popular. Even the volunteer lists are struggling. General lack of interest."

That got Ryan's attention, and he looked at his friend in surprise. "Seriously? What's happened? There's never been a lack of interest in Lost Creek—they've even done a Santa rodeo before and had a waiting list."

"Rodeo is old hat now," Caleb said with a shrug.

"Between SHCC starting to host college events more, and the regular circuits coming through, they can get a rodeo just about any time they like. Why bother?"

"Why bother?" Ryan sputtered before pinching the bridge of his nose and exhaling slowly. "Rodeo is part of the culture of Lost Creek. The guys and I didn't put the rodeo team at Sam Houston Community College on the map for it all to be ignored. What is the matter with everyone?" He dropped his hand and glared at Caleb. "This ain't right, Caleb."

Caleb raised a brow and folded his arms. "I know it ain't. Didn't say I was in with them, did I?"

Ryan scowled, letting his hands droop over the rail. "It was always a full house growing up. Always."

"I know, man. I was there for most of them." He watched Ryan for a long moment, then tilted his head. "So what are you gonna do about it?"

"Me?" Ryan shook his head and looked away. "Really not my business anymore."

Caleb barked a hard laugh. "Look me in the eye and tell me that again. You about took my head off when I said numbers were down, and now you're going to pretend it's not your business?"

"It isn't," he insisted, shaking his head once more.

And it wasn't.

He wasn't on the rodeo circuit anymore. Hadn't competed in eighteen months. Hadn't ridden a bull since the injury. Didn't even race his horse across the ranch anymore.

He didn't even have a competitive spirit anymore.

He could complain all he wanted about lack of interest and attendance, but he hadn't gone to any events, either. Hadn't shown up at the SHCC rodeo events. Hadn't reached out to any of his former teammates or competitors, most of whom had come through Lost Creek at least once since he'd been back and recuperating.

He hadn't even cared about rodeo since his injury.

Not really.

Ryan bit his tongue now at the lie. Of course, he cared. He cared so much, he couldn't face it. Couldn't deal with pitying looks and prying questions. Didn't want to see the disappointment in the guys that he had given it up.

Because he hadn't given it up.

It had been taken away.

"When you're done roaming the open range of Denial," Caleb mused as he unlatched the gate and swung it open a little, "let me know. I'm ready for some real ideas to keep Lost Creek in the rodeo business." He moved into the corral, whistling a little as he moved amongst the cows.

Ryan watched him do so, gnawing on the inside of his lip. Caleb was right, and he had no trouble admitting it.

He was in denial about Lost Creek's rodeo, and there was no point pretending he wasn't. What's more, he knew full well why.

He was scared of getting back into rodeo in any way, shape, or form.

What if being around the competition made the pain of being out worse? What if he couldn't find satisfaction in his work at Broken Hearts because he was still dying to ride? What if volunteering or being on a committee or showing any interest in the rodeo events brought back the months of darkness he'd felt after the word had come that he couldn't return? What if . . . ?

What ifs are worth as much as tobacco spittle, and they're a lot less satisfying.

Ryan smiled at the phrase echoing through his mind, perfectly recollected in his grandfather's gravelly twang. He'd have hated that Ryan was out of rodeo, but he would have been ashamed of the way Ryan had cut himself off from everyone and everything in the world he'd once lived for. Grandad would have hated nothing more than a retreat, and there was no doubt, that was exactly what Ryan had done.

He exhaled heavily now, tapping the edge of his hat down a touch. "Caleb?"

The larger man turned, hands at his belt, looking at him. "Boss?"

Ryan made a face, then groaned. "Do you think it might help things if I got the Original Six back together? Not all competing, obviously, since I can't, but at least back in town? Maybe do a clinic or something?"

Caleb pursed his lips, his head bobbing as he nodded in thought. "Yeah, I think that'd do something. You get your guys down here, get them to compete, and we might get somewhere."

"Might?" Ryan pressed, narrowing his eyes. "What else do you think needs to happen?"

"Well, I think it might help a lot of people if a local hero proves he's bigger than his career-ending injury and leads the way in doing something for the rodeo besides showing up for it." Caleb tipped his hat back a bit and grinned his version of a dare at him. "What do you think?"

It was the worst sort of pressure, and it clawed at Ryan's stomach with a determination that left him a little queasy.

But, if he was going to jump, he might as well leap.

"Fine," he grunted, waving a hand. "Tell Tom I'll do it, and I'll see what I can do about getting the guys in. Now, which of these beauties do you think we can get the most for?"

CHAPTER 4

I MAY HAVE FOUND something.

Grizz's text had taken her by surprise, considering Talia had only been off for one day. It had been the longest day in a while, and she'd hated every moment, but she had survived by the skin of her teeth. She'd made herself a list of things to accomplish, given that the day was at least thirty-six hours long, if the day before was anything to go by.

She hadn't started a single one yet.

Hadn't even showered until Grizz had texted that he wanted to meet up.

It would have been embarrassing, had she been meeting anyone else, but as it was Grizz . . .

Well, she couldn't see how anything could be more embarrassing than crying snot all over his probably expensive sweater.

He'd told her not to worry about it, said his wife cried on his shirts all the time, but Talia had never quite seen the powerful and perfect Rachel as the blubbering type.

Talia hadn't been, either, before all of this.

She used to be a bit of a fashionista, for a single mom on a middling paycheck, but the last few months had been an exercise in the use of lounge pants and leggings in her workplace wardrobe. No one had said a thing about it, but Talia was sure they'd noticed.

Made no difference now.

She and Grizz were meeting at a quiet cafe not far from her, at his insistence, and Talia had jumped at the chance to do so. She couldn't bear to have people over at the house these days, not when the place still had fall decorations and even her lame Christmas tree up.

She couldn't bear to take any of it down.

Austin had done the decorating in October, loving the colors of autumn, and he'd begged her incessantly to let him put things up. She'd reluctantly relented, and while it wasn't the job she would have done, it wasn't half-bad. He'd been well on his way to putting the Christmas tree up, which she'd put a stop to, but he'd sworn that he would make it an autumn tree, he just wanted the lights to help make it magical.

Talia had gone with it, with the underlying hesitation all mothers everywhere understood, and secretly planned to take it down once his fascination with it had faded.

The accident had come before he'd lost interest, and the tree had never come down.

Maybe it never would.

She shook her head, bringing herself back to the sunshine of the day. It was warmer than it had been lately, but the wind still held the same cutting edge to it. Would spring and summer be warmer for her as well? Had the last several months been more miserable because of the natural chill and gloom of winter? Could she find rays of hope in the sunshine that would gradually increase in the world?

It seemed too much to hope for, but Talia needed help

somewhere. Or from someone. She couldn't do this by herself—she'd failed too many times to try further. It had taken her long enough to admit that, which seemed momentous, and she hoped it meant she would be open to whatever suggestion Grizz had.

He was one of her favorite cousins, and he now knew full well how she was struggling, so anything he offered would be worth serious consideration.

She'd keep that in mind.

Reaching the cafe, Talia paused, seeing Grizz at a table by the window. He saw her and waved, grinning in his usual way. She waved back, managing a smile she didn't have to force, then moved to the doors and pulled them open. It wasn't crowded, which wasn't surprising, as it was barely lunchtime—more like brunch.

She wondered if he chose this time partly on purpose.

She moved around the scattered tables and found Grizz, leaning over to kiss her cousin's cheek fondly. "Hi there."

"Hey, kiddo." Grizz winked, still grinning as she sat down. "Hungry?"

"I could be." She shrugged a shoulder. "More like I need coffee."

Grizz chuckled at that. "Can do. Get whatever you want, it's on me."

Talia gave him a playful look. "Well. In *that* case, I'm starving."

His chuckling deepened, the sound rolling across the table and creating a smile that Talia hadn't meant to form. It was just the nature of his laugh, and the familiarity of it. She'd missed this, and even the sudden pang of regret at shutting everyone out for so long couldn't shrink her smile.

"It's good to see your old self, Talia," Grizz told her. "Even if it's just a quick glimpse."

She nodded, having come to the same conclusion herself. "I know. I can almost feel her, but it's like seeing a stranger rather than myself."

Grizz cleared his throat. "Which brings me to my idea." He paused as their waitress came by, and they quickly gave her their order, Grizz opting for the lunch side of brunch, while Talia stuck to the breakfast side.

Once Talia had her coffee poured, the waitress moved away, giving Talia the chance to look back at her cousin. "You were saying?"

He surprised her by pulling out his phone. "I'm sending you a link," he informed her, tapping at the screen of his phone. "And I want you to seriously consider it."

"You're sending me a link?" Talia repeated before snorting softly. "Grizzy, you could have sent me a link without taking me out to lunch."

He gave her an exasperated look as he set his phone down, his piercing blue eyes widening. "Look, I wanted to see you, check on you, and actually discuss this with you like real family members, okay? I can send you links to my Amazon wish list or stupid videos of goats whenever you'd like, but this is worth being in person."

Talia snickered and held up her hands a little. "Fine, okay, I'll listen." She reached for her now buzzing phone and clicked on the link in the message he'd sent.

A website popped up with a picture that was straight out of a John Wayne film, complete with dirt roads. All it needed was an empty Main Street and a saloon, but at least it was out in the countryside.

Sort of.

There were hills, which was nice, as she'd always thought of the Wild West as being flat, and the house was absolutely gorgeous, in a rustic, homestead sort of way. A row of trees lined the road up to it, and there was a gate bearing the same logo as the top of the page.

"Broken Hearts Ranch," Talia read aloud. Her eyes flicked up to Grizz. "They don't beat around the bush, do they?"

He smiled at her. "Keep reading, smartie."

She did so, scrolling past the picture. "It's in Lost Creek, Texas, which means nothing to me... A therapeutic retreat?" Her brow furrowed, and she read more closely. "For women needing a place to heal and time to do so. Specialized therapy based on individual needs, incorporating the structure and work of ranch life to help reset the broken pieces of life."

Grizz said nothing, for which Talia was grateful.

She was too busy staring at her phone in stunned silence.

Why stunned, she didn't quite know. But her thoughts were hard to put words to, so all she could do was stare.

She scrolled back up to look at the picture, pushing the snarky first impression out of her mind. There were at least three shades of green on those hills she'd mocked, and four shades of yellow, which seemed an odd thing to notice, but it was true. She'd never imagined Texas as a place of color in nature, but she had never been, so that impression wasn't founded on anything except those John Wayne movies that always showed more dirt than anything else.

Even now, she wondered if there had been filters placed on the picture to make it look prettier.

She forced her thoughts to move onto the purpose of the place, and found herself swallowing with some difficulty. "You think I need to go away to have therapy?"

It wasn't a fair question, and she knew it the moment the words left her mouth.

Grizz's brows shot up. "Is that what you think I'm saying? Really?"

She could only shrug again. "It's therapy, and it's away."

"Talia..." He sighed and sat back in his chair, drumming his fingers on the table. "Look, I got this info from Rachel when we talked after pancakes. She jumped out of bed and ran to get her phone, and with three kids, I don't need to tell you that she never gets out of bed for anything less than a fire alarm."

She would have smiled at that had she not been so confused at the moment. Not about Grizz's intentions, or his wife's, as they'd always been very generous where Talia was concerned. The issue was more how she felt about what he was suggesting, if she could seriously consider it, and if such a place, with such a purpose, could actually do anything for her.

"Rach says," Grizz went on, oblivious to Talia's internal debates, "that someone in her dance company went to this place after a car accident ended her dance career. Her body eventually recovered and endured the rehab to get her functional, but it didn't do anything for the loss of her passion in life. She went to Broken Hearts after it was recommended, and came back completely changed. She's the technical advisor for their company now and regularly fields job offers from New York companies."

"Wow," Talia murmured, impressed despite herself.

That wasn't something to be ignored, but every person's situation was so different. How could she possibly expect such a place to work for her specifically?

Was there a therapy to be applied for a woman who had spent her entire adult life, almost from the day of high school graduation, devoting her life to her child, working purely to provide for her child, spending every day loving her child, only to then lose him on a snowy day in a crosswalk?

"I looked through the details," Grizz said after a long pause, no doubt waiting for Talia to respond, "and it's solid.

Run by a licensed, credentialed therapist, individual sessions and group sessions, working on her family's ranch, a beautiful setting away from a big city . . ." He reached across the table and tapped his fingers on her forearm almost anxiously. "Rach is convinced this will help you."

"Help me?" Talia asked softly. "Or fix me?"

"Hey."

She met his eyes, her own beginning to water. "What?"

He gave her a sympathetic smile. "You don't need to be fixed. Rachel knows that, I know that, Clint knows that, and I think you know that, too. You need to heal, and you need to reset. And since your job conveniently wants you to do so . . ."

Talia scowled at the mention of it. "My job is just that. A job. I'll probably find another one after this. Doesn't matter if I have flexible hours now." Her lower lip trembled, and she looked away, squinting her eyes in an attempt to keep herself from crying.

"That's what I'm talking about, kiddo." He tapped her forearm again. "You need a reset button for your life. Lots of change has happened, and lots of change will continue to happen. This place could help you get yourself squared away so you can make sure you're headed in the best direction for your future." He waited another moment, then added, "We want you to smile again, Talia. Really smile, and for more than three seconds at a time."

She nodded, her thoughts lining up a bit more. It was sweet, what he said, and she wasn't going to pretend it didn't touch her. She wanted all of those things, too. Wanted her life back. Wanted any life back. Wanted to feel something when she woke up in the morning instead of feeling nothing.

But would she have to go through hell in this place to get to that reset she so desperately needed? She'd shut down after Austin's funeral, and had never really come back from that. If she felt anything, it was despair, and it was exhausting to face that day in and day out. So much easier to feel nothing, so she'd settled into a routine of nothing. Become addicted to nothing.

Could she go back into the ugly, heartbreaking, gut-wrenching truth of her life as it was?

She didn't know.

She honestly didn't know.

"Think about it?" her cousin pressed gently, yet somehow with a root of firmness that prompted a response.

"Okay," she conceded, nodding again. "I'll think about it."

With perfect timing, their food arrived then, and they moved on to the safer subject of Grizz's kids and home life. It stung a little, reminding her of Austin, but she could sting a little for this gentle giant she so loved.

Hours later, back home on her couch, she pulled up the website for Broken Hearts Ranch again. She couldn't deny that her heart was broken, that it had been broken since November, and that she struggled to even find all the pieces, let alone manage to put them back together. She barely managed to get out of bed in the morning—how could she possibly fix anything about herself when she had zero motivation for her life?

Was it possible that this place could actually pick her up from the cold, hard ground and give her some semblance of a life again?

Scrolling through the pictures, Talia got the impression that this wasn't a soft, fuzzy sort of retreat. She wasn't going to be handled with kid gloves and given tropical drinks after a massage. This was a place designed to put you to work on your road to recovery, not hold your hand and hug you.

Granted, there might be hand holding and hugging, but there would also be a swift kick to the pants, in a way.

She might need that.

Who was she kidding? She absolutely needed that.

She made a face as she looked through the application requirements, biting her lip as the prospect of going became more of a possibility.

It could be an awesome sort of vacation, in a way, though she suspected she would be put to the test emotionally, if not put through the wringer. But it would be away from home, away from her job, and away from reminders.

That was a serious win.

Her phone buzzed in her hand, her mom's picture popping up.

Talia sighed once, then pressed the green phone icon. "Hi, Mom."

"Hey, sweetie," the warm, familiar voice sounded, hesitation palpable. "What are you doing?"

"Looking at a therapeutic retreat on a ranch in the middle of nowhere, Texas, that Grizz found," she replied without any of her own hesitation.

There was silence for a moment. "Okay," her mom said slowly, "I didn't expect that."

Talia chuckled and opened the website again, looking through pictures. "It's called Broken Hearts Ranch. Looks like they do therapy sessions, let you do chores on the ranch, and really focus on finding structure and purpose in daily life. It's a beautiful place, if the pictures haven't been doctored."

"You're considering this, aren't you? I mean, you are seriously thinking about it."

Her mother's voice was soft, and there was a hint of excitement there that would have broken Talia's heart had it not already been so. She'd lost her dad years ago, before she ever got pregnant, and her mom had given her everything, had been there for her constantly, had never let her down. She had struggled along with Talia in all this, and maybe even because Talia had struggled so much. It had to be painful to watch, but she'd never pushed Talia to do more or be more. She hadn't ever made her feel that she should grieve differently, or that she should be better by now.

Surely, she had ached for her daughter, though.

Talia would have done the same for Austin.

If she had no other motivation, the chance to alleviate her mother's distress and anxieties would be enough.

"Yeah," she murmured, finding herself smiling. "Yeah, I'm seriously thinking about this. I don't know why; it should be something I just roll my eyes at and crack jokes about. But something about the idea of a retreat specifically designed for broken hearts that doesn't involve a beach, a spa, or the mountains..."

"You have to do this," her mom interrupted briskly. "Talia, baby, you have to. I'm looking at it now on the computer, and this could be so perfect for you. Working through your pain with actual work, like physical labor, and engaging with a therapist regularly... Oh, sweetie, this just answers all of my prayers."

Talia jerked at that, staring at the phone, though she couldn't actually see her mom. She had no idea, no inkling, that her mother was even remotely religious, beyond a few holidays. She had been praying?

"You're praying, Mom?" she asked quietly, unable to help herself. "Really?"

"I've prayed for years, hon," came the equally soft answer. "Years and years. Ever since we lost your dad, and even more when we lost Austin."

There was no helping the tears that sprang into Talia's eyes, though she'd never been religious or spiritual herself. She didn't think Austin was gone forever from her life, would like to think he was her guardian angel now, but had never really considered what she actually believed, in that regard. Knowing that her mother had faith of any kind, and that she used it on Talia's behalf...

"Momma, I want to go," she managed to squeak, nodding for the benefit of absolutely no one. "To this ranch, I mean. I want to go."

"Then apply! Get Grizz to write you the letter, and start working on the application. I'm covering your plane tickets."

Talia coughed a surprised laugh, wiping at her damp eyes. "No, Mom, I can afford that."

"I don't care if you own a plane," her mom retorted, sounding a little emotional herself. "I'm buying your plane tickets when you get accepted, and that's final!"

"Yes, ma'am." Talia grinned at her phone as she clicked over to the messaging app, and began a quick text to her cousin. "Fingers crossed I actually get accepted."

"You will," came the confident reply. "If any broken heart deserves healing, it's yours."

CHAPTER 5

"KELLIE! KELL, I KNOW you're in there! Kellie!"

Ryan shook his head as he stood outside of his sister's house, intentionally not going up on the porch to knock. His boots were caked in particularly damp, sticky mud that would earn him buckshot in a butt cheek if he trespassed any farther in such a state, so bellowing from the safe boundary was his only option.

Grinning at the lack of response, he inhaled deeply, threw his head back, and hollered, "KELLIE!"

The familiar barks of Frankie and Casper echoed from somewhere nearby, and he had no doubt they would come bounding around the house shortly. The dogs had the worst case of Fear of Missing Out he had ever seen outside of a human, and they'd knock him over in a heartbeat.

"Are you crazy?" his sister demanded as she stormed out of the house from the kitchen door, stomping down the wraparound porch toward him, screen door slamming ominously. She wiped her hands on the half-apron she wore, leaving streaks of flour on the navy fabric. "We are not back on the ranch the way it was when we were kids. I've got guests here!"

"Are they sleeping?" Ryan asked without much concern, hooking his thumbs into his belt loops.

Kellie frowned a little. "No, of course not. None of them are."

He shrugged his shoulders. "Then my bellowing shouldn't be a crime."

"Watch it, buck," she warned, her eyes narrowing, no hint of a smile on her face. "Now, what do you need so badly?"

Ryan smiled up at her, feeling almost mischievous. "We're gonna have company for dinner tonight."

Kellie blinked without her expression changing at all. "Are we? Who? And why am I just finding out?"

"We are," he confirmed, shifting his weight into an easier stance. "Some guys. And because the last one just said he was in."

"Some guys?" She rolled her eyes and heaved a sigh. "Ryan, you know how I feel about having more guys on the property than we have to. Especially ones who might not respect the boundaries and rules we have to have. What am I supposed to tell the guests? They can go out and eat in Lost Creek?" She rubbed a hand at her brow, which left a faint streak of flour there as well. "Who did you invite?"

Ryan made a face, trying not to grin at his own private joke. "Oh, you know, just . . . the Original Six."

It was hilarious, the way his sister's eyes widened in time with her mouth dropping open. He half-expected her to gasp dramatically or faint against the smooth planks of the porch beneath her feet.

But she did none of those things.

"The Original Six?" she repeated slowly. "Seriously?"

He nodded, grinning freely now. "Seriously. Reid just

confirmed, and he was the last one. They're all going to be here."

Kellie matched his grin, her irritation with him gone now. "That's fantastic! Are they competing? Did you invite them or did they . . .? You know what, I don't even care. It'll be so great to see them!" Her brow creased in thought. "I should make another loaf of bread. I've got one rising now, I could do another. They'll wolf down dinner. I was planning on a roast—do you think they'll eat a roast? Maybe I should do chicken fried steak . . ."

"A home-cooked meal? They'd eat anything short of leather," Ryan assured her. "And why are you making the bread? What happened to what's-her-name? The cook lady?"

His sister snorted softly. "If you came to the homestead more often, Ry, you'd have noticed she's been gone for three weeks now. She found being here too remote and unsatisfying, so we're back to meal duty. I'll give the ladies a night off from that, and the new arrival can settle in."

Ryan's ears perked at that. "New arrival? I didn't see that on the schedule. I thought that was Friday."

"She could get a cheaper flight today," Kellie explained, her hands folding in the fabric of the apron and wiping off. "She asked if it was all right, and since Amy left ahead of schedule, we have the room ready." Her eyes raised and narrowed as she looked at something behind him. "That might be her now. How tacky would it be to greet her wearing an apron?"

Ryan turned to look, and saw the blue sedan kicking up dust on the drive in. "Nah, it's life on the ranch, right? We're rustic, or something."

"You can be rustic, cowboy. I'm hostess and therapist, and I need to look professional," Kellie huffed.

He glanced behind him to see her scrambling at her

apron ties before succeeding and tossing the thing back toward the kitchen. "You're wearing jeans and a flannel over a tee, Kells. That's pretty rustic."

She stuck her tongue out at him quickly.

"Ah, there's the professional." He exhaled and squinted up at the roof above her. "Want me to get out of the way so you can greet her properly?"

"Yes, please," she said without shame, smiling with sisterly fondness. "Don't want the poor thing to get the wrong idea of this place."

Ryan nodded in thoughtful consideration. "That it's a dude ranch filled with single, attractive, willing men?"

An even more sisterly expression of derision flashed across her face. "That it's some pathetic, poor, mud-swamped farm in desperate need of money and upkeep."

"Nice, sis." He clicked his tongue and tapped the brim of his hat, turning to move around the house. "See ya later."

"Don't go too far," she called as he walked away. "She'll have luggage you might need to help with."

"That's not in my job description," he yelled back, though he stopped and turned back, leaning against the railing of the porch lazily while he waited to be summoned.

This place wasn't designed to be a holiday destination. Why in the world would anyone need to bring so much that it couldn't be managed by herself and Kellie? They had a washer and dryer in the house, and they worked fine, so there was no need to overpack. They were remote out here, so there would be no need for fancy wear, aside from what they might wear to go to the bar or dance in Lost Creek, but that certainly wasn't a place for formal stuff.

All of the ladies would have their work clothing supplied for them, if nothing they brought was worth getting dirty, so that negated that issue as well. Really, were they supposed to have a concierge at the homestead? They hadn't had anyone all that high and mighty since Ryan had been back, and he suspected they likely wouldn't unless word got around. How could the pictures of their place on the website tempt anybody used to caviar and pearls to come stay with them?

Something cold and slightly damp touched the dangling palm of Ryan's hand, and he jumped a little, looking down. Casper stood there, tail wagging, tongue lolling, while Frankie sniffed an apparently fascinating patch of grass nearby.

"Hi there, buddy," Ryan murmured, scratching the mutt between his ears. "You catch any rabbits yet today?"

Casper didn't reply other than to lick his muzzle and lean into Ryan's scratching.

"I'll take that as a no," Ryan chuckled.

Not to be ignored, Frankie caught onto the attention his brother was getting and trotted over to take part.

Ryan pushed off the railing and scratched Frankie's ears with his other hand, laughing when the dogs mirrored each other beneath his fingers.

"You two are ridiculous," he told them in no uncertain terms. "I think we'll do a tick check tomorrow, what do you think, hmm? You been romping in the brush and trees? Maybe we'll check you for burrs, too, but I think you take care of those on your own."

Neither dog seemed interested in addressing his questions, or showed any concern for what he was suggesting. He suspected he could say the word "vet" while he was scratching them and not hear a peep.

The sound of tires crunching against gravel brought him up, looking toward the front of the house, where the blue sedan was pulling up.

He couldn't see the driver, but the back door opened, and a petite woman with dark hair got out, trim legs encased in slim-cut jeans that somehow didn't seem to quite fit. She tugged at the waist of them, hiking them up a bit, then shook the tail of her baggy green T-shirt out a little as she looked up at the house.

There was something about her expression that Ryan instantly liked, the curiosity mingled with hope, which was a nice change from the reluctance and distaste he'd seen on the faces of a few other women who had come to stay. Those expressions tended to change the longer they were here, and especially after they had started in with Kellie's therapy sessions, quite a few coming to view the ranch as a home away from home.

Would this one?

He watched her take in a deep breath, then release it, and he wished he could tell what color her eyes were as she narrowed them at something he couldn't see on the roof. Her lips quirked into a small smile, and she ran a hand over her long braid, her fingers lingering at the end to toy with the hair there. Her bottom lip tucked under her teeth briefly, and she rocked on the balls of her sneakers.

This woman was broken?

She looked fine to him.

Mighty fine.

Ryan took the liberty of slapping the back of his own head for that, given his sister would have done so and knocked his head off with it.

Rules were rules.

He'd never had a problem with that, and he certainly wasn't going to start now.

"Hi!" he heard his sister drawl as she came out of the house, though he wasn't sure when she had gone back in or what in the world for. "You must be Talia."

"That's me," the woman replied, her smile remaining in

place, though somehow it changed. It was hard to tell from his vantage point, but strain of some kind seemed to come into it.

He didn't like that.

"Welcome to the ranch," Kellie continued, almost skipping down the steps.

Ryan would have flicked his sister's ear for her tone, so peppy and bright. Did she always greet her clients that way? They were broken, if the brief for coming to the ranch was right, and surely hearing a tone like that wouldn't help matters. And this woman in particular probably needed an arm around her shoulder, not a greeting card in her face.

Broken people didn't need parades.

His sister should know that.

"Aren't you gonna call it Broken Hearts Ranch?" Talia asked Kellie as she came to her, hand outstretched.

Kellie shook her head firmly, smiling at her, not seeming the least bit bothered by Talia's slow response to her. "We rarely call it the full name while we're here, hon. Nobody needs reminding of broken hearts when we're trying to mend them. I'm Kellie Prosper, and it is so good to have you here."

"Is it?" Talia asked, taking Kellie's hand and shaking it, though she suddenly looked very young and very insecure.

Ryan suddenly wondered what her age was, and her situation.

He never wondered those things, and he wasn't supposed to care.

Ever.

"Yes. It is," Kellie assured her new guest, putting both of her hands around Talia's. "Come on in, let's get you settled." She looked over Talia's shoulder, nodding once. "I'll get my brother to help with your bags."

"Oh, no, I can . . ." Talia tried to protest.

Ryan was already heading that way when he heard his sister holler, "Ryan! I need you!"

"Yeah, I figured, Kellie," he grumbled as he came around the corner of the house, making sure to smile so Talia could see his affection for his sister.

Kellie gave him a warm smile as he reached them and tilted her head toward the single suitcase Talia had packed. "Would you please take Talia's bag to her room for us?"

"I can do it," Talia insisted firmly, gripping the handle of her bag. "Really, it's fine."

Ryan ignored her, but politely, standing in front of them both, hands at his hips. "Which room, Kells?"

"The only open one," she shot back. She rolled her eyes and looked at Talia. "I swear, I do tell him these things, but the man just doesn't listen."

"I don't need help with the bag," Talia told her, apparently not caring about the sibling banter.

Kellie grinned at that. "I know that, hon. But we might as well make use of Ryan while he's around. Gives him something to do."

Talia finally looked at Ryan, and he was struck by the amber color of her eyes, something he had never seen before and could have studied for ages. It was like watching butterscotch cook on the stove, swirling round and round in the pot while it neared perfection. Her long, dark lashes were a perfect curtain for such eyes, and he struggled to remember how to speak for a second.

He touched the brim of his hat. "Ma'am."

She blinked, then managed to smile just a little. "I don't suppose it would do me any good to argue further, would it?"

"No, ma'am," he replied, his throat scratching on the words. "I make it a point never to argue with my sister. She's more stubborn than any mule I've ever met."

"We won't be seeing much of Ryan during your stay," Kellie assured Talia in a slightly louder voice, widening her eyes for effect. "He's really very busy running the ranch part of the place."

Ryan glanced at her with a crooked smile. "If you say so, sis." He moved over to the suitcase and took one side of the handle, though Talia still had not released it. "You're gonna need to let go, ma'am, or I will be superfluous to this whole thing."

"Big word, cowboy," Kellie praised as she looped her arm through Talia's. "Playing Scrabble?"

"Triple word score," he shot back, wishing she would let the woman talk to him rather than interfering.

Talia surveyed him for a moment, inhaling shortly before exhaling in a rush. "I'm not very good at letting things go," she admitted.

Ryan raised a brow, wondering if she might have more than one meaning there. "Need help?"

"Probably."

Though nobody had asked him to, he reached out and gently pried each of her small fingers from the handle, ignoring how soft her skin felt against his calloused fingers. When only her palm remained, he lifted that off and let it rest by her side, cursing himself when his hand brushed very lightly against the denim of her leg when he did so.

He hadn't meant to do that, didn't want her to think anything, prayed she hadn't noticed.

He noticed, though. Every stupid bit of skin that had touched her burned like a hot iron, and he could feel some of that heat going to his face now.

Perfect.

"Right," Kellie said, completely oblivious to Ryan's soon-to-be blistering skin issue as she led Talia up the steps of the porch. "Let's head in. Are you exhausted from your trip? You must have had an early flight."

"It wasn't that bad," Talia replied easily, though she still seemed uncomfortable somehow. Could have been being here, could have been Kellie's nature, could have been whatever had broken her enough to send her here.

Ryan could see the tension and the strain, and he would bet a fortune Kellie could, too.

He'd never seen his sister at work, though she'd certainly done enough to help him out of his own personal mess. He wondered how she planned on helping Talia through her mess, and what would work for the spitfire.

He frowned at himself as he hauled the surprisingly heavy suitcase up the stairs. How in the world did he know she was a spitfire? She hadn't barked, sniped, glowered, or fought in any way yet—she'd only said she couldn't let go of things. She could have been the gentlest soul on the planet for all he knew.

But that wasn't right. Couldn't be.

Somehow, deep in his bones, he knew Talia was a spitfire, just like he knew he was gonna have to watch out for this one.

He could be in a whole heap of trouble if he wasn't careful.

He entered the house with the suitcase in tow, closing the door and habitually wiping his boots on the thick mat there. Glancing down at it, he saw the remnants of his earlier muddy excursions and grinned to himself.

His sister would have no one to blame but herself for this mess. He was just doing as he was told.

And now, whistling to himself as he wheeled the suitcase in, he wouldn't mind just leaving a bit of mud and dirt wherever it pleased his sister to lead him.

He was just being helpful, after all.

CHAPTER 6

TALIA HAD NEVER SPENT any time on a ranch or a farm, or in any place remotely resembling Texas in her entire life, outside of field trips she'd taken as a kid. She hadn't even been a chaperone on Austin's field trip to a farm in the first grade, which hadn't seemed to matter at the time, but now she wished she had. It might have come in handy being on this ranch now if she had managed to develop any sort of real appreciation for it.

She didn't dislike the place, and actually liked the charm of the big house, but she had the unsettling feeling of being very, very small in a place where she would get lost in a heartbeat if she wasn't trampled by angry cows first.

Did cows get angry?

It was a stupid thought to have as the chipper and friendly Kellie led her down the cozy halls of the place. How it was possible to have cozy halls in a house that was this large was astounding, but it managed to do so. It wasn't ornate in any way, and Talia was actually looking forward to wandering the place later to look at every picture and examine every little detail of its arrangements. The decor resembled everything she'd thought a ranch house would have, though there were no hay bales being used as furniture, and she'd glimpsed a fantastic stone fireplace in the main room that she was dying to sit by.

But she wasn't here to explore a house and sit by a fire that was completely unnecessary in the Texas heat.

She was broken, and she needed help.

She was broken.

Admitting it was probably the first step, right? She could admit it until she was blue in the face—that wasn't her problem.

Doing something about it was the problem.

Doing *anything* about it was the problem.

"I hope you don't mind," Kellie was saying as she led Talia down the hall, "but we keep the rooms pretty simple. Feel free to put up any pictures or personal touches you like. Whatever you need to make it home."

"Thanks," Talia murmured, though she had nothing to put up. She hadn't cared about personal touches in a long time, and any bed would do at this point. She glanced behind her to see Ryan following with her suitcase at a respectful distance.

There was something about the guy that she liked. Whether it was his soft drawl or his crooked smile she couldn't tell, but he had been gentle as he'd pried her fingers from her bag, and there was the same warmth emanating from him as from his sister.

If nothing else, the Prosper siblings could make this trip worth it for her.

His blue eyes rose to hers, and she forgot to look away or pretend she hadn't been eyeing him.

A small, crooked smile curved his lips, and something in

Talia's rib cage fluttered. She swallowed and turned back, shifting the leather strap of her purse onto her shoulder. "Is there a schedule for today, Kellie? I've never been to a place like this. I'm not sure..."

Kellie shook her head as she turned into a bedroom, stopping just inside and gesturing for Talia to enter. "Nope. First day is always more about settling you in than starting anything. We will have an intake interview at some point today. It's..." She paused to check her watch. "It's eleven now. Do you want to meet after lunch?"

"I'm not hungry," Talia told her as she looked around the room, the single twin bed covered in a quilt looking more inviting than anything else she'd seen. "I grabbed something at the airport."

"All right," Kellie replied without seeming too concerned about it. "What about a rest? You deserve that, no question."

Talia smiled at the sweet suggestion, and even more that it wasn't in the least bit patronizing. She got the sense that there wouldn't be many opportunities to rest during the day while she was here, so that might be something to take advantage of. "I'd love a nap, but we can talk first. I might sleep better after that."

"Talkin' with my sister would tucker anyone out," Ryan drawled from behind them, his voice curling as much as his smile had done.

Talia glanced over just in time to see Kellie whack Ryan across the chest with a satisfying thump, though it sounded as if what she had hit was pretty solid.

Interesting.

Ryan chuckled at his sister and looked at Talia, laughter still in his eyes. "Where would you like this, ma'am?"

There was something about the way he said "ma'am" that was ticklish, which was a strange sensation. She'd hated that word, and hated being called it even more. It always sounded like something you said to an old woman who needed help to cross the street or who couldn't reach the groceries she needed. It wasn't something you called a woman who was turning twenty-six in a matter of weeks.

But when Ryan called her ma'am, there was nothing old-sounding about it.

It sounded more like a one-word country song.

"On the bed," Talia told him quickly, resisting the urge to clear her throat. "Please."

Ryan nodded, then gave his sister a dramatically thoughtful look. "This one says please. Nice."

Kellie hit him again, this time on the arm. "Boy, I will tan your hide if you don't get out of here the moment that suitcase hits the bed."

In the process of moving that way, Ryan paused a step, looking back at her. "Well, then, it just might take me a minute to do that . . ." He exaggerated the next step, which was miniscule in comparison to the strides he had been taking.

Talia clamped down on her lips hard, a laugh rising up.

This was the easy banter between siblings she had always seen in her cousins, but being an only child, she hadn't had that herself. She could banter with Grizz and Clint like they were siblings, but it wasn't regular. Nothing could have made her feel more at home than this, and though Kellie had said they wouldn't see much of Ryan while she was here, Talia was hoping that wasn't actually true.

She'd enjoy seeing Ryan whenever she could.

"Knock it off," Kellie said with a laugh. "Come on, Ry, we've got things to do before Christmas."

He looked at his sister with a crooked grin again. "It's March, Kells."

"Exactly." She gestured for him to get on with it. "Come on."

Ryan relented and easily swung the large suitcase onto the bed, then set his hands at his hips, which emphasized his slender build, though his chest and torso seemed maxed out enough . . .

Talia's cheeks flushed, and she looked down, pretending to brush a hair behind her ear, though everything was still neatly contained in her thick braid. "Thanks, Ryan."

"No problem, ma'am. No charge, either."

She glanced up at him and found him smiling at her, which didn't help the flushing.

At all.

He dipped his chin in a small nod. "See you around." Then he walked past her out of the room, patting Kellie's arm fondly as he did so.

Ryan Prosper smelled like hay, leather, spice, and molasses cookies.

What in the world?

Talia *did* clear her throat now, and turned to face Kellie. "Did you want to do that interview now or . . . ?"

Kellie smiled and nudged her head toward the suitcase and bed. "Go ahead and get unpacked, freshen up, what have you. I don't have anything on my schedule for a few hours. Just head back down the hall and go past the living room down the same hall. Can't miss it. My name's on the door."

"Right. Thanks, doc," Talia replied, trying for the teasing nature that came so easily to Kellie and her brother.

Kellie nodded, not correcting her, though the smile was still in place. "One rule. Wear comfy shoes."

Talia blinked. "What? Are we working out or walking or . . . ?"

"None of the above," Kellie assured her. "I've just found that people have a better intake interview experience in comfy shoes." She shrugged and winked before turning to walk out of the room, tucking her hands into her jeans pockets.

It didn't take Talia long to unpack and get her shirts and pants into the dresser and all. She hadn't brought all that much, aside from several jackets and different pairs of shoes. She hadn't been sure what sort of footwear would be needed on the ranch, as the description of "ranch duties" hadn't been very specific. She had brought tennis shoes, hiking boots, dirty "backyard only" shoes, and a sturdy pair of rain boots, plus a pair of sandals and three pairs of flats, just in case they might come in handy.

Considering she'd only brought two shirts that couldn't be classified as T-shirts, it wasn't likely she would get out much aside from the regular stuff she'd have to do as part of her therapy.

She'd never had a shoe problem, per se, but a healthy appreciation for footwear was definitely in her nature.

Comfy shoes for her intake interview, though . . .

She really didn't want to wear shoes at all right now, not after hiking her way through the airports to get here. She moved to the small drawer at the top of the dresser and pulled out a thick pair of socks, which she had tossed into her suitcase at the last minute, and quickly tugged those on.

Comfy meant no shoes for her, but she was polite enough to cover her feet when in someone else's house.

At least she had that going for her.

She crept out of the bedroom, feeling the sudden urge to tiptoe, though she had yet to see any other people in this house except the Prosper siblings.

Was she the only guest at the ranch right now? That would be some really direct attention, and she wasn't ready for that.

Biting her lip, Talia paused and knocked gently on the nearest door. When she heard nothing, she opened the door and peeked in. The bed was made, though it could barely be called that, and three pairs of shoes were at the foot of it.

She nodded to herself and closed the door, resuming her walk to Kellie's office. She didn't want to be the only broken heart on the ranch, so having at least one housemate was a relief. It wasn't that she intended to suddenly become best friends with whoever she was, or that she wanted to spill all her secrets. She actually thought any sort of confessions on her part would be hard to come by. The facts were easy enough to admit, but as for the rest . . .

Nope. Not happening. And not to any strangers she was sharing a house with.

She just wanted to make sure there was enough mortification to go around rather than enduring target practice from a trigger-happy therapist.

She might be heading into her intake interview, but Talia had every intention of taking stock of Kellie Prosper as well. She had endured a therapy session or two in her life, especially after her dad had passed, and it hadn't been a great experience. If this was going to head that direction, she'd shut herself off and play the game to endure her time at the ranch.

There was no way she was going to let herself get more broken than she already was just to fill someone's quota.

Passing the living room, she stole a glance at the stone fireplace, smiling to herself as she picked the exact spot she would sit when it was cool enough to have a fire going.

Was it ever cool enough in Lost Creek for that?

She moved ahead, her eyes tracking the doors and seeing the slightly ajar one on the end. "Ten bucks says . . ." Talia murmured to herself as she neared.

Sure enough, a simple door plate had been fastened there, and it read, "Kellie Prosper, PhD, LPC, NCC, CCHMC."

Not much simple about that alphabet soup, but Talia supposed that was good enough.

She exhaled softly, then knocked on the door.

"Come on in," the warm Texan accent answered in an equally soft tone. "It's open."

Talia pushed the door open, smiling hesitantly. The room was a light green, something that reminded her of spring, but when the day was cloudy. It was soothing somehow, something mossy and fresh—she could almost smell the forest this color belonged in. There were no waterfall sounds, no divan for her to lie on, and no imposing bookshelf displaying tomes of knowledge and various awards.

There was, however, a tidy desk, an oversized chair, a perfectly manicured fern, and a neatly scripted quote on one wall. It was impossible to tell from her place if it had been painted on, or if the words were vinyl lettering, but her attention was drawn there.

A single step is enough.

Her brow furrowed at that. A single step was enough? A single step didn't get anyone anywhere, wouldn't accomplish anything. Why would a therapist who had opened a live-in clinic on a ranch, and had her clients work on said ranch, embrace the idea of a single step?

Images of the moon landing popped into her head, but she was fairly certain Kellie wasn't living or modeling her patient care after the platitudes of astronauts.

But what did Talia know?

"Hi, Talia," Kellie said simply, her smile suddenly gentle. "Ready?"

Talia nodded once, but said, "Not really."

"I figured." Kellie gestured at the oversized chair near the wall. "Have a seat."

Legs suddenly shaking, Talia complied, folding her knees into her chest when she had done so. "Is this where you ask me to tell you my problems?" she tried to quip, feeling exposed and raw somehow.

Kellie laughed quietly and leaned her elbows on the desk, lacing her fingers. "Nope. I have a general idea of your situation from your application. We're not going to talk about those particulars right now unless you want to. Do you?"

Talia shook her head, her throat tightening.

"Didn't think so." Kellie looked at her computer screen, narrowing her eyes for a minute as she clicked her mouse three times, then pushed away from her desk and rose, pulling her chair around the desk to remove any obstacle between her and Talia.

It was all Talia could do not to lean farther back in her chair, to get as far away as she could from such close attention. She liked Kellie so far, but she wasn't sure she was ready for this.

Kellie's slight smile told Talia she knew full well what had happened, and she sat back in her own chair, not at all put off. "Has anything changed from what you had in your application?" she asked without any sort of introduction.

Talia thought back to the process applying to this place had been. She'd needed to provide a medical history, have a background check, include a reference letter, and basically write a pitch for why she needed to come to the ranch and what had caused her broken heart. There had been a full questionnaire to accompany all of this, and she was pretty sure applying to college was an easier process, though she'd never done so.

What had she said? How had she phrased things?

Did it actually matter?

"No," Talia replied simply, shaking her head. "My son is still dead, and I'm still not over it."

Kellie's expression didn't change. "That isn't what I meant."

"I know." She managed a swallow, blinking hard. "I don't

feel anything anymore. I can't. I'm just as broken now as I was the day he died. Broken is normal."

"But broken is not permanent," Kellie insisted. She leaned forward, her eyes searching Talia's. "I ask our guests two questions at every intake interview, and the answers help me guide our therapy sessions and goals. The first is this: Why did you want to come here?"

The question caught her off guard, given she had written an entire essay explaining why she should come to the ranch and what her situation was. Kellie had the paperwork on her desk, Talia could see her name on it. Yet she was asking Talia why she wanted to come?

Then the word choice struck her.

Want. Kellie asked why Talia *wanted* to come to the ranch. Not why she needed to or deserved to, but wanted to.

Why did she *want* to come?

"I didn't," Talia admitted in a hoarse whisper. "I didn't want to come. I basically lost my job because I'm not really there—I'm just a robot going through the motions in my life. I know I need help, I've known that for a while. I just don't want to be anywhere. Do anything. And running away from all of that to retreat like this makes me feel weaker." Her voice broke, and she looked down at her hands. "And more broken."

"You're confusing retreat with desertion or surrender," Kellie told her in a soft but firm voice. "A retreat isn't a sign of cowardice. It's a sign of acknowledging you do not have the strength to presently accomplish your goals. A retreat is a means of regaining ground or strength, of going back to the drawing board, or finding a new strategy. A retreat is an intention to face the difficulty when better prepared to do so."

A flicker of something positive lit inside Talia's chest, but she didn't dare acknowledge it, just in case it turned out to be heartburn or something. "Why doesn't it feel that way?"

Kellie's hand reached out to touch Talia's sock-covered foot, though she didn't go farther than that. "Because you've just taken the first step toward finding that strength, which is allowing yourself to accept that you don't have it right now. And there is nothing wrong with that. We think we should always be fine, no matter what happens to us, but that isn't fair to our bodies or our minds. We are meant to feel things and experience things, and that drains us more than we realize. Seeing that isn't a bad thing. It's one of the most honest realizations we can have."

"A single step," Talia murmured, feeling moisture gathering at the corners of her eyes.

"A single step," Kellie repeated. She released Talia's foot and sat back silently.

When she didn't say anything else, Talia looked up at her. "What's the second question?"

Kellie's mouth curved. "What do you want to gain out of your experience here?"

"I'm stuck," Talia told her with more honesty than she usually allowed with someone she wasn't related to. "I don't want to be stuck."

"Good." Kellie nodded slowly, still watching Talia, and waiting.

Was she supposed to say more?

Talia wet her lips. "I want to breathe without hurting. I want to feel again. I want to care that the day is sunny and that I'm alive."

"Excellent," Kellie praised in that gentle tone she used so well. "And this retreat? What does it mean to you?"

"That's three questions," Talia pointed out, trying for a smile.

Kellie laughed in a warm way that belonged in a conversation by a fire with hot cocoa in hand. "I didn't say there were *only* two questions, just that there were always two questions."

Talia would give her that, and she would further admit that it felt good to make her laugh. Kellie might be her therapist while she was here, but she suddenly felt like she had known her for ages, and thought that, if given a chance, she could have talked to this woman for hours without ever feeling ashamed of it. Like they were old friends who just needed to catch up.

"I don't know what it means, honestly," Talia heard herself say. "I don't know anything except that I'm here."

"That's fair. So let me ask you this: Do you want to regain strength? Find better ground for your battles? Do you want a new strategy and new resources to face the enemy at your particular door?"

"Yes." Talia nodded repeatedly, swallowing hard as her chest began to tighten. "Yes, I want to face it all, and I want to survive facing it."

Kellie's warm smile spread, and she reached out a hand for Talia to shake again. "Then welcome to your retreat, Talia James. Let's see what we can do for you."

Chapter 7

"Is it supposed to be bubbling like this?"

"Ryan, step away from the stove before I hurt you."

"I'm just saying, it looks suspicious when it boils like that."

A sharp corner of a hand towel snapped against the back of one thigh, making Ryan yelp and jump back from the slightly bubbling gravy. "I said, step away!" his sister barked, striding over with a furrowed brow.

Ryan held up his hands in surrender, then rubbed at the tender spot on his leg. "I forgot how good you are with that."

She widened her eyes, shooing him away. "Yeah, I am, and yes, the gravy is supposed to have those little bubbles, unless you want it to be lukewarm and basically curdling."

"That sounds disgusting, and I may lose my appetite," Ryan proclaimed as he made a face, turning away from the kitchen to pat his stomach.

"With the aromas comin' from that oven, you must have the intelligence of a gnat," drawled the annoyingly fit form of Westin Farr from farther down the counter, where he was almost gleefully mashing potatoes.

Ryan scowled at his old friend. "Just because you're the biggest brownnoser this side of the Mississippi doesn't make you right."

"You leave West alone," Kellie scolded as she opened the oven to check on the chicken fried steak. "He was nice enough to offer to help, unlike someone else."

"Yeah, Reid," Ryan barked, turning to scold the dark-haired guy standing by the table, watching the scene in the kitchen like it was some sporting event. "You could have offered."

Reid Browning flicked a crooked smile in their direction. "I know where my skills lie, and they are not in the kitchen. Kellie knows she can ask me to carry this or hold that, but unless otherwise instructed, I'm gonna stand right here."

"Yeah, where it's safer!" Kellie laughed, tossing a grin over her shoulder. "I haven't forgotten the scrambled eggs incident, Reid. I think there's still soot from that fiasco around here."

West snorted a laugh as he continued his mashing. "Did you lose both eyebrows on that one, Chute Boss, or just the left one?"

Reid returned the laugh with a mocking one of his own. "Very funny. Can we just agree that I'm doing the most helpful thing I'm capable of by being over here? Ryan's just being a pest."

"Supervising," Ryan corrected, picking up the basket of bread and bringing it to the table as though he had intended to do that all along. "Very important." He looked down at the basket, then turned to look at his sister with folded arms. "What happened to making another loaf, Kells? This ain't your work."

"You really gonna talk to a lady like that, Prosper?" another voice drawled from beyond the screened porch door. "I see your manners ain't improved much."

Ryan felt his mouth spread in a wide grin before adopting the doleful expression of a younger brother. "My sister is no lady to me, Lars, and that's just the way it is."

The porch door opened, and three men walked in, each face a more welcome sight than Ryan could have predicted.

It really had been too long.

"Hats off, boys," Kellie hollered without looking, and they all complied in smooth motions.

"Hey, boys," Eric Davis greeted, his towheaded blond hair slightly matted from the hat. "Kellie."

Ryan strode over to them, shaking hands and clapping them on the back. "Thanks for showing up, guys. Good to see you."

"It's better to see your sister, I reckon," Eric admitted, his gaze moving to the kitchen. "Lookin' good, Kells. Been a long time."

Kellie came around the counter, smiling as though the gang had come just for her. "Sure has, Eric, but your flirting hasn't improved. Good gravy, y'all look exactly the same."

"Beggin' your pardon, Miss Kellie," Ford Hopkins grunted from behind the other two, "but I have put on a good twenty pounds since I saw you last, and it's all muscle."

"Between the ears, maybe," Lars Jackson guffawed, slapping Ford on the back. "Not anywhere else." He looked at Kellie and sobered a little, nodding. "Thanks for having us here, Kellie. 'Specially on short notice. I know Ryan probably didn't warn you."

"Not much has changed there, that's for sure," Kellie confirmed. She smiled at them all, sighing just a little. "I never thought I'd say it, but you are a sight for sore eyes."

"I know," Reid admitted soberly. "I have that effect on people."

Ryan coughed a laugh, and the others chortled along with

him, the dynamic between them so familiar, it was as though no time had passed since they'd last rode or competed together.

They'd been at a lot of the same rodeos since leaving college, so their paths had crossed more often than not, but since his injury, Ryan had taken no pains to stay in touch. That sort of thing didn't matter too much, all things considered, but it bothered him now. They'd been close once, but the years had given them some distance. There had been a close camaraderie in their days as a team, and that sort of bond didn't have an easy definition. It was a brotherhood of sorts, even on the days when they couldn't stand each other. Even when they competed against each other, they always had a mutual respect and understanding that you couldn't find anywhere else.

There was a kinship between almost all rodeo riders, really, but what the Original Six had . . .

Well, it was different, and that's all Ryan knew.

And he'd missed it.

A motion beyond the kitchen caught his eye, and he watched the petite figure of Talia James move into the great room just beyond the dining room. Her eyes darted to their gathering, though she wouldn't have seen all of them, given the angle and the doorway, but it was clear she was trying to be discreet for whatever reason.

Maybe to give them privacy? Or to go undetected? Whatever it was, he found it oddly adorable that she was actually tiptoeing into the room like it was Christmas morning, her fuzzy socks pulled up over the leggings she wore. With the distance from here to there, they wouldn't have heard her unless she marched in, but the effort was cute. Why she thought she needed to be so quiet and unobserved was curious, though. There were rules at the ranch, but not involving the actual rooms of the homestead. She could come and go as she pleased, and they were well used to guests coming into the kitchen during all sorts of family dinners.

Not that Talia would know that, or the guys, for that matter. Kellie's takeover and renaming of the place had happened well after their college days, but none of them would care if Talia wandered in. Heck, they'd probably invite her to sit down with them and start trying to make her blush with compliments.

But it was clear she had no intention of coming into the dining room and kitchen area; she just sat on the hearth of the stone fireplace. There wasn't even a fire going, but she sat there, looking into it as though the hypnotic motion of the flames captured her attention.

"I thought the guests went out for the evening," Ryan murmured to his sister as the guys joked with each other about something.

She followed his gaze and made a noncommittal noise. "Talia's new, and one therapy session with the others hasn't been enough to make her comfortable. She just wanted a quiet evening here. I offered to have her join us, but . . ."

Ryan frowned just a little, though he shouldn't have been surprised.

He had seen and met and worked alongside enough of the ranch guests to understand that time was always a key factor, as was patience. His sister was well trained, well educated, and damn good at her job, if the praises sung by her former guests were anything to go by. She had found a way to help all of them, and she would do the same with Talia.

He'd be interested to see what would change in Talia when she did.

"Right, I need the honey butter taken to the table, and the green beans as well. I don't care who does it, so long as they both get there," Kellie announced as she returned to the kitchen.

Lars and Ford moved to help her while Reid and Eric finished setting the table. West proudly brought forth his mashed potato masterpiece as though he had raised the potatoes himself, and soon enough, all of them were sitting around the table, including Kellie.

"How long are we staying in Lost Creek?" Eric asked as he eyed the feast before them. "And how many times can I come for dinner?"

Kellie laughed and propped her elbows on the table, folding her fingers together. "This is a special occasion, and it doesn't happen often. But I'll tell you what: You guys stick around and do the rodeo, you can come round for dinner the night before."

Reid's eyes narrowed. "All three nights?"

Ryan smiled as his sister remained completely unruffled by the question. "Did I stammer, Reid? The night before the rodeo, we can have a family dinner here."

Family.

Ryan looked around the table, at these guys who had been part of his life through some of his most growing moments and understood his passion like few others would. Lars and Ford had actually been there when he'd had his accident, and had shown up at the hospital for him. Reid, West, and Eric had been on another circuit, but they'd called him repeatedly.

They'd probably have been there alongside him during his recovery, if he had let them. But he'd shut everyone out from the moment he'd heard the worst, and missed out on keeping this going. Even now, no one was asking him why he'd cut them out. They were just hanging out around the table as though no time had passed.

The questions might come later, but with how things were now, he knew there wouldn't be any accusations in it, just curiosity.

He couldn't blame them for that; he just didn't have an answer.

"Ford," Kellie suddenly said with a smile, "would you say grace, please?"

"Sure." He bowed his head, clearing his throat. "Lord, we're grateful for this home and this food, and for being all together again. We're grateful for our health and our safety, 'specially with what we do to risk it. We ask for a blessing on this meal, and on us all. And particularly for the ladies Kellie's helpin' here on the ranch, that they may find the healing they need in their lives. In Jesus's name, Amen."

"Amen," they all echoed.

Kellie surreptitiously wiped at the corner of one eye, which made Ryan's throat tighten. She so rarely got acknowledgement from people who weren't actually on the ranch, and while she would never complain about what she did, given how she loved it, the strain of it all took its toll. The only reason Ryan knew about any of that was because he knew his sister better than anyone, and he knew when she was worn down.

Those were the days she got out of the homestead and threw herself headlong into ranch chores again, though she had a couple she did regularly. On those days, she could outwork any two of his ranch hands, and himself.

Then she'd sleep hard and wake up the next day energized.

She was getting close to another hard ranch day, he could see, so he made a mental note to save some good work for her.

But Ford's praying for her guests . . .

That saw into the heart of Kellie perfectly.

"Thanks, buddy," Ryan murmured to the broad-shouldered man beside him, nudging him with his elbow. "I mean it."

True to his reserved nature, Ford only shrugged.

"All righty, y'all, dig in!" Kellie said brightly, picking up her fork.

"Don't hafta tell me twice," Lars announced as he reached for the platter of chicken fried steak. "I haven't eaten a meal like this in years."

"Tell that to your gut," West suggested, taking the bread basket. He glanced at Ryan. "You said Kellie didn't make this, right?"

Ryan groaned as he handed off the bowl of potatoes, the rest of the table chuckling at the reminder. "Nice, West. Thanks a lot."

Kellie snickered from her place at the head of the table. "I'll have you know that I did bake bread today, but I remembered how you boys down loaves like it's a challenge, so I picked up some more fresh bread from Mariah's Bakery in town."

"In *that* case . . ." West pointedly took two large slices of bread from the basket and placed them on his plate. "No offense, Kells, your bread is good and all, but Mariah's is the bread to end all breads."

They all continued to laugh as the food got passed around and they began to eat, catching up with details about people they all knew and teasing each other, just like they used to.

"So, Ryan," Reid said suddenly, sitting forward and looking up from his second helping. "What's the plan?"

Ryan stared back at him blankly. "Plan?"

"Yeah," Eric chimed in, cocking his head as he looked at Ryan now. "You got us all here, even though only West, Ford, and I were entered for Lost Creek. Said you needed our help."

"I did say that, didn't I?" Ryan pressed his tongue to his front teeth in thought. He hadn't really thought all that much beyond getting the guys in, figuring their names would be enough to get some attention going for the rodeo. Clearly, he would need a little more thought and a decent chunk of action.

What exactly either of those might be was still to be determined.

"Oh, good," Lars mused in a slow drawl. "He's thought about this carefully."

Ryan gave him a hard look. "I'm not running any kind of show here, Lars. I just said I'd get you boys in. Tom Hauser says numbers are down in the events, so they could probably use more guys to compete."

"Easy enough," West grunted, drumming his fingers on the tablecloth. "We can make some calls. Ford can be pretty convincing when he wants to be."

Ford snorted softly, but lifted his palm from the table in a sort of shrug. "Threaten to tie down a guy or two, suddenly they listen to you."

"Never works for Eric," Reid pointed out with a grin.

"Ha ha, Chute Boss," Eric shot back, rolling his eyes. "They'll make a clown out of you yet." He looked down the table at Ryan. "What about SHCC? They love an alumni thing. We could talk Buddy Powers into setting something up down here. That would help, right?"

"Definitely." Kellie nodded firmly, taking a sip of her water. "Numbers have been down at events, but the SHCC rodeos still get the best turnout." She frowned before looking over at Lars. "What if you did a mutton bustin' clinic? They haven't had one of those events in a few years—you'd probably get a decent turnout."

"You want me to teach kids?" Lars made a show of rearing back a little, shaking his head. "I'd do it, but I can't promise it'll be good."

"Better you than us," Eric said simply. "You and West could do it. The rest of us could do some roping and tie-down demonstrations. I've got the YouTube channel, plus sponsorship from King Spurs, so that might help."

Ryan nodded in thought. "Yep, they'd go for that. And if we make it known that we still need volunteers, with all these new ideas, maybe numbers will go up?"

Heads bobbed in nods around the table. "Worth a shot," Ford grunted.

"What are you gonna do, Ryan?" West asked around a bite of green beans. "No offense, buddy, but I know you're unable to compete."

Normally, talking about this would make Ryan shut down and change the subject, but at the moment, he only felt a twinge of discomfort. He'd been thinking about this himself, after all, and as long as he didn't dwell too much on the "they versus him" situation, he'd be fine.

Hopefully.

He shook his head. "Not sure. I thought about being a pickup man, since I probably wouldn't pass as a barrelman, either. Better to be on the horse supervising and escorting the animals back to gates than keeping an agitated bull distracted, right?"

"Now that's a solid idea," Lars praised, his eyes widening. "You know they're always looking for a good pickup man. Your average rancher would work well enough, but a skilled rodeo man would always be a better candidate."

"Why not run the thing, Ryan?" Reid suggested. He shrugged, making a face of consideration. "You've been around the circuit enough—you could run the Lost Creek rodeo."

Ryan hissed, shaking his head. "I don't think so. I've got a ranch to run, and Kellie's last manager didn't know a hammer from a hay bale."

"He wasn't *that* bad," Kellie grumbled, looking down at her plate and going slightly pink in the face. "I didn't have a say in hiring him; he'd been running it for Mom and Dad before I bought them out, and it had been okay up until then."

"Kells, stop," Ryan told her as gently as he could from across the table. "That wasn't a jab at you. The guy was practically a crook, and you couldn't have known how bad things were when you're focused on the important stuff here. Those few months you did both jobs after firing him almost killed you. If you had a clone of yourself, you'd be able to run both the retreat and the ranch flawlessly, but you've got me, and I call 'em like I see 'em."

Kellie looked up, meeting his eyes with a fond smile. "Which just proves my excellent taste in hiring you."

Ford cleared his throat and leaned forward, looking up the table at Kellie. "We can pitch in, if it would help, Kellie. If we're gonna be in town for a bit anyway, we might as well be useful."

"Absolutely," Lars echoed, nodding fervently. "I'd love to take a look at the place for real, give my two cents."

"I'd take five cents if you had them to rub together," Ryan muttered, shaking his head. "She owns the place, but I run it, and I know what I'm doing." He pushed up from his chair, plate in hand. "Kells, did you set pies out to cool?"

"Of course." She nodded, gesturing toward the porch. "Just sitting out there, as usual." She got up as well, taking her plate. "I'll get these dishes in the sink to soak, and you can go get those."

Westin was up like a shot. "We'll do the dishes, Kellie. You stay right there."

"What?" Kellie said with a laugh. "No, Westin, you're my guests, I can't have you do the chores."

"No, ma'am, I'm with West on this one," Ford agreed as

he picked up his own plate and reached for hers. "No guests here, and we can do the washing up in return for that meal."

"You're both terrible," Ryan informed them, setting his plate in the sink. "I'll never live any of this down, you know that?"

Reid perked up. "Oh, are we making Ryan look bad? In that case, I'll do the drying."

"Unbelievable." Ryan shook his head and headed for the porch. "I'm uninviting every one of you." Still shaking his head, he pushed open the screen door and strode out into the evening chill. There was a bench their dad had built for their mom specifically for cooling baked goods, and Kellie had kept the tradition alive in her own way.

Whistling to himself, Ryan turned to the two pies cooling there and tapped the pans with a finger to test the heat.

"Perfect," he murmured when he wasn't singed by them. He picked them up and was moving back to the door when he stopped, looking farther down the porch.

Talia was there, leaning against the railing and looking up at the sky as stars began to appear. A breeze caught loose tendrils of her dark hair, though most of them were still contained in her braid from before. Still, the hours had loosened and relaxed it all, and there was something about this more casual look that he liked better.

Twisting his lips, he changed direction and moved out toward her. His footsteps brought her head around, and she straightened up.

"Sorry, are you guys coming out here?" she said quickly. "I can go back inside. I just wanted to see what the stars looked like so far from a city."

"No, you're fine, stay here," Ryan insisted, inclining his head back toward the railing. "You should look at the stars, they're great." He hesitated a moment, then asked, "You're from a big city?"

She nodded, moving back to the railing. "Chicago."

Ryan whistled low, squinting out at the darkening horizon. "Wow, yeah. That's a big city."

"You ever been?" she asked.

"Nope. Been to Dallas, though, which is kinda the same thing. Less windy, though."

Talia looked at him in confusion. "What?"

"Windy," he said again. "You know . . . Windy City?"

As he'd hoped, she rolled her eyes and looked back out at the sky. "That's bad."

Ryan smiled to himself. "Yeah, sorry. Bit out of practice. My sister banned my jokes."

"I can see why." She glanced back at him, leaning her arms on the railing. "You should get back to your guests. I'm sorry, I didn't mean to take you away from them. I was trying to be super quiet and not disturb anything."

"Disturb?" Ryan laughed once. "Did you hear us in there? Ma'am, you could have run a bulldozer through there and not disturbed us."

She smiled just a little, but it was enough to encourage him. "I mean, I did come out here for more quiet, so . . ."

He hissed through his teeth, shaking his head. "Why didn't you just holler at us to keep it down? I do apologize. Reid has a mouth the size of Texas, and Eric can't shut up anymore, now that he runs his own YouTube channel."

"You don't have to call me ma'am, you know," she said, either avoiding his statement or not hearing it. "It's cute, and it's sweet, but really, just call me Talia."

Ryan's smile returned at that, and he nodded once. "Can do. I'd shake your hand now that we've been informally introduced again, but they are presently occupied. You can call me Ryan, unless you're more inclined to follow my sister's path, in which case you can just whistle like I'm one of the cows."

Talia laughed softly, and it had a warmth to it that Ryan loved, though it was faint. "Well, I don't know how to whistle. Not like that, anyway. I can whistle a tune, but I can't do the really loud, really piercing whistles."

"I could teach you," he heard himself say, which surprised him into a momentary silence. But a brief glimpse of an imagined scene where he spent time with her specifically to teach her to whistle was enough to spur him on. "It's not so hard, once you know how."

"You want to teach me to whistle?" She scoffed and gave him a wry look. "Is that part of the package here at the ranch?"

He shrugged. "Could be. Could also just be our thing. Might help you out when you graduate to the advanced chores on the ranch."

"Advanced chores? Hmm." She tilted her head at him. "What are remedial chores?"

Ryan sniffed and looked out at the dark fields. "Picking up rocks. Hands down." He cocked a crooked grin her way and started backing toward the screen door. "Welcome to the ranch, Talia. And if you're in the mood for pie, you're welcome to join us."

She waved a hand, smiling at him in return. "Thank you, but you go ahead. Enjoy your friends, I don't want to impose."

"Not an imposition. It's an invitation. And it's always there. But if you're against being around people, I'll make sure there's a spare piece for you in the fridge. Come get it after we leave. I won't tell," he added in a loud whisper as he reached the door.

Her smile lit something within him, and it zinged something down his left leg as he reached for the screen door, entering the kitchen again. "Okay, who wants pie?"

CHAPTER 8

PICKING UP ROCKS WAS the worst thing Talia had ever done, and she'd had a decent chunk of miserable chores as kids.

This beat them all.

It was easy enough to do, but wandering the fields up and down over and over again just to get rocks had to be a form of torture the government had considered inhumane and done away with. She had rocks of all sizes in her bucket, and she wanted to dump them all back onto the ground. Caleb, her foreman of sorts for the day, had told her which sorts of rocks could stay and which had to go. Most of the time, she wouldn't have to dig at all and could just pick up a rock and toss it in. Other times, the rocks were large enough and stuck out enough that she had to pry them out with her fingers.

Texas was dry and flat, and there was no other way to describe it, which meant working the rocks out was annoying in the extreme.

She had a trowel in the strange holster of sorts she'd been given, along with gloves and a little baby rake, but she had so far refused to use it.

Why in the world hadn't someone invented a machine for this?

She reached the edge of the field, as marked by the fence, and stopped, shaking her head. "Five," she muttered, counting the number of passes she had made. She turned to her left, took one measured step forward, then turned to face the field and began to walk again.

Torture. No other word for it.

Still, it was better than sitting in her room at the homestead doing nothing. At least she was guaranteed a time limit so she could attend her first session of group therapy before lunch. She'd briefly met the other ladies yesterday when they'd come in from their chores and tasks, but they'd hurried to head into Lost Creek, and she had opted to stay at the homestead, intending to call it an early night.

That hadn't happened, as she had sat by the fireplace she'd been so fascinated by and then moved out to the porch to stare at the night sky, but she didn't regret that, either. The stars had been incredible, unlike anything she had ever seen. If it was as clear tonight, she fully intended to put shoes on and walk out to really see them, maybe even lay on the ground to look up at them.

And then there had been Ryan.

She had been awkward and embarrassed, feeling like an intruder in someone else's home, but Ryan had immediately put her at ease. His jokes needed work, but they had made her smile, which was kind of a big deal. He had to be used to having guests roaming in and out of the homestead, but it had meant a lot that he had gone out of his way to say hi.

And true to his word, he had saved a piece of pie for her, which had tasted amazing at 11:35, when she went to get it.

She hadn't seen him yet today, but she was curious to see what it was he did on the ranch. This huge ranch that seemed never ending and was way more impressive than she'd thought when she arrived. She was so far from the homestead house out in this field that she'd never make it back without getting lost, and the fact that this place was that large baffled her. She was the only one on rock duty today, which might have been a hazing ritual, but she had signed up for irrigation maintenance for the afternoon, which no one else had picked.

There might have been a reason for that, but Talia didn't know enough to say no.

Ryan was in charge of the ranch part, she knew that much, but what did all that mean?

She'd heard some of the conversation at the dinner the night before, mostly about rodeo, but she didn't know what any of it meant or who the other men had been. None of this was any of her business, but she was curious just the same.

"How you doing, Talia?" Caleb called, riding up on his horse, grinning like she was doing something amusing.

"Great!" She held up a thumb, but made a face.

She could hear his laughter as he neared her, and he thumbed back his hat just enough that his face was clearer. "Yeah, this isn't anybody's favorite chore. Except for one lady a few months back who was really OCD. This was her happy place, and the fields just have not been the same since she left."

"Maybe she should be hired on," Talia suggested blandly, swinging her bucket beside her. "Might solve your problems."

"Don't think I haven't suggested that," he told her with another laugh. "How's it coming?"

Talia exhaled and looked around the land. "I've just started my sixth pass. I think I figured out which rocks need to go. Can I ask you a question, though?"

He nodded once. "'Course."

"Why am I doing this?" she asked point blank, one hand going to the base of her neck.

"Because chores build character and give structure," he recited like a well-practiced parent. "Daily satisfaction with your work does a lot for your mind."

Talia fought a smile. "Yeah, I get the idea behind the chores, and I fully support that. I meant, why am I clearing rocks from a field? Why is anybody clearing rocks from a field?"

Caleb stared at her for a second, then threw back his head on a loud laugh. "Sorry, ma'am, I'm so used to guests complaining about working at the ranch before they're used to it that I don't even think about it anymore." He cleared his throat and pointed to his left, Talia's right, to the area she hadn't gotten to yet. "So you see how about twenty yards away, there's some decent-sized rocks?"

"Uh-huh, and plenty of little ones." She shielded her eyes, looking more closely. "It makes the ground a little . . . unsightly, but is that the problem?"

"Not unless we're having a photoshoot," Caleb retorted with a chuckle. "No, the issue is that our horses or cattle can turn an ankle on those, and while that sounds minor to you or me, the ankles on horses and cattle aren't as easily healed. It can be pretty bad, so we tend to make sure every pasture gets a turn getting cleared. Then there are the fields for planting, where the rocks cause other issues, so . . . Basically, however you look at it, rocks on the ranch are bad."

Talia nodded in thought, then peered up at him. "Gotcha. Makes sense, and suddenly, I don't hate this with quite the same passion."

Caleb gave her a surprised look. "Seriously?"

"It still sucks," Talia assured him without hesitation. "Not my preferred hobby of choice, but it doesn't seem like a hazing ritual now."

"You thought a retreat for broken hearts based out of a

ranch would engage in hazing?" he asked flatly, expression unreadable.

Talia had known the man for all of three hours, but she took a chance. "Yep."

Caleb stared, then he snorted a soft laugh, his face erupting into a smile. "Yeah, you're right, we do. It's not this, though, and we only do it to the ones who are in a good head space. We're not messing anyone up. Usually, it happens before you go home, though, not new arrivals. I think Jessica leaves next week, and she's doing good. Once I get the OK from the boss, we'll set her up. You'll see."

"Jessica is the one with the dark, curly hair?" Talia asked, twirling her finger in an imitation of the tight curls on the woman in question. "Fantastic green eyes? Dimple?"

"Think so," came the unconcerned reply. "When I see her, the hair is pulled back, and she's mad at me for giving her a bad chore. But she always gets it done, and gets it done well."

Talia smiled at the praise, which was probably the best it got from this hardworking rancher. "What's the hazing ritual? Something traditional?"

"Nope, varies from person to person and depending on the season." Caleb chuckled as he rested his wrists on his saddle horn. "Boy, I can't wait to see what we cook up for you, Talia."

"Good headspace, remember?" She pointed a finger at him, then shook it. "Not yet. Still broken, okay?"

His smile turned surprisingly gentle. "Hey, I know. But I got you smiling, didn't I?"

He had a point there.

"Come on, I'll give you a ride back to the homestead." He held out a hand to help her up.

Talia blinked at it. "Uh, what about the field?"

"My kid loves clearing rocks," Caleb assured her, "and

my wife just texted me that he's driving her up the wall, so they'll be out here within the hour. Come on."

She looked at the horse uncertainly. "That's not a banana bike, Caleb. No second seat. How's that supposed to work?"

"Simple. You get on, and we ride." He shrugged, his hand steady. "I'm driving, you just have to hold on. Now hurry up, or I'm going to lose feeling in my hand."

"I cannot believe I'm doing this . . ." Talia muttered, setting down her bucket and closing the distance between them to take his hand. "Okay, so on the count of three or . . .?"

Before she could finish the thought, the burly man had pulled her up and had her straddling the saddle just behind of him. "Right, ever ridden a horse before?"

Still out of breath, Talia shook her head. "Not even once."

"Great. Just don't scream. They hate that." He clicked his tongue, and the horse moved beneath them, starting toward the gate of the pasture.

Her nerves faded fairly quickly, the skill of Caleb matching perfectly with the nature of the horse, and while they weren't doing a wild gallop like she saw in the movies, they moved pretty fast. The wind blew across her face with a refreshing edge that was exhilarating, and she wondered what it would feel like to be on the horse alone, to feel the power of the animal she rode propelling her forward to whatever destination she had in mind, or to no destination in particular. To feel the complete freedom of the ride, fully embracing the wide-open land and sky. To let her mind be wiped clear of what bogged it down in the place she left behind . . .

This was magical.

She exhaled roughly, trying to find thought in the midst of her epiphany. "So it doesn't bother the horse to have double the weight?" she asked Caleb over the sound of hooves.

"You think you double me?" She could feel him laugh

more than hear it. "You're a lightweight, Talia, so no, it doesn't bother him."

She hadn't thought of that, and it made her laugh when she *did* think about it. What was more, she could learn how to ride while she was here, and maybe by the end of her time, she would be able to take rides to clear her head and find herself.

Would Kellie take that as a goal she wanted to get out of her time here?

Caleb reined the horse in when they reached the barn, the homestead house within easy walking distance. "You good from here?"

"Yep," Talia answered, eyeing the ground and the distance it was from her position in the saddle. "Now if I could figure out getting down without breaking something..."

"Here, I've got it."

She glanced up to see Ryan coming toward them, black T-shirt tucked into his jeans, well-worn cowboy hat atop his head, stripping off work gloves. "Where did you come from?"

He grinned up at her, shoving his gloves in a back pocket of his jeans. "Texas, ma'am."

Caleb groaned behind her. "You sure you want to get off here, Miss Talia?"

Ryan ignored him and held up his hands, his fingers beckoning. "Come on. Easy peasy."

Talia looked at his hands uncertainly. "Am I supposed to take your hands or...?"

Ryan laughed, the sound somehow holding the same soft twang his voice had. "Here, I'll come closer. Put your hands on my shoulders, okay?"

"Okay..." She leaned over and did so, her hands flexing against the surprising amount of muscle there, considering how trim he was.

"Ready?" he asked, his voice low and warm, rippling down her spine despite the heat of the day.

She nodded, more out of instinct than answer.

Ryan's hands went to the tops of her hips, his fingers hooking into her belt loops. Before she could even register that sensation, he had lifted her off the horse and settled her safely on the ground, giving her the same feeling of breathless exhilaration she'd had riding moments before.

"Oof," she muttered as she tried to find the ability to swallow.

"What?" he said at once, stooping to look her over. "You okay?"

Talia hastily nodded, jitters suddenly running up and down her arms and legs. "Yep. Totally great. First time on a horse."

Ryan made a clicking noise in his cheek. "Yeah, that's a doozy. It gets easier."

"Great." She pinched the fabric of his shirt between her fingers, finally swallowing, then froze, realizing her hands still sat on his shoulders. She tugged them away and backed up two steps, hitting Caleb's horse as she did so. "Sorry. Awkward."

"Yeah, he is, but he'll grow out of it," Caleb chuckled above her. "I'm heading out to the west pasture to check the new fence. You good, boss?"

"Yep," Ryan answered, tapping the bridge of his hat, his eyes still on Talia.

She twisted her lips, the toe of her left foot digging in the dirt. "Good morning."

"Hey." He grinned quickly. "Practically afternoon now, isn't it? I've been up since five."

"Sounds like a personal problem." She bit down on her tongue, wishing the words back with a wince. "Sorry, I bite..."

He shrugged easily. "Doesn't bother me, no apology needed. Ranch life starts early. It doesn't even register that everybody else doesn't. You headed up to the house?"

Talia nodded. "First group therapy session. Care to give me some pointers?"

"Can't, I'm afraid. Kells doesn't let outsiders in." He tilted his head. "Can I walk you?"

"Sure, yeah." She turned and started in that direction, Ryan falling into step beside her. "I'm not really a touchy-feely person," she admitted as almost another apology. "This might all blow up."

"Well, that happens," Ryan told her, not seeming concerned. "Just try not to actually blow up the house, I'm kind of fond of it."

Talia snorted softly, shaking her head. "Again with those jokes, Ryan. Gotta work on those."

"What do you call this? I'm trying to practice!" He laughed again, then sighed. "Don't worry about it—the session. Kells is great at what she does, and nobody gets a push they can't handle."

"I've heard that." At his curious look, she explained, "My cousin's wife knows someone who was here once. That's how I found out about it. They thought it would be the perfect solution to get me unstuck from my life, but I don't know." She looked over at him in hesitation. "Maybe don't tell your sister that?"

He shook his head slowly. "Not a peep. And I'm pretty sure you don't have to spill your secrets in the first five minutes."

Talia exhaled heavily, her eyes falling down to the gravel beneath her feet. "It's not that, I don't really have secrets. It's more being open with strangers, you know?"

"Sure do." He didn't say anything for a moment, then asked, "Why not practice with me?"

"What?" She laughed in surprise, her eyes flying over to him. "I thought your sister was the therapist."

His crooked grin reappeared and made her chest tighten.

"She is, but you said there's no secrets. Just a thing with strangers. So, start with me. It won't go anywhere, and might warm you up before facing the group."

If she had been in Chicago, Talia would have told him off for being nosy and interfering. She'd have shut down and ignored him, probably striding into the house in a temper or something. But being here was different, had a more genuine feel to it, and Ryan was . . .

Well, he was comfortable. He didn't have a mean bone in his body, as far as she could tell, and his idea didn't seem like such a bad one.

She bit her lip slightly, then nodded. "Okay. Um . . . I'm Talia James, I'm from Chicago, and . . . my son died last year."

Ryan winced audibly beside her. "Oh, shoot, I am so sorry. I shouldn't have pushed you to say anything, I'm an idiot."

"It's okay," Talia told him softly, managing a sad smile. "You didn't know, and I need to work on saying this." She took a deep breath, then let it out quickly. "I'm stuck because Austin was all I had. I got pregnant my senior year of high school, and decided to keep the baby, which didn't interest his dad, so it was just us. Had Austin three weeks after graduation, and that's all I've done ever since."

"Wow." Ryan cleared his throat, looking away. "I can't even imagine." He waited a beat. "Well, I'm Ryan Prosper, born and raised here, and I used to do rodeo."

"What are you doing?" Talia asked, stopping to look at him. "You don't have to share anything."

He raised a brow at her. "Do, too. Group therapy is group sharing. Part of that is listening, I think. So if we're gonna have this trust between us, we gotta walk the two-way street. You share, I listen; I share, you listen. Builds trust, or something."

"Or something," Talia murmured, her smile turning less sad. "Okay. So you used to do rodeo. Why'd you stop?"

Ryan started walking again, Talia joining him, their trip to the house almost done. "Bad injury. Super bad. All recovered now, but bad enough that I can't compete anymore. Huh."

Talia caught that. "Huh?" she repeated. "Huh, what?"

"I think that's the first time I've said I used to do rodeo. Everybody else already knew that, so I never had to use the past tense before." He glanced over at her, something different in his eyes. "Thanks, Talia."

The use of her name in his particular voice and twang was magical, way more than when he said "ma'am," and sounded way more like a country song she would have on repeat and never get sick of.

"You're welcome, I guess," she replied, uncertain how she felt about something that momentous happening while he had offered to help her. But she knew she liked it.

A lot, potentially.

"Ryan, can you teach me to ride a horse?" she asked before she lost her nerve. "Like, really ride?"

"Of course, yeah." He nodded repeatedly. "What are you doing this afternoon?"

"I'm on the irrigation team."

"Perfect," he told her as they reached the porch, leaning on the post while she started up the stairs. "That doesn't take long, so I'll switch to riding out with y'all and take you over to the stables when it's done."

Talia turned on the second step, sliding her hands into her back pockets. "It doesn't have to be today, I know you've got to be super busy."

He shrugged again, his crooked grin in place. "Might as well be today, and I'm not *that* busy. It's fine." He squinted as his grin spread. "Maybe we'll even get some whistle practice in."

He was ridiculously cute when he was teasing like this,

and a little, baby dimple appeared on his left cheek when he smiled this big, visible even amongst his dark scruff. He probably hadn't shaved this morning, but it couldn't be more than a day old. She'd always been a fan of scruff, though she hadn't thought about that in years. Hadn't dated for years.

And she would *not* be thinking about dating Ryan Prosper while she was here to work on her grief over Austin.

Besides, he might just be a nice guy, and not interested in her at all. It could be part of his job to take care of her like this.

"Okay," she murmured, smiling almost shyly. Her eyes traced his shoulders, and her smile faded. "Oh my gosh, Ryan, I got dirt all over your shoulders from picking up rocks. I am so sorry."

He glanced at his shoulders, then made a face. "Nah, it's fine. Dirt happens on a ranch. It's good for me, kinda like our own special moisturizer."

Talia burst out laughing and clapped a hand over her mouth.

Ryan's almost painfully blue eyes fixed on her then, his smile softening. "You've got a beautiful laugh, Talia. Hope that Kellie can help you do it more." He tipped the brim of his hat in her direction, then pushed off the post and turned to head back toward the barn.

She watched him go, then went up the rest of the stairs and headed into the house.

Kellie sat in a chair by the stone fireplace, two of the other ladies settling into other places in the room, where the furniture had been turned into a large circle.

"Hi, Talia," Kellie greeted with a little wave. "Feel free to wash up if you like. We'll get started as soon as Amanda, Jill, and Cassie get back."

Talia nodded, moving into the community bathroom to wash her hands and splash some water on her face. There was no sense in taking a full shower and changing, not when she had more work to do this afternoon. And with everyone else being involved in ranch chores and work, there really wasn't a reason to do so.

The furniture might get dirty, but if that's what Kellie wanted them to do . . .

She looked in the mirror, taking a moment to prepare herself. She could trust Kellie, she knew that much, and the other guests had done this before. It would be fine. She wouldn't have to talk about everything right now—no one expected her to talk about Austin in depth today.

A single step, Kellie's wall had read.

She could do a single step.

Exhaling slowly, Talia left the bathroom and returned to the great room, taking a seat next to Jessica with a slight smile. "Hi."

"Hey there," Jessica returned with a smile. As if she could see into Talia's nerves, she patted her knee. "Don't worry, this isn't all that bad."

Talia nodded once and looked over at Kellie as the other three they had been waiting for came in and took their seats.

"Okay, guys, welcome back." Kellie flicked her pen in Talia's direction. "Has everyone had a chance to meet Talia?"

Nods bobbed around, and smiles met Talia's gaze as she looked at them.

"Talia, can you do a quick intro?" Kellie asked her, her natural warmth on full display. "Whatever you feel like telling us is fine."

"Okay . . ." Talia cleared her throat and straightened in her chair. "My name's Talia, and I'm from Chicago. I . . . don't really have a career, and um . . ." For some reason, she couldn't understand, her eyes began to water, her throat constricting. "And I've been broken since my son died in November."

CHAPTER 9

"What are you doing, Ryan?"

Ryan didn't even glance up from his work. "I know it's been a while, Lars, but as a reminder: I'm saddling a horse."

Lars didn't find that funny, which wasn't a surprise. "Why? That's not your horse, even I can see that."

"Because one of our guests wants to learn to ride," Ryan replied, tightening the cinch across the belly of Moonshine, who was their easiest-mannered mare and the best one for beginners. "I offered to teach her this afternoon when she's finished with the irrigation team."

"Can't one of your ranch hands do that?" Lars asked, coming to lean against the stable. "I wanted to take a look at the ranch with you, see if I can offer some advice, that sort of thing."

Ryan shook his head, looking up at his old friend. "Sorry, pal, I can't hand off this one. The guests that come here . . . well, they have a hard time opening up about a lot of things, and if one of them asks me specifically to help . . ." He shrugged his shoulder and patted Moonshine fondly. "I'm not going to minimize that trust by not valuing their request. I may not have letters after my name like Kellie does, but this is my ranch now, too. It's not this or that, it's this *and* that."

Lars raised his brows at the explanation, smiling slightly. "Nice to see you grasping your sister's vision. I shouldn't have asked, sorry."

"It's fine." Ryan jerked his head toward the stable entrance. "Feel free to saddle up and ride out yourself, though. Free rein, take a look. Caleb's the most senior worker, probably knows the place better than I do, so he'll talk your ear off."

"Great." Lars looked at Ryan more closely. "How are you doing, Ryan? I mean, really? Getting the news that you were done had to be tough."

He was not about to have this conversation with Lars, not standing in the stables prepping to teach Talia to ride, and not when he hadn't talked to the guy in a year-and-a-half. Anyone with a passion for rodeo would feel the way Ryan had felt, like his knees had been cut out from beneath him and every day felt off. He should be training and planning his season, but instead, he was looking at the numbers for new machinery for the ranch and brokering deals for heads of cattle.

Part of him wanted to get rid of the ranch life permanently to completely avoid anything related to his former life, but he wasn't that determined.

Plus, he had Kellie to think about, and she needed him here.

"Well, it was no picnic, that's for sure," he told Lars with a more carefree edge than he felt. "But I could be flippin' pancakes down at the diner, so this is better than that." He clicked his tongue at Moonshine and tugged on the reins, one hand near the bit in her mouth as he started to lead her out to the pen. "Have fun looking around."

Lars called out something about heading into Lost Creek that night to meet the guys, but Ryan didn't pay attention enough to hear it. He didn't want an invitation, didn't want to relive the glory days, considering the rest of them were at the height of their rodeo careers. He didn't want to be the awkward footnote of the conversation. They were already meeting up tomorrow to talk business and their efforts to improve attendance this year, and he couldn't bring himself to go constant rodeo mode when he'd only be watching.

At least being a pickup man would have him on a horse in the ring, even if he wasn't the one competing.

He exhaled slowly, shaking his head as he began to walk Moonshine around the pen while they waited for Talia. It could all get to be too much, his hanging around the rodeo so much after so long away. It had become a habit to avoid everything, and he'd gotten used to it. Comfortable with it. Settled in it.

It was easy to not miss doing rodeo if he was never around it.

Would being thrust back into it make everything worse?

He was going to have to start talking to Kellie professionally sometime soon if he didn't shape up. She'd offered more than once, but he'd always brushed it off, saying something about not needing to talk to his sister about his feelings. But the truth was he'd been feeling a nagging prickle in a corner of his gut that knew Kellie would be able to help him.

He'd just gotten really good at ignoring that thing.

Why, then, was he going to help out in Lost Creek?

The roaring of an ATV brought his head up from his moody moseying. He recognized Tim, one of their employees, as the driver, slim frame and tiger-striped helmet making him easily identifiable, but who could be behind him was another question entirely. Any of the guests at the ranch could drive the ATVs, once they had proven they could do so safely, and it wasn't uncommon to see them roaring about the land here and there, either for work or for a bit of fun.

But seeing just one of them wasn't common, and seeing arms around the driver was even more uncommon.

Ryan squinted, wondering if one of the guests had needed something, struggled with the work, or had bad news. Most of the guests left their phones in their bedrooms while out on the ranch for work, though it wasn't a requirement to do so. The only regulations with phones were to protect the privacy of fellow guests and to not have their phone during sessions or structured group activities. Daily work didn't count.

He hadn't had to deal with any of the guests having a breakdown yet, though his sister had told him it was entirely possible. He'd walked through some basic training for dealing with that, but the prospect of suddenly facing one made him want to do a refresher.

"Listen," he recited under his breath. "Breathe. Validate. Encourage. And . . . what is that other step? Shoot . . ."

His apprehension faded when the ATV pulled over to him, and the helmet on the rider came off, a mass of dark brown waves tied back suddenly coming to view, with an accompanying pair of amber eyes.

Flashes of the image of them driving up with her arms locked around Tim replayed in his mind, and he burned in irritation. It was a good thing he didn't carry a gun while he was working, or Tim would have been run off like his sister's ex.

It usually took more for Ryan's temper to erupt, but not this time.

Not with her.

"Hi!" Talia called, waving a little.

He pressed his tongue to his front teeth and held a hand up in greeting, moving to the fence and leaning on it, Moonshine's reins in one hand.

"We finished early, boss," Tim hollered over the sound of the ATV. "She did great! Gonna keep the crew on their toes when we really get going out there!"

Ryan nodded, keeping his mouth pointedly closed to keep the curse words in check.

"I'm gonna check the berry fields," Tim announced, jerking his thumb toward them. "It's getting close to that time."

"Right," Ryan muttered, though his employee wouldn't hear it. But he held his hand up again to signal his acknowledgement, and Tim took off with an annoying rev of the ATV.

Idiot.

Talia came toward him, bobbling the helmet almost playfully in her hands. "What am I supposed to do with this? Any ideas?"

Ryan smiled and pointed to the fence post nearby. "Just pop it on the top there. Tim can get it when he comes back to park."

"I can put it away," Talia insisted. "I don't mind."

"Tim can put it away," he countered, cocking his head. "For making you hold onto him like that."

Her eyes widened as she slowly set the helmet on the post. "He didn't . . . I was just trying to hold on, and it seemed like a motorcycle, so . . ." She gave him a strange look. "Why do you care if I was holding onto Tim, anyway?"

Feeling a bit like a rat in a trap, he gestured a shrug of sorts with his hands. "I'm protective. You know, ranch rules."

It was true, in a way. Not *the* truth, not *his* truth, but it was a true statement.

"What, hanging onto a guy on an ATV ride?" Talia asked, not buying it. "Is Tim even single?"

"Don't know, don't care." Ryan smiled almost smugly at her spirit. "Not supposed to have any sort of relationships or feelings between guests and ranch workers. Even the appearance of feelings is a no-go. Not that I'm suggesting you do, but Tim knows the rules, and I gotta keep him in line."

Talia pursed her lips a little, which was probably the most distracting thing he'd ever seen. "So this isn't a dude ranch."

"Correct."

"Hmm." She looked along the fence as though in thought. "I knew I should have gone to that other place in Oklahoma."

Ryan groaned loudly. "You did *not* just wish to be in that Okie-dokie-hokey wannabe up north instead of the United State of Texas. How dare you!" He chuckled and slapped the fence rail. "Hop on over, we'll get started."

She placed a foot on the fence rail and rounded the top of the fence far more easily than most of the guests that came through the ranch. "You know, in Chicago, it's generally frowned upon to hop fences."

"Uh-huh." He eyed her and the fence pointedly. "You did that too well for me to buy that."

Talia slipped her hands into the back pockets of her jeans again, shrugging without actually shrugging. "Didn't say I listened, did I?"

He chuckled, nodding in approval. "Very nice. Talia, I'd like you to meet Moonshine. Moonshine, this is Talia."

As though they had scripted it, Moonshine nickered and tossed her head, nudging a little forward.

Talia didn't look particularly afraid, but it was clear she wasn't exactly comfortable, either. "Hi."

"Kinda hard to meet her over there. Come on." He ran a

hand over Moonshine's mane gently. "She's a love, I promise. Enjoys having her nose scratched."

"Who doesn't?" Talia closed the distance between them and brought the tips of her fingers to Moonshine's muzzle.

Ryan smiled, trying not to laugh. "Little bit higher up. Between the eyes and the nostrils. Long strokes."

Talia listened to him, her fingers tracing up and down softly, and he watched as a small smile appeared on her lips.

Moonshine seemed to appreciate the gesture, too, dipping her head farther into Talia's touch.

"Hey there, Moonshine," Talia murmured, flattening her palm against the horse to rub rather than scratch. "You're not going to turn crazy and buck me off, right? You got me, right? Just between us girls..."

Moonshine blinked, then sighed a deep, contented sound that had Ryan staring at the horse in surprise.

"What?" Talia asked. "Did I bore her?"

"No..." Ryan told her, smiling and patting Moonshine's neck fondly. "No, that's a good sound. She's relaxed and comfortable." He gave Talia a look, still smiling. "She doesn't do that for me."

Talia brightened, her smile wide, crinkling her eyes. "Really?" she all but squealed.

Ryan nodded his confirmation. "Really. I think we're ready. Come here, I'll help you up."

They moved to the stirrups, and Ryan tapped them with a finger. "Left foot here. Reach it up."

"I'm not *that* short, Ryan," she grumbled, hoisting her foot up into the stirrup.

"Not what I was saying," he informed her without any hint of remorse. "Now I'm not going to just shove you up there, okay? We're all about teaching you. So. Grab the saddle horn, make sure you have it in a good grip."

"Saddle horn," Talia recited. "That's the handle-looking thing?"

Ryan dropped his head, chuckling. "Yes, it's the handle-looking thing."

"Got it."

He glanced up, nodding in approval. "Okay, now this is the odd part. I need you to hop and scootch yourself over a little bit, just until you're practically facing forward, hips open to the horse, okay? And grip the saddle with your other hand."

"You want me to what?" She looked at him like he was insane, though her hand gripped the saddle as he instructed.

Ryan exhaled shortly. "Okay. Excuse the hand placement." He put his hands on her hips and applied pressure to indicate how she should move. "Hop, okay? And scootch. Like turning scootch."

She hesitantly did so, and he did his best to adjust her position to turn more fully toward the horse. When she had come enough, his fingers tapped the front of her hips as a sort of signal.

"'Kay," he began, "I'm leaving my hands here for safety. Now you push up. Use the foot in the stirrup to bring you up to level. When you get there . . ."

"Can I just get there first?" she all but barked, her fingers gripping the saddle and pommel with obvious anxiety.

He shook his head. "Sorry, no. If you stop there, you won't make it all the way over. Push off, or jump, if you like, and swing your leg up and over. The momentum helps."

Talia shook her head softly. "Oh, boy. Something's really wrong with me."

"What? Why?" Ryan asked, trying to look over and around her shoulder at her.

She flicked her eyes to him, but nothing else. "I'm about to get on an animal that could easily squash me, and I'm doing it at a ranch in Texas where snakes probably gather, and getting on this animal requires some agility and flexibility that I may not possess, and if I don't do this right, I could completely fall off the other side, hit the ground, break something, and be embarrassed for the rest of my life that I did all of that in front of a really attractive cowboy who talks like a country song, and I'm just not sure I can handle that. Best of all, I asked for this, so yeah, something's wrong with me."

Ryan blinked, wondering if he should have undergone training for nervous rambling, but clinging to the admission that she found him attractive. "Right," he said slowly. "That's why my hands are still here, to keep all of that from happening." He cleared his throat. "And remember that this animal is your new BFF Moonshine. She wouldn't squash you."

Talia nodded once, which meant she heard him, even if she didn't really listen. "Okay. Can you give me the instructions again?"

"Yep." He adjusted his hold on her and scooted in. "Jump. Swing. Settle."

"That's not what you said before."

"I just summarized."

"Couldn't have done that first?"

"Didn't think of it first. Ready?"

Her chin bobbed. "Ready."

Nothing happened, and Ryan grinned, but bit it back. "'Kay, darlin', you're running this show, so you're the one who's gotta do something."

"Sorry," she mumbled. Again, she adjusted her grip on the pommel and saddle, then, holding her breath, she jumped from the ground, pushing up with her left foot in the stirrup, and swung her other leg up and over the saddle, settling perfectly into it.

Ryan grinned fully up at her, laughing once. "Nicely done, Talia! Moonshine didn't even twitch, and it's rare for a first-timer mounting to not get a walk-off."

"I have no idea what you just said," Talia replied, sounding breathless. Then she beamed down at him. "But it sounded amazing."

He laughed again and patted her thigh. "It was." Then he realized what he'd done, and moved his hand down to Moonshine's back. "Sorry. Don't tell Kells."

"Why?" Talia asked pointedly. "Because she'll think you're making a play for me?"

He snorted once. "Well, I'm not the one who said someone is really attractive and speaks like a country song, so if anybody is getting in trouble . . ."

"Let's just pretend I said you're a cuckoo clock and that Chicago dogs are awful, okay?" she said quickly, her cheeks coloring.

"Why would we pretend that?" he laughed.

"Because that's nonsense, not true, and Chicago dogs are king. So it would be less believable." She cleared her throat and held up the reins. "How do I hold these?"

Ryan cleared his throat as well, smiling to himself, and moved the reins. "Well, you don't need to today, since I'll lead, but when you get there, beginner's hold is the English style. So stick your pinky in there, then palm up . . . and let the reins fall across there . . . Uh-huh, and grip."

"Huh." Talia showed him her hold on the reins, making a face. "Not bad, right?"

He allowed himself to smile up at her, genuinely and freely. "Not bad at all, Talia James. Let's get you riding." He moved to the front of the horse and gently took the reins, clicking softly. "Come on, girl."

With a snuffle, Moonshine began to move, shuffling at

first, but then settling into something actually resembling a comfortable walk.

"Group therapy was interesting today," Talia announced as they began to round the pen.

Ryan glanced back at her. "Good. I'm glad. But you don't have to tell me, you know. Privacy and all that. I'm . . . I'm happy to listen if you want to talk, but my sister's the therapist, not me."

Talia rolled her eyes a little, smiling. "Yeah, I know, but it's like . . . Well, I think we're kind of friends now, so I might need to talk things out."

He returned her smile, nodding more to himself than to her. "Yeah. I think we're friends. Not just kind of."

Her amber eyes crinkled again. "Okay. So group therapy. Awkward moments at first, but once we hit our groove, it felt more like a bunch of gals just talking. All that was missing was wine."

The image made Ryan laugh to himself. "Yeah, Kellie doesn't let alcohol on the premises when there's guests. Masking the truth of emotions and enabling unhealthy coping mechanisms, or something."

"Wow," Talia said, sounding impressed. "You know the speech by heart."

"I know it," he said with a slightly superior look up at her, "because when I was recuperating at her house and feeling the worst, I wanted a drink, and I heard the speech myself."

There was a beat of silence, where Ryan wanted to kick himself for saying anything about it, and normally, he would have been a heck of a lot more guarded about it, but he didn't have any guards with Talia.

It would have been unsettling if he hadn't felt comfortable with her.

"From your rodeo injury?" Talia asked softly.

Relief washed over him, and he swallowed as he thought about the phrasing of his next words. "Yep. I was a bull rider, which basically means I ride a really pissed-off bull and try to stay on for eight seconds. I was having the ride of my life when he tossed me sooner than I thought on a run, and I lost my grip and my balance, and flew off. He . . . well, he got me good, which happens sometimes. It just so happened that this time, it affected some internal organs."

"Holy crap . . ."

Ryan smiled slightly, though relief and humor weren't anywhere near this conversation. "I was in the hospital for a while, rested up a bit once they took out that kidney, and the fractures started healing, and then as soon as I could, I was back to figuring out a training schedule and working on my strength. But in my follow-up doctor appointments, the doc was adamant that I don't ride again competitively. Something about being too high a risk now that I only had one working kidney. And . . . my family agreed."

Talia didn't say anything, which should have put him off, but he could also feel some confusion there. As if she wanted to ask a question, but didn't know how.

"Rodeo isn't like a fair coming into town," he tried to explain, keeping his attention on the dirt ahead of his boots. "It's a career, and a way of life. It was my job, and I worked hard for it. I was good at it. I made a decent living, was living my dream. We might be a crazy bunch of cowboys, but we're professional athletes, sure as the guys who play baseball and basketball and hockey and all the other sports are. Except now, just like that, I was a has-been." He exhaled slowly, then cleared his throat. "So yeah, I wanted a drink. Didn't have a drinking problem, still don't, but I knew alcohol could numb the pain I was feeling, and I'm not talking about the injury."

"I get that," Talia murmured from the horse. "I tried that,

even. It just burns a lot, gives you a roaring headache in the morning, and doesn't do a darn thing. Just so you know."

He glanced over his shoulder at her again, smiling in sympathy. "Took one for the team, did you?"

Her throat bobbed, and she nodded. "Something like that. When Austin died . . ." She paused, exhaling slowly.

Ryan stopped the horse at once and moved to put his hand over hers. "Hey."

She looked at him quickly, her eyes wide and already swimming.

"You don't have to do this," he told her softly, squeezing her hand. "This isn't one of those 'I share, you listen; you share, I listen' exercises. I don't expect a thing in return when I tell you something, okay? This isn't part of the ranch experience—I'm just here. I'm your friend, Talia. If you wanna talk, we can talk. If you want to just shut up and ride the horse, we can do that. I'm not gonna pretend that losing my career compares with losing your boy, and you don't need to, either. Got me?"

She swallowed again, a tear escaping and moving down her cheek quickly. "Gotcha." She sighed and wiped the tear away, sniffling. "So weird, I haven't really cried about that in a while. I mean, I did when I was talking to my cousins, but they're like brothers."

Pleased she was at least coherent, Ryan smiled and nodded, moving back to lead Moonshine around. "Cousins in Chicago?"

"Yep, that's where we're all from." There was a beat, and then she exhaled roughly. "My cousins are Grizz and Clint McCarthy."

Ryan frowned at that. "The one rings a bell, but can't say I know the other. Should I?"

The laughter that erupted from Talia contained a

thousand rainbows and the magic of Christmas in its sound—no music in the world ever reaching this thing of beauty.

It was all he could do to continue putting one foot in front of the other while she laughed.

"Ryan Prosper, you have just made my day, my week, and maybe even this entire year, who knows? We're only in March." She all but cackled, tossing her gorgeous hair back to laugh more. "Oh, it hurts to laugh. I can't breathe. Oh my gosh. Oh, bless, that was amazing."

"Was it?" He made a face, pretending to consider that. "Good. Congrats to me. What exactly was amazing?"

Talia beamed, laughter still making her more radiant than he'd thought any woman could be. "My cousins are professional athletes, Ryan. Grizz plays baseball, and Clint plays hockey. Both pros, both can be watched on TV, and I've spent so long thinking everybody in the world knew their names that I had no idea that on a ranch in Texas, their names mean nothing, and I am beside myself."

Ryan winced dramatically. "Not gonna offend a whole family of intimidating Chicago dwellers with my ignorance?"

She shook her head, giggling again. "Not even close! I've been trying to take some air out of their big heads for ages, and even Austin used to say they were getting too famous. He was their biggest fan, though. We never missed a game for either of them. For his birthday this year, we were going to . . ." She paused, her eyes widening.

"Talia," Ryan murmured, something in his chest cracking a little. "Don't."

"No, it's fine . . ." She wet her lips, her brow furrowing. "That's what made me stop. I just mentioned him so casually, and his birthday, too . . . It takes the breath out of me, but I don't think I'm gonna cry." She looked at him with some concern. "Does that seem normal?"

He nodded slowly, smiling gently. "I think so. He doesn't need to be tucked up on a shelf in your head, only to be brought down when you need a cry. You can tell me anything you want about Austin—good, bad, or ugly, and with smiles or tears—and it'll be fine by me."

Talia smiled back, exhaling. "For Austin's birthday, we were going to go to Clint's game in St. Louis and sit front row, right up against the glass. He'd always wanted to. Said it would be as good as being on the ice, right up in the action, and then he could heckle the other team while wearing his uncle's jersey."

"Sounds like my kind of kid," Ryan said with a nod of approval. "Something to be said for being in the thick of things. Never was very good at heckling, though. Look at me, I'm a twig, nothing intimidating."

"You're not a twig," Talia laughed. "I've felt those shoulders, remember? You've got muscle, all right, Ryan Prosper. You just hide it better than most."

He frowned, squinting up at her. "Is that good or bad?"

Her smile was something bordering on tender, and it made his stomach and one kidney flip. "It's good. It's really good." She gave an almost laugh, and then made a show of looking at Moonshine. "But I tell you what, this pony ride of yours is boring both of us, so how about we take it up a notch?"

Ryan rubbed at the back of his neck. "All right, if you say so, but don't say I didn't warn you."

CHAPTER 10

RYAN PROSPER WAS THE most distracting man Talia had ever met.

Also, he had the cutest butt she had ever seen, which may have been part of why he was distracting, but she hadn't noticed that their first few meetings. Riding on top of a horse for a while as he led the animal around gave her a pretty good view, though, and now it was impossible to *not* notice.

Whatever he was, the man was no twig, and if his shoulders could be as secretly muscled as they were...

Whew. Was it always this hot in Texas?

"How are you settling in?"

Talia jumped, turning away from the window of her room, where she had been blatantly checking out Ryan as he and a few of the ranch hands worked with a new horse in the pen. "What? Settling? Fine."

Kellie narrowed her eyes, smiling slightly as she leaned against the doorway. "I'm glad to hear it. Want to tell me what's caught your eye out there?"

She was *not* about to tell her current therapist that she

was checking out her brother, so she managed a quick swallow. "They're training a new horse out there. Ryan . . . well, he was teaching me to ride earlier today, and I thought I was getting pretty good until I saw this." She pointed out the window, relieved that her cheeks were beginning to cool in the face of a not-quite lie.

"You can't compare your day one with a calm horse to a wild horse no one's really ridden yet," Kellie assured her, coming into the room. "You can make huge strides for you compared to where you started, and still not be close to a bronc rider at the rodeo."

Talia frowned slightly. "Bronc rider. Is that like a bull rider, but with a horse?"

"Almost exactly." Kellie folded her arms, smiling. "You know rodeo?"

"Not even a little bit," Talia told her without shame. "Ryan told me he used to ride bulls, and something about eight seconds."

Kellie nodded, her smile turning sad. "Yeah, the longest eight seconds on the planet start when the clock does. Ryan doesn't ride anymore."

Talia raised a brow. "Uh, is this where I tell you that he's actually riding the wild horse right now? And it's doing crazy things?"

"He's doing *what*?" Kellie was to the window in a heartbeat, pushing the sheer curtain aside and glaring out at the pen.

They both watched as the horse reared, Ryan still on its back, Talia gasping while Kellie remained silent. Ryan had it all perfectly managed, of course, never losing his cool or his balance, and didn't even flinch when the horse bucked a few moments later.

He was astonishingly good with the horse, and you didn't have to know horses to see that.

"I'll kill him," Kellie growled under her breath. Without a word, she turned from the room and stormed out.

"Uh-oh . . ." Talia murmured, smiling a little as she watched Kellie march from the house toward the barn. Ryan had gotten off the horse and was letting it run around the pen freely, which it seemed more than happy to do.

All of the men looked at Kellie as she approached, and if the flying state of her hands was anything to go by, she was speaking her mind without filter or volume control. Ryan approached the fence and leaned his arms over the top of it casually, as though his sister wanted to discuss dinner. He didn't smile, which was probably smart, and while Talia couldn't see Kellie's face, she could see Ryan's reactions. He was calm all throughout, clearly listening to whatever she was saying, and when he spoke, it was without any sort of temper or excitement.

It was revealing, and yet Talia already knew that Ryan listened well. That he was calm. That he cared.

He wasn't like any other man she'd ever met, and it had been so long since she'd even gone out . . .

Evidently satisfied with the conversation, Kellie turned from the fence and walked back to the house, her expression satisfied, but hardly happy.

Ryan, on the other hand, broke his somber demeanor and grinned at the retreating form of his sister, which made Talia laugh. As though he heard the sound, his eyes flicked to the window where Talia stood.

There was no way he could see her, was there?

He tipped the brim of his cowboy hat, his smile spreading further still.

Talia's heart skipped, as though it was waking her up from years of sleeping, and helplessly, she waved a little, still not convinced he could see her.

Ryan slapped the fence once, then pushed off and returned to the horse.

After taking a minute to appreciate that particular view, Talia left her room and headed out to the great room. Kellie was curled up on a couch, reading over some notes, her irritation with her brother apparently forgotten now. She glanced up when Talia came in, and her smile reappeared. "Hey there. Sorry, I got distracted after yelling at my brother. I was gonna ask you if you wanted to chat."

Talia cocked her head. "We had a session this morning before chores. Am I supposed to have more than one?"

Kellie's smile spread. "Perks of living with a therapist, even for a short time, is informal sessions can happen at any time and as often as you like." She sat up and patted the couch cushion on the other side of her. "Come sit."

Feeling that same sense of knowing Kellie for years, Talia returned her smile and sat where she indicated, tucking her feet beneath her.

"How was your first day working the ranch?" Kellie asked gently.

"Tough," Talia laughed, rubbing a hand along the denim on her lower legs. "I haven't even done the hard jobs yet, and I already know I'll be sore tomorrow!"

"You seem to be handling it well," Kellie said with a laugh. "I know it's not for everyone . . ."

Talia shook her head quickly. "Oh, no, I loved it."

Kellie blinked at that. "You did? Seriously?"

"Seriously . . ." Talia's smile turned hesitant. "Was I not supposed to? It's just . . . I haven't done anything that productive in a long, long time. It felt so good."

"Good." Kellie reached out and put a hand on Talia's arm, squeezing gently. "That's what I hope for when guests are here. It's not about the chores themselves, it's about hard work and finding a little victory in accomplishing them. Being forced to step outside of yourself can do a world of good, and sometimes, we need help doing that."

Talia eyed this woman in thought. There was more than just professional training and experience at work here. Her ranch was so specific, so original a setup, and with such particular aims, that there had to be something personal driving her.

Did Kellie have her own broken heart? Even if it had healed now, there had to be moments . . .

"Why did you start this place?" Talia asked quietly, hoping Kellie could feel enough of the same sense of kinship between them to trust her. "I'm not trying to pry, I just . . . I just want to know."

Kellie's smile was sad and strained, which shifted her appearance into something that made Talia hurt. "I was married once. To the love of my life, I thought. We wanted kids, and we were trying . . . After my third miscarriage, he left. Turned out, he'd been having an affair since the first miscarriage."

Talia hissed in sudden, sympathetic agony and covered Kellie's hand with hers.

"I had moved away from the ranch when I married him," Kellie murmured, feeling cold beneath Talia's hand, "so when I was suddenly single and brokenhearted, I came back to my roots. Threw myself into ranch work, and wound up buying out my parents. I realized that working that way helped me process my grief, and I also realized my ex had thrown himself into an affair for his grief. Not exactly a good coping mechanism there, but it made me see that we don't always know how to process what breaks us, or how to keep going while living with it. So I started this place."

Kellie paused, looking all around her, smiling softly. "It

was so strange. I knew all of these things from my education and training, all of these tools and principles, and I couldn't find comfort in any of it. I needed more. So . . . I made more."

Talia took a deep breath, letting it out slowly. "I told you in my application that I lost Austin," she said in an almost raw tone. "I told you I got pregnant in high school. I decided to keep my baby, and raise him on my own. I got a job as soon as I could after having him, and I had my mom for free childcare. I worked my tail off to provide for us both, and devoted my entire life to that boy. I never went to college, but I worked the best jobs I could find that gave me time to be with him while making a living. Everything became about giving my son the best life I could. And then he was gone . . ."

Kellie turned her hand on the couch to bring her palm flush with Talia's, lacing their fingers. "It's okay."

"He was my whole world," Talia whispered, the words choking her as she said them. "Everything I had done from the day I found out I was pregnant was for him. Absolutely everything. I think a lot of moms lose themselves in their children, raising them and caring for them, and everything all of that means, but I didn't have anything else in my life. I lost the light in my life when I lost my son, and in a way, I lost my own life as well."

"Grief is a powerful expression of love, Talia," Kellie told her, turning more fully toward her. "We can't lessen the pain of our losses without diminishing the joy we felt while we had them. That's why we need to find ways to turn reminders of our loss to reminders of our joy. It won't stop the tears, but maybe it will help us smile through them."

"I've shut all of that out," Talia admitted, staring off at nothing. "I don't go into his room, but I haven't changed anything about it. His shoes are still by the front door. His backpack is still on the floor in the laundry room because he could never remember to hang it up. I drive the long way to the grocery store because I don't want to drive by his school. I dodge calls from the mom of his best friend because I don't want to know what else we have in common when our sons were the reason we met. I'm . . . I'm avoiding everything, but I'm still stuck in it."

She trailed off, the ticking of a clock somewhere the only sound in the room. Her pulse began to match it, the sound of both pounding in her ears.

"You're in a grief cycle," Kellie murmured, though her voice sounded muffled somehow. "Over and over and over. It becomes like an addiction, or a habit. Feeling miserable, or feeling nothing, becomes our normal, our comfort zone, even though there is nothing comfortable about it. Feeling something got us into this mess, so not feeling something is bliss."

"Yes." Talia nodded with a hard swallow. "But life still goes on. I don't know how, but for everyone else, it does."

Kellie shifted closer. "Talia, do you want *your* life to go on?"

"I don't know." Tears welled and began to fall, rolling almost painfully slow down her cheeks. "I want to feel alive, but I don't want to move away from him."

"He's not one place in time. Not one memory, not one day, not one pair of shoes. Moving forward isn't moving away from him, because he is with you."

"But the more time goes on, the more time passes since my boy was here with me." Talia sniffed loudly, congestion beginning to well in her sinuses, her forehead, and the base of her throat. "I . . . can't remember how it sounded when he slept. I checked on him every night for seven-and-a-half years. I heard that noise every night for 2,749 days, and now I can't remember it. I need time to freeze so I don't lose any more of him."

Kellie tugged on Talia's hand and pulled her into a tight embrace, her hands rubbing soothing circles on her back. "Oh, sweetie... I'm sorry you're going through this. I won't say I'm sorry you hurt so much, and now you know why."

Talia nodded against her. "I loved him so much. So much it broke me."

"Broken things mend, Talia," Kellie said softly, the pressure of her hug almost painful, but comforting in its way. "They won't be the same, but they do mend."

"It hurts to be happy without him," Talia whimpered. "To laugh. To smile. I feel so guilty every time."

Kellie sat back, her hands on Talia's arms. "I'm gonna be a straight shooter, okay? You are clinging to your grief and that guilt instead of your memories of him. I didn't know Austin, but I'm pretty sure he'd hate that you feel shame in finding joy when he's not here."

Talia wiped at the tears on her face. "He would. He'd find a way to make me laugh any time I was sad or grumpy, and it worked every time." She laughed a watery laugh, swallowing. "One time, he made me a silly mask out of paper plates to hold up in place of my sad face, and we started singing songs with that mask until we were crying from laughing."

"Now that's the kind of story I want to hear." Kellie squeezed her arms, then released them. "I'm going to give you a challenge. I want you to take that journal I gave you when you arrived, and I want you to write about how you can find joy even though Austin is gone, and how you can include him in those moments so you won't feel that guilt." Kellie stooped a little, trying to meet Talia's eyes. "Will you do that?"

Sniffling again, Talia nodded. "Yeah. Might take me a few days to figure anything out."

Kellie smiled at that. "Why do you think this retreat isn't a one-week course? You have all the time you need. And while you're at it, start thinking about that guilt you have. You don't have to work it out yet, but when you're ready, write about that, too."

"Okay." Talia sighed, sniffing once. "Sorry, I seem to be crying more here than I have in the last month."

"That's actually great," Kellie insisted, scooting back to lean on the arm of the couch. "It tells me you aren't beyond feeling anything, you're just out of practice." She looked at her watch, then back at Talia, sighing. "They'll be starting dinner soon. I think Amanda and Jill have it tonight. It's usually pretty good when they do. But they are loud, so if you want some quiet . . ."

Talia was up before she could finish the thought, and headed to her room. "Thanks for the heads up!"

Kellie's laughter followed her out, and Talia inhaled deeply, then exhaled slowly as she returned to her room. She hadn't felt this raw in weeks, yet she wasn't distraught about it.

That had to be progress . . .

She pulled open the drawer of her nightstand, which held the Broken Hearts Ranch journal she'd been given at her intake interview. Technically, she was supposed to have written a welcome entry about her thoughts and goals for while she was here, but she hadn't done that yet. There was something very first day of school about that, and she hadn't felt up to engaging in that way.

This new challenge for her journal, however, might be worth trying.

After all, she wanted nothing more than to be able to find joy in her new normal and not have the crushing guilt that pressed on her as she lay in bed at night trying to sleep.

Austin would have wanted her happy. When he had been alive, he had made it his mission to always cheer her up, if not lighten the mood entirely, and remembering that only made her feel more guilty. She wanted to live in a way he would like, but she didn't want to give the impression that she could live a full life without him.

She was positive there could only be a half-life at best.

But how did she tell Kellie that?

Or Ryan.

Twisting her lips to one side, Talia started writing, jotting down her feelings on finding moments of happiness in her life as it really was, not how she wished it was. On what Austin would do to make her happy if he were here. On why being happy made her feel choked by guilt.

The entry morphed into an entirely new one, no topic in sight and full rambling mode, spilling everything in her head and her heart onto the page. She didn't care if it made sense, and the more she wrote, the worse her handwriting became. Her emotions rose and fell, swirled in forty directions, and waved back and forth between several of them. She ignored the knocks announcing dinner, frantically continuing this stream of emotional upheaval through her pen as though it were some stroke of genius she would lose if she stopped.

Page after page filled with thoughts, with feelings, with questions she couldn't answer, with memories and details about Austin she hadn't thought of in years. The more she wrote, the closer he felt, and that alone would have been enough to keep her going.

Except it was agony. An addictive, possessive sort of agony mixed with ecstasy, knowing that the rising emotions and memories would not bring her boy back, nor would it end with his laughter echoing in the room.

But with the pain also came the sensation of a dam bursting, and a rushing of something pent up within her that had been building and applying pressure to her weakest spots.

It wasn't a good feeling, exactly.

It was more exfoliating.

Could a heart and soul be exfoliated?

They had to be. She had never felt so scrubbed raw in her life, didn't know it was a possibility, and by the time her cramping hand registered in her mind, her entire body seemed to echo with the same aching.

She dropped her pen, staring at the words on the page, oddly feeling as though they had been written by someone else, despite the proof in her own handwriting and the pulsing muscles in her palm. But the sensation of complete exposure, leaving her without any of the walls she had spent so long building up, was too real to have been anyone else writing what she had.

Had her entire body been covered in scabs, and had they all torn off at once, she could not have felt more tender across her skin and all the way through her.

Laughter from the dining room and kitchen areas met her ears, and she looked up at the sound, a faint part of her brain telling her to go and join them.

But the last thing she needed was other healing women. Her experience was too fresh to share with them, didn't quite fit with her recovery in an obvious way. She couldn't have anyone jump to conclusions, or grow overly supportive, or tell her about their experience with something similar.

She needed a walk, and she needed to talk things out with someone who wouldn't judge her any way the conversation went.

Pushing up off her bed, Talia slipped into some shoes and all but tiptoed out of her room, remembering a back door to the ranch house that didn't pass the kitchen. It would have made things much easier the night of that dinner with Ryan's friends, but it would be more useful to her now.

She needed to find Ryan, and she didn't know where his house was. She knew that none of the ranch employees live at the house, and that Ryan stuck with that rule, despite the place being his family's, but she had neglected to ask where he lived.

Hadn't thought she'd need that information up until now.

But she could start with the barn. It was safe enough.

It was almost sunset, which cast the land of the ranch with a deep golden color that she instantly loved. An almost rosy hue rested on every surface, giving her the desire to stand in place and breathe in the smell of hay, grass, dirt, and something sweet she couldn't decipher. She wanted to stand on top of the rise she'd seen while looking at the irrigation that afternoon and look out on as much of the land as she could see, then sigh with the beauty of it.

Not that she had time to do any of that right now. She needed to get to Ryan fast, get all of this off her chest, and then go back to the homestead house before anyone noticed she was gone. She hadn't heard of there being any punishments or consequences for things like that, but she didn't want to get a reputation.

Sneaking out of the main house to see a guy was risky enough.

Yikes.

"Don't think about it, don't think about it, don't even think about it," she muttered to herself as she hurried toward the barn.

The sound of a car ignition sent her into a full sprint around the front of the barn, and a dark, mud-splattered pickup truck sat at the fence, the bed half-full with various pieces of equipment, rope, and buckets. It could belong to any one of the ranch workers she had met since arriving, but she secretly crossed her fingers it would be the one she needed.

She slowed her step to approach, fingers rubbing together at her sides.

The driver's side door opened, and Ryan stepped out, brow furrowed, no hat in sight. It was kind of adorable, how matted his hair was without the hat on it, and she wanted to ruffle it to see what he'd look like then. Not in any kind of romantic sense, just . . . just to see.

He was attractive enough as it was.

"Talia? You okay?" he asked, starting toward her.

She nodded hastily, forcing a smile. "Yeah. I just wanted to catch you before you went back to your place, wherever that is on the ranch."

A corner of Ryan's mouth lifted to one side, though he still looked concerned. "It's just down that road a bit. You probably passed it during irrigation."

"Nice." Truth be told, she couldn't remember anything about that, and it wasn't the point.

"So what's up?" He gave her a searching look, which felt scorching in her oversensitive state.

Perfect.

She exhaled quickly. "When Austin died, I shut down. Completely. Didn't let myself feel anything I didn't have to. Went through my days like a robot, nothing coming in and nothing going out. Strictly survival, because staying in bed just wasn't my style."

Ryan's brows slowly rose, and he folded his arms loosely. "Talia, you don't have to tell me any of this. You don't have to do this to yourself."

"Yes, I do," she ground out. "I need to talk about it, I need to feel it. And I can't do that yet with them, but I think I can with you."

"Okay," he said softly. He nodded in encouragement. "I'm listening."

She swallowed hard, suddenly terrified of losing the strength she'd felt surging through her all the way here and in her journal exercise. "I tried drinking," she hissed through tightly clenched teeth. "But it just soured everything. I guess I should be grateful for that, but all I wanted was to be as numb as humanly possible. My baby was gone, and my heart went with him. Did you know you can live without a heart?"

Ryan didn't answer, and blessedly, didn't touch her, either. She might have crumpled into a million pieces if he had, and then she would recoil back into the version of herself she had been earlier. How she knew that, she couldn't say, but it was true.

"And I have been like that," she went on, "from the day I buried him." She shakily took in a breath, then released it with as much control as possible. "Until today. Until now."

"What changed?" Ryan murmured with the gentleness of a breeze.

"Nothing. I just took a step, and that step exploded into the wall of emotion I had forgotten existed." She met his eyes, her hands becoming fists at her sides. "I hurt everywhere right now, and I haven't really hurt in months. I haven't felt *anything* in months, but now I feel everything. It's the most terrifying feeling I've ever had, because I didn't want this, and now I can't stop it."

Without a word, Ryan calmly closed the distance between them, wrapping his arms around her and pulling her into a hug that felt like home. He didn't say anything, but the slow motions of his hands on her back rippled warm against her, soothed an ache that had begun to spread.

"I think this is me getting unstuck," she whispered as she brought her curled fingers to her face, "but why does it hurt so much?"

"I don't know," Ryan admitted, his voice rumbling in his chest. "That's the damndest part, isn't it?"

She nodded against him, sighing heavily. "I need to find joy somehow. Instead of walking in my grief, I need to find some joy."

"Okay." He waited a beat, then asked, "How?"

This was the question she had been avoiding, but an idea came to her fully framed, somehow exactly where she needed when she needed it. "I want to live for Austin instead of without him. I'm not sure what it means yet, but I want . . . If Austin were on a ranch like this, he would want to find a creek or a pond and skip rocks on it first."

"I can teach you how to skip rocks," Ryan said at once. "We've got a reservoir on our land—it'd be easy enough."

Talia lifted her head, pulling back to look at Ryan. "Really? You can?"

"Of course." He brushed a bit of hair from her brow, and her skin tingled with the contact. "Anytime you want, we can do that. And anything else you think Austin would have done here or wanted to do here, I will make it happen."

She almost cried again, and those tears would have nothing to do with grief. "But what about your work?"

"Hey." He gave her a crooked smile and brushed his thumb along her cheek. "I'm the boss here, remember? I tell other people what to do, not the other way around."

"What about Kellie?" Talia ventured, finally smiling as a warmth started in her toes.

Ryan made a face. "Okay, she can tell me what to do, but that's it." He grinned as Talia snickered, then sobered a little. "But seriously, Talia, I'll do anything to help you. Anything I can."

"Thank you," she whispered, feeling the tears beginning to well again. She laughed through them. "Where have all the guys like you been when I needed them?"

"Only one guy like me, ma'am," Ryan drawled easily,

sliding his hands from her back and leaving fire in their wake as they grazed her sides. "And that's all you need."

"So it seems." She smiled almost shyly and hooked her index fingers into the pockets of her jeans. "I'm making jam tomorrow, so I probably won't see you . . . unless we could do another horse-riding lesson before dinner?"

Ryan's smile returned in its glory. "You got it. I'll plan a trip to the reservoir for us, say Saturday?"

Talia nodded with a jolt of energy she hadn't been prepared for. "Okay, if you're sure you can spare the time."

"I'm sure," he said simply. "I've got Lost Creek Rodeo meetings in the morning, and the afternoon is all yours."

"I'll take it," she quipped without thinking. Then she blushed, and her throat tightened. "I better get back. Thanks, Ryan." She turned on her heel and started toward the house, her arms swinging hastily at her sides.

"Talia?"

She whirled, much too fast for any act of calmness. "Hmm?"

His crooked grin was still there, and he didn't need the cowboy hat to be the most charming sight she'd ever seen. "Good night."

For a woman used to not feeling things, she sure felt near to combusting with that sweetness. "Good night," she responded, not sure the words would actually reach him with how softly she'd said them.

She couldn't bear to watch, though, so she turned back around and continued up to the house, adamantly refusing to look over her shoulder at him.

But there was a strange burning spot on her back, if that told her anything at all.

CHAPTER 11

RYAN WAS NO EXPERT in meetings and the format they should follow, but he thought that a meeting of the rodeo committee a few days before said rodeo ought to be a recap of what was going to happen, and not a brainstorming session.

That was not happening here, and it was taking forever. If this meeting wasn't over in the next five minutes, Ryan would plan a revolt and throw a circus instead of the rodeo.

How many times could they talk about the same thing and get nothing done? No, he wasn't going to be a barrelman purely to entertain the crowd. No, the Original Six were not going to do an exhibition in team roping. No, they were not going to play bull pinball. No, they would not pose for pictures with fans.

They wanted to *compete*, not be a sideshow.

Well, the others wanted to compete. Ryan just wanted to watch without having to wave at the crowd.

They had all come to this meeting to prove they were willing to help, and had reported on the other rodeo athletes they had convinced to come in, only to discover they had been practically the only ones working in any real capacity to improve numbers. The rodeo committee was made up of people who had been around the block more than once, and ought to have been contributing a lot more than copping out by hinging on big local names. Committee chair Tom Hauser looked as though he had been spoon-fed pig slop as his entire committee pitched ideas that solely focused on the Original Six and no workable actions.

Ryan felt for the guy. No one had been a bigger proponent for rodeo in Lost Creek than this guy as long as he'd known him, and here his plan had all but fallen apart due to either laziness or ignorance.

But this was Lost Creek. Ignorance in the rodeo world shouldn't have existed here.

Glancing around the room, Ryan wasn't the only one getting irritated with this. Lars and Reid, in particular, were looking sour.

"Look, fellas . . ." Lars broke in, effectively cutting off Bill Perkins's blustering about a Lost Creek bake sale. "We're not gonna headline your entire rodeo series. We've got careers to factor in and opportunities we're already slated for. We're here to help, but we're not the show. This hokey-dokey, ho-hum you're doing might work for a single rodeo, but it's not going to help turn any kind of profit for your rodeo, or your town."

Reid straightened up, clearing his throat. "I'll second that. We've been calling every rider and roper worth beans to join us out here, and y'all haven't matched that."

"Now wait just a minute," a beefy man Ryan didn't know interjected, red in the face and almost strangled by his bolo tie.

"Can it, Harry," Tom barked in a tone that wouldn't get any pushback. "I was thinking the same thing, but in less polite terms. Please go on, Reid."

Reid nodded, momentarily turning into the spitting

image of his big-wig lawyer dad. "With all the years this town has hosted a rodeo, there's got to be some regulars who are in your network. Have you pushed them to help out? Have you reached out for more sponsors, put out feelers for new ones? What about vendors? What about Mrs. Harland, for Pete's sake? She's not even on your list, and no rodeo should exist without that stamp." He shook his head, seeming a little hesitant, then exhaled. "If you're gonna do this, you gotta actually do it. Actually put in your time, and make that time worth putting in. You're not gonna get those minutes back, so make them count. Otherwise, what are any of us doing here? I know I've got other options, and so do the other guys."

Nods ran up and down the table, and Ryan wished like hell he could nod with them.

He had other work to do, but no other circuits.

Ever.

Lost Creek might be his only shot at ever being part of rodeo again. Up until this moment, he hadn't known he wanted anything to do with it if he wasn't riding, but he realized he did.

And badly, too.

"We're willing to help," Ryan added, leaning forward and resting his elbows on the table, giving each man on the committee a hard look. "Otherwise, we wouldn't be here. But we aren't the committee, you are. And don't be looking at Tom, because I know for a fact that he's been making calls himself when he should be able to delegate that stuff. If you don't wake up, neither will Lost Creek, and that's the truth."

There was a beat of silence, then Tom cleared his throat. "Any questions? No? Great. Thanks for coming in, guys. We'll be in touch." He was up and moving to shake their hands before any of them had managed to so much as get to their feet.

The man looked like he needed a stiff drink.

Ryan was at the end of the line of guys and rose, shaking Tom's hand firmly. "We'll figure this out, Tom," he assured him. "It shouldn't all rest on you."

Tom gave him a flat smile. "Any chance I could bribe you into joining the committee and then staging a coup to take over?"

There was nothing to do but return the smile, as laughing in his face would be rude. "Nope. I've got my own problems."

"Yeah." Tom exhaled, shaking his hand again. He moved to the door and held it open, an unspoken invitation for the guys to get outta dodge.

None of them needed a verbal invitation.

They filed out quietly, moving down the hall and heading down the stairs of Town Hall before anyone said a word.

"Nice speech, Chute Boss," Eric said, nudging Reid with an elbow.

Reid shook his head in disgust. "I sounded like my dad, and I could hear it as it was coming out." He made a face and looked around. "Got any soap I can use to wash my mouth out?"

They chuckled, knowing that Reid and his dad had issues, though none of them really knew what they were. They'd googled the guy once, his law firm in DC being pretty high on the food chain, but Reid was determined to go his own path. Maybe that was the issue.

But it could be anything, really. Family was complicated.

Not Ryan's—his parents had retired to San Antonio when Kellie had bought them out, and they'd been the team parents for the Six in their college years—but he was lucky. He knew it, too.

"That was a bust," Ford grunted, jerking his thumb back up toward the conference room. "Was it supposed to be worth something?"

Ryan sighed heavily. "Probably. Sorry, guys, I may have brought you out here for nothing."

"Not nothing to get the gang back together," West told him without sentimentality. "And I think we'd all have made it out here at least once this season."

"Yeah, but I thought . . ." Ryan trailed off, shaking his head. "I thought we were part of the solution, not the only solution."

Eric grunted once. "That's what happens when you get non-rodeo people planning a rodeo. Seriously, Ryan, why not just take over?"

Ryan glanced behind him as they moved out of the building. "Because I have a life?"

"You do?" Reid looked shocked. "How did I miss that?"

Ford reached forward and flicked the back of Reid's hat, which tipped it down to nearly cover his eyes. "Hey," Ford grunted.

"Thanks, Ford," Ryan said, scowling at Reid. "I'm trying to pick up the pieces of my family's ranch and make it profitable again, remember? We don't make much off of Kellie's guests, so the ranch needs to provide for itself. It's better than it was, but it's still a mess."

"Here's an idea," Ford mused, his low voice clearer than normal, his brow furrowed. "What if we park ourselves on the land instead of just around Lost Creek? We pay you rent for the space, and additional for whatever amenities we wind up using. And board for the horses, of course. Standard rates."

Ryan was shaking his head before his friend finished. "Absolutely not, no way. You guys can park yourselves on the land for free, I'm not charging you for that."

Westin nudged him hard. "Who said charging? Dude, we'd pay to park anywhere in Lost Creek, and personally, I'd rather pay you than some local I don't know. And you'd better believe I'll pay you to board my horse, just like I would anyone."

"Does it count as staying there if you sleep under your truck, West?" Eric asked with a teasing grin.

"Shut up," West barked, not looking at him, which made them all laugh. It was one of West's more unusual habits, sleeping under his truck, but it oddly suited his Old West kind of nature.

Still, nothing about this conversation made Ryan comfortable. Good, honest hospitality didn't usually include payment, and he'd been raised well.

Some of his ancestors were bound to roll in their graves about this one. But he couldn't afford to fight the idea for long, considering what it could bring in for them.

"Look," Lars told him with a laugh, "let's grab a bite, then head back to the ranch and talk about this. It's a good idea, and a great deal for you. Given what I saw on my drive through the place, I've got some thoughts for building up your profits."

Ryan shook his head again, this time smiling to himself. "Can't, sorry, boys. I've got plans."

The beat of silence was unnerving and telling, but he refused to look at them all.

"Plans," West repeated. "As in . . . socially?"

"It's not that unheard of," Ryan grumbled, finding himself feeling both snarky and amused by the disbelief of his friends.

Reid barked a hard laugh. "Who can count the number of girlfriends Ryan had during college?"

Now Ryan did look around, and saw every hand up. "Guys . . ."

"Zero," Eric announced, as though it was helpful. "And what about in all the professional years we've known him?"

"Big fat goose egg," Ford added, smiling in his subtle way.

If he was jumping on this bandwagon, things were getting out of hand.

Before Ryan could change the subject, Lars jumped in the mess. "Wait, is this the same gal you taught to ride the other day instead of showing me the ranch?"

"He did WHAT?" West gaped openly. "Ryan, you hate doing riding lessons!"

Ryan scoffed loudly, which probably wouldn't fool anyone. "I do not."

Reid held up a finger. "Uh, pretty sure I have emails from our days at SHCC where you refused to do the community riding lessons."

The others all nodded their agreement.

"Well," he told them by way of explanation, "when you have to learn how to ride all over again, it's a little different, and it changes things."

Not a single one of them bought it.

Ford folded his arms, making him look even more imposing. "Probably helps that this woman is gorgeous, right?"

Ryan nodded immediately and without shame. "Doesn't hurt, yeah." He grinned as though he had something to do with that, making them all explode with more laughter.

"Right, so tonight, let's round 'em up together and do a bonfire or something. We always think better around a fire." Lars gave Ryan a scolding look. "Think you can wrap up your wooing by dark?"

"I make no promises," Ryan shot back. "But feel free to use the fire pit by my house all night if you want to wait up."

Eric applauded, grinning outright. "No hint of denying his ulterior motives. Nicely done."

"I think they're his primary motives," Reid said out of the corner of his mouth. "Don't tell."

Ryan debated between glaring, scowling, and being outright condescending, but settled for adding a touch of coolness to his gaze and tone. "For your information, it isn't my primary motive, not that it matters. I offered to help her with something she thinks will be helpful to her, and I mean to do it right."

Westin blinked at that. "Wait, she's one of your sister's guests?"

"So many red flags," Eric muttered, shaking his head.

"Knock it off, will ya?" Ryan snapped. "I told you what I'm doing, and I don't need y'all turning that into some opportunity to make a move like I'm the bad guy in some B-list movie. I'll have you know I cleared this with Kells, and she's real pleased I offered."

Ford frowned a little. "Yeah, but does she know you think that gal is gorgeous?"

Ryan felt his temper fade and a little amusement come back in before looking at his friend with gratitude. "Not exactly. I'm saving that conversation for a better time. Like Christmas."

"Sounds about right." Lars shook his head. "Okay, maybe we see you tonight, maybe we don't. But she can come, too, if you want. You're both invited. So is Kellie, and really, any of the guests. It's a bonfire, not a committee."

"I love being invited to my own fire pit," Ryan grumbled. "But I'll let Kells know. The ladies might like it—a few are leaving next week. Can I go now?" He gestured to his truck, against the bumper of which he had been leaning for the past few minutes. "Like I said, plans . . ."

"Fine," Lars told him, rolling his eyes, while Ford and the others just waved him away. "Have fun, and don't do anything Reid might do."

"Hey!" Reid squawked.

Ryan rolled his eyes. "Bye, Dad." He pushed off the bumper and rounded the front of his truck to open the driver's side door. "Don't make trouble."

"Who, us?" Eric gasped in mock offense.

Pointing a finger directly at him, Ryan glowered. "Don't put videos of my ranch on your YouTube channel."

"You're leaving for a few hours. Not days." Westin chuckled and waved him off. "Get outta here."

Ryan didn't need any further encouragement. He jumped in the truck, turned it on, and was backing out of his parking spot all within fifteen seconds. There was no looking in his rearview mirror as he pulled away, and zero hesitation about what he was about to do.

He'd been looking forward to it all week.

It wasn't as though he hadn't seen Talia regularly since she'd come to his truck the other day. In fact, he had seen her every single day since then for riding lessons, though they wound up talking more often than not. Riding, but talking. For a guy not used to much social interaction, that was quite the change.

But talking with Talia hadn't felt like being social for the sake of it.

It felt like . . . summer.

Not the hot, nasty sweat and grit mingled with humidity that could choke a man, but a clear summer morning before the heat was unbearable, and the warmth of the sun just felt like perfection. Or the evening after a hot day, when everything began to cool, and you could watch the sunset with a peaceful contentment that was hard to find anywhere else. Or the nostalgia of sitting around a fire and staring into the hypnotizing flames . . .

Being with Talia felt like the best sort of losing his mind he'd ever heard of, and he wasn't sure what to do about it.

Her sense of humor kept him laughing, and her quick responses kept him on his toes. She kept her emotions close to the vest, but so did he, and it worked for them. Just being together was enough.

For him, at least. Talia had never given him an impression that he was annoying her, and she had allowed him to hold her while she cried . . .

That had been a powerful moment for him. Impulse had taken over, concern for her outweighing any sense or control. Taking her in his arms had been the most natural thing in the world, and it scared him to death.

Because he loved it.

Not her tears, but being the one to comfort her. The one she turned to. The one she trusted enough. And the feel of her in his arms went beyond any description.

Sometimes, they talked about Austin, and those moments were really something. For a woman who didn't show much emotion outwardly, she'd sure loved that boy fiercely. He'd never seen someone with so perfect a broken heart, and it was taking everything he had not to ask his sister to go the extra mile for this woman.

Kellie would have smacked him upside the head. She *always* went the extra mile, and he knew that. But extra miles for everybody weren't really extra miles, were they? Talia was special, and he wanted everything for her.

He would have sold his soul to get Austin back for her.

Heck, he was teaching her to skip rocks today so she could feel closer to the boy. They'd been practicing whistling, which she was terrible at, and he thought Austin would have loved that. He'd take her out riding away from the pen this week, and he thought maybe she'd find Austin there, too.

Whatever would make Talia happy, Ryan would do.

But would anything be enough without Austin?

It was a question that terrified him. She didn't cry every time they talked about him, but the air changed when they did. Became heavier, and cooler.

Maybe today would change that.

He clicked his tongue in disappointment at himself. It was sounding like he was jealous of her grief over her son, and nothing could be further from the truth. He wanted her happy, and happy with him, but he wanted her to have her son, too. There was no competition. There was not one without the other.

There was just continuing grief and a budding hope in the middle of it.

If he could make it so that Austin was somehow always there in their minds, in a happy way, then maybe there wouldn't be second thoughts about any of it. More outings like this, as though he were taking them both to the reservoir. More times where she didn't have to choose between Ryan and the memory of Austin. Where she could have them both.

Dang. He needed to talk to his sister. This was taking complicated to a whole new level.

He liked Talia. He liked her a lot. And heaven help him, he'd like her a heck of a lot more if he spent more time with her, which he planned on doing. At what point was he allowed to be more selfish and less altruistic?

Not that he minded being altruistic... Not with her.

But a guy wanted to think seriously about kissing a woman he really liked once in a while.

He tapped the roof of his truck out the window as he turned onto the drive, a habit born from childhood, and exhaled slowly as he rubbed at his chin in thought, his elbow resting on the open window.

He'd spent so much of his time lately thinking about Talia, about what to do for her, how to help her, that he'd forgotten he was supposed to be moping about missing out on the rodeo with all of his friends in town. It had taken over most of his absent thoughts for the last eighteen months or so, and yet he hadn't thought about it even once in at least three days. The feelings hadn't gone away, they'd just been replaced by something of greater interest to him. Something with more promising returns than indulging in regrets.

Something . . . happy. Pleasant. Hopeful.

Real.

That was it. Talia was real. She didn't try to impress, she didn't fake anything, she was a straight shooter, and she smiled without seeming to realize it. If either of them were gamblers, he would have called that her tell, and everything he needed to know would be right there in her smile, depending on the version of it that appeared.

He knew she loved riding Moonshine without her saying a word. He knew she'd enjoyed making jam as part of her ranch tasks. He knew she liked his sister more than she let on. He knew she was cautiously optimistic about her fellow guests. He knew she adored her cousins, and valued their input highly.

And he knew she liked s'mores a lot more than she'd ever admit.

He should invite her to the bonfire after they were done this afternoon. She'd love the opportunity to sit around a fire and laugh in easy company, especially if he could talk Kellie into bringing s'mores stuff.

She could also meet the guys.

Less of a great prospect, but it had to happen at some point. Better she do it when there was no pressure for anyone to pretend to like each other. And if she liked rodeo . . .

He smiled to himself. Talia admitted herself she didn't know anything about rodeo, and he'd have to warn her about bringing the subject up in that company. Maybe he ought to encourage her to watch some videos on YouTube.

Not Eric's channel, but others were good enough.

He blinked as the barn and house came into view, bringing him back to his task at hand. He turned down the road toward the barn and grinned at the sight of Talia leaning against the fence, waiting for him.

All she needed was a hat, and she would have been any cowboy's vision.

She was a vision anyway.

He pulled up and shifted his truck into park. Talia came to the passenger window, leaning her arms on it and giving him a smile. "Hey, cowboy. You know the way to any reservoir around here?"

If she kept talking to him like that, he'd wind up kidnapping her and driving off into the sunset.

He thumbed his hat back, his grin only growing. "I think I could find my way to one. You need a ride?"

"Yes, please." She opened the door and hopped up, smiling more easily than he'd seen her do yet as she shut the door and buckled in. She brushed back her dark hair behind her ears, and turned her amber eyes to him. "Hi."

Feeling as though his lungs might gallop like a wild colt, Ryan managed to keep his smile in place. "Hi. Would it be weird, or too much, to say it's really good to see you?"

Talia's smile could have brightened any sky beyond the sun, and he knew she was pleased. "Nope. Not weird, not too much. It's really good to see you, too."

A lesser man would have kissed her then.

Ryan, however, nodded, his face ready to break from his smile, and shifted the truck into drive. "Glad to hear it. Let's get to rock skipping, shall we?"

CHAPTER 12

TALIA HADN'T FELT THIS ticklish inside since she was seventeen years old.

She'd wound up pregnant from feeling this ticklish, and not thinking clearly when she felt this ticklish. She wasn't going to make that mistake again, no matter how much she'd loved Austin.

Still, it was good to feel something like this again, and Ryan Prosper was definitely a better option than Cory Kilgore had ever been.

Riding in Ryan's truck was a strange kind of torture. She tingled all along her left arm, like a sunburn she could feel coming on, though it seemed to seep into the center of her chest as well. Her fingers itched with the desire to reach out and curl into his where they dangled from the armrest. And she wanted to make him smile.

He had the most dangerous smile she had ever seen.

Which was hilarious, as Ryan was the most approachable, kind, comfortable, charming man she had ever met in her entire life. There wasn't a mean bone in his body, let alone a dangerous one. Oh, sure, he was strong, and probably ripped like crazy, but he wasn't going to send anyone running from the room in fear or by power of intimidation.

She'd been fighting the temptation to watch videos of his rodeo days online, more to keep herself sane than anything else. If she saw Ryan in action, it might turn her into a complete fangirl, and she needed to keep her head somehow. Ryan could be her friend, could be the net that caught her when she fell, could be anything in the world.

Just not the man she loved.

Talia gripped her right knee with her hand, her nails digging in. Where had *that* thought come from? She liked Ryan and was attracted to him, like any other red-blooded woman would have been, but love . . .

That needed to get out of her personal dictionary fast.

"You all right over there?" Ryan asked at exactly the wrong time. "You got quiet."

"Yep," Talia quipped, her voice tight and too high. "Just thinking."

It wasn't a lie. She was thinking.

Sort of.

The truck turned down a faded gravel road and through a brief tunnel of trees. "Hmm," Talia said with a soft laugh. "Tree tunnel."

"A what?" Ryan laughed.

Talia gestured around them. "Tree tunnel. That's what Austin and I always called these."

"So did we." Ryan grinned at her, flipping her stomach over with that crooked tilt that he had perfected so well.

She had to smile back. "Does everyone?"

He shrugged, chuckling. "Probably." He turned the steering wheel, slowing the truck. "All right, we're here."

Talia looked out the windshield at the calm surface of the water, the edges of the reservoir dotted with brush and the occasional tree. A wall of large rocks supported one side, but the rest of the borders were sloped with the natural surroundings around them. On the other side of the rock wall, she could see out onto the ranch land, though the elevation hadn't changed enough for her to call it a vista or anything. Still, it emphasized the size of this place.

And this was no tiny pond here.

"Wow," she said, impressed at seeing such a large body of water in a place where the only water she'd seen had come from the faucet or sat in a trough. "Did you guys do this yourselves?"

"Yep," Ryan confirmed with a nod. "I mean, not me personally, but my grandpa, dad, and uncles did. Ask any of them, they'll say it was the worst summer of their lives."

Talia laughed and got out of the truck, sighing as though she were on the top of a mountain and looking at an incredible view. "It's really something. You'd never know it was man-made."

"It was a pond originally," Ryan explained as he, too, got out and walked over to the water's edge. "They just dug it deeper, took it wider, threw a couple of fish in there for good measure, and we've never had a problem with it since. I mean, every now and then, I gotta check that rock dam, but it's solid." He glanced over at her with that same crooked smile, taking out her left kneecap. "Don't tell my folks, but Kells and I used to come up here after really hard days of working the ranch and go for a dip."

Gasping dramatically, Talia stared at him with wide eyes. "Ryan Prosper, you never! I am shocked at you!" She giggled and made an X over her heart with a finger. "Cross my heart, not a word." She scrunched her face up a little, looking around the ground by her feet. "So what kind of rocks do we need for this? Probably pretty flat . . ."

"Oh, don't worry about that. I brought some with me." He turned to move toward the back of his truck, whistling some absent tune that made her smile.

"You did what?" Talia laughed, running a hand through her hair as she watched him.

Ryan hefted a large bucket out of the truck bed without straining at all and grinned at her as he came back. "Got rocks. Just in case we have to go through a lot while you get the hang of this. I wanted to make sure we have plenty. Save us the time of having to look around for rocks."

"Ugh, looking for rocks." Talia shuddered for effect, making a disgusted face. "Worst chore ever."

"No arguments here." He came over to the water's edge and set the bucket down, muscles in his forearm shifting as he did so.

Talia didn't know forearms were sexy, but suddenly . . .

Ryan tipped the bucket to show her the contents: a bunch of flat, smooth rocks that could fit in the palm of her hand. Tons of them, some cleaner than others, and all clearly picked specifically for today.

How did that happen?

"Alrighty," Ryan began, straightening and grinning at her, rock in hand. "Ever throw a Frisbee?"

"Successfully?" Talia quipped before shaking her head. "Only at Clint's head to get his attention."

Ryan made a soft clicking sound. "Doesn't count. Okay, so what you want to do is keep the rock as flat as you can. That's how the skipping works." He curved his index finger around the edge of the rock, showing her. "Easiest to do it this way. Gets you a nice angle and a good flick that helps with the bounce."

"Uh-huh," Talia said without emotion, not actually comprehending what he was talking about.

He turned slightly, flicking his wrist toward the water without releasing the rock. "Keep it nice and flat," he said again. "Use your finger to kind of spin it as you release. And don't throw the rock."

Talia looked at him in surprise. "Wait, what?"

He flicked a quick smile at her. "Throw your arm and let go off the rock." He looked back at the water, and sent his arm flinging out in front of him, releasing the rock at the farthest point with an impossibly quick flick of his wrist and finger.

Talia watched in amazement as the small rock skipped six times before disappearing beneath the surface of the water. She shook her head, trying not to gape before looking at Ryan with narrowed eyes. "How did you make that look so easy?"

Ryan laughed and picked up another rock. "Luck, princess. Pure luck." He paused, then craned his neck from side to side, considering something. "And a little bit of skill."

"There it is." She snorted to herself, shaking her head. "Princess. What am I, six? And do you see any kind of tiara or twirly dress over here?"

He gave her a surveying look. "Not six. Definitely no tiara, but I wouldn't mind seeing you in a dress and twirling."

Talia's cheeks flamed instantly, and she lowered her eyes, nudging at pebbles with her shoe. "I may be a city girl from Chicago, but I'm no dainty princess."

"Didn't say so, even if you are the size of my pinky finger." He shrugged his shoulders, jabbing his fingers into the pockets of his jeans, which seemed to be his standard stance. "Besides, I'm pretty sure my sister was a princess a few times as kids, and she always managed to whoop me while she was, so I think you could just as easily wear the tiara while in boots and skipping rocks. But if you don't wanna be, pick something else. I'll call you Sam, if it does the trick."

She met his eyes again. "What trick?"

He hesitated, his jaw working like he couldn't decide on the words. "The one where you come to a bonfire on the ranch with me tonight. And maybe come out to Lost Creek with me on Monday night. I wasn't kidding about the dress, though I only want you to twirl if I can spin you myself."

It had never hurt to not smile before, but her cheeks burned fiercely with the impulse she refused to allow. "Are you asking me on a date, Ryan? Two of them?"

He shook his head slowly, and her heart plummeted.

"You're not?" she prodded, a hitch coming completely out of nowhere.

"Just one date," he told her carefully, not smiling, even if his eyes were on fire. "The bonfire doesn't count. I never call it a date when both my sister and Reid Browning are present."

The rush of air that came from her was embarrassing and obvious, but she couldn't help it. Relief had never tasted so sweet, and she beamed at this incredibly attractive, maddening cowboy. "That makes sense. Awkward, am I right?"

He nodded, his lips curving with a dip that caught her breath. "Everything's awkward with Reid. Comes with his personality. So . . . is that a yes?"

"Yeah," Talia told him softly, feeling suddenly shy and a little weak in the knees. "It's a yes."

"Great." His smile spread further for a moment, like the sun peeking out from behind puffy clouds in a blue Texas sky. "Now, my non-princess, would you care to try a rock?"

"Oh, why not?" She moved to the bucket and plucked a smallish, smooth rock from it. She turned to the side, cocking her arm at an angle the way he had, and frowned as she moved her wrist in the flicking motion. "So it should skip? If I do this?"

Ryan laughed and came over to stand behind her. "It's not a remote, hon. Doesn't do what it's told. Try it once, and we'll see what needs to be adjusted."

Talia shook her head, exhaling to herself. "This isn't maddening enough—now you're actually watching me."

"You should be used to that by now, Talia."

Goosebumps ran up and down her arms and legs despite the heat of the day, and she did her best to ignore him, though she could suddenly feel every inch of distance between them. "Watching me ride is not the same thing as watching me throw a rock pathetically," she assured him with as much firmness as she could while burning alive, unsure if she wanted to be right about her subtle accusation or not.

"Just throw the rock."

No easy answers, then. Fine.

Biting the inside of her cheek, Talia did her best to mimic Ryan's throw and released her rock, only for it to plop through the water with a single, deafening sound.

"Hmm." She turned to face Ryan with a quirked brow. "Now what, Coach?"

He was smiling at her, just a little, and she wasn't sure why, but it was insanely cute. He unfolded his arms and gestured for the bucket. "Get another one. We'll work on it."

Talia shrugged and picked another rock from the collection, then moved to face the water. "Okay."

He put his hands on her arms and twisted her a little. "Turn. Feet, too."

She obeyed, matching her lower half with her upper half. "Check."

"Arm, please."

Talia smiled to herself, and held her arm out to the side, rock in her palm.

Ryan took her elbow in one hand and her wrist in the other, his hold on her gentle and ticklish at the same time. "Bend the elbow."

Her arm obeyed, almost going limp with his touch. It

buckled, and would have tucked into her side had he not been putting it into position just away from her body.

"Uh-huh, hold that about here." His hand at her wrist shifted, fingers tapping at the back of her hand. "Loosen your wrist. Bend."

Her wrist obeyed and moved with his every pressure to her hand. "Like that?" she asked, her voice sounding like a pant even to her own ears.

"Yep." He bent her wrist back and forth like it was an exercise to warm her up. "Gotta flick your wrist to get the good spin. Can't do that if it's locked."

Talia swallowed, each press of his fingers against her hand creating a similar sensation in the back of one knee. "Makes sense."

His hand moved up to cover hers, his fingers sliding between her own as he adjusted her hold on the rock. "It's not a pencil, hon. Think of your finger as the catapult, and it's gotta launch the rock. Move these to prop the rock into your finger. See?"

Nodding was the only reply she could give, especially since her eyes had glazed over, and she had no idea what her hand was doing at the moment. All she knew was that he held it, and that was enough to make her mind go blank.

"So when you throw this," Ryan told her, somehow seeming perfectly fine while she was dying, "kinda guide it with the direction of your throw. Don't step so much and shift your weight from back foot to front foot. And throw with your arm to the side, not at an angle. Like the worst way ever to throw a baseball."

"Trust me, I know how to throw a baseball," Talia insisted with a hoarse bark of a laugh. "Grizz made sure of that before I was eight."

Ryan made a soft sound behind her. "Not sure if that's better or worse for you now. This isn't like that at all."

No, it wasn't. Grizz teaching her to throw a baseball was nothing like this.

But she was pretty sure that wasn't what Ryan meant.

Then again, he was still standing close to her and cupping her hand in his. There was no way she could hope to throw the rock and have it skip with any kind of success. But it was entirely possible that she would turn in his arms and kiss the son of a gun, no matter what happened.

That would make an interesting entry in her Broken Hearts journal.

Broken hearts . . .

Austin . . .

Like a bucket of cold water had been dumped over her head, Talia shivered, and not because of Ryan's touch. Getting wrapped up in him was taking away from her purpose for being here. Today, that was doing what Austin would want, and he would have loved skipping rocks. He would have laughed at her failure to skip rocks.

And he would have told her to keep trying no matter how many times she failed.

"Am I ready now?" she asked Ryan in a clear voice, doing everything she could to put distance between them without actually shaking him off.

She liked Ryan. She liked him a lot. She just couldn't let that define her time here.

He would get that, wouldn't he?

"Should be," Ryan said with a squeeze to her elbow, as though he knew exactly where her thoughts had gone. Then he stepped back, giving her blessed space and air to breathe.

Now if only she could actually skip the rocks.

She frowned at the water. "Please cooperate." Then she threw her arm, just the way Ryan suggested, and flicked her wrist, doing her best to use her finger to press the rock where she wanted.

It bounced once, then plopped beneath the water.

"Shoot," Talia muttered with a scowl. "Not quite."

"Are you kidding?" Ryan cried coming to stand beside her, putting a hand on her arm and laughing. "You got one! That's fantastic!"

There was nothing to do except grin up at the guy for that. "That's exactly what Austin would have told me. I can hear him saying, 'Mom! You did it! Do it again!'" She laughed and put a hand to her heart, smiling at the thought of her sweet boy and his toothy grin.

"And would you do it again?" Ryan asked, grinning over at her. "If he said that?"

"In a heartbeat," she replied, nodding her head fondly. "Just to hear him laugh again, and until he lost interest. I couldn't refuse him something like this." She smiled back out at the water. "And he would turn it into a contest between us, and beat me. And I wouldn't let him, it would just happen."

Ryan laughed softly, bending to pick up a rock from the bucket and tossing it back and forth in his hands. "Well, I won't make this a contest, but I'll skip rocks until you lose interest. Or we lose the light. I'll just assume Austin is on my side if I beat you."

"You're going to beat me anyway!" Talia protested, whacking him on the arm even as her heart swelled at his offer. "You're like a pro rock skipper!"

He held up a finger. "Am not, and I can safely say so because there is such a thing as a professional rock skipper."

"There is not."

"Yes, ma'am, there is." He tossed the rock again. "Look it up. Watch some videos. They're crazy good. I'm just a hobbyist who has too much time to think these days. Practice, Princess Chicago, and you'll beat me soon enough."

Talia snorted and picked up a rock, carefully positioning

herself again to try for more than one skip. "Do you come out here to think a lot?"

Ryan nodded once. "Used to. Little busy now with the ranch, and a certain little lady's riding lessons." He winked, then sent his rock sailing out over the water, getting at least four skips on it.

"Show off," she grumbled, still aiming hers. "What would you think about?" She threw her rock, getting maybe a half bounce out of it.

"Try throwing flatter," he suggested as he picked another rock for himself. "This and that, I guess." He paused, shaking his head. "No, I'm gonna be straight with you. No minimizing." He straightened, rock in hand. "I thought about my career, and everything I'd lost with it."

He said it so simply, almost casually, but there was an unmistakable weight to such a thing, and she bit the inside of her cheek as she debated how she would phrase her next question. She wanted to be there for him, as he had been there for her so often in the last few days, but she didn't have a career, a passion she had brought to life, or a life's work . . .

She had made her life about Austin, though.

And now her life didn't have its focus anymore.

Maybe that wasn't so different.

"Did you feel lost yourself?" she murmured, reaching for a new rock, running her thumb over the smooth surface.

"Oh, yeah." He looked at his rock, still in his hand, apparently in no hurry to throw it. "I'd been practicing for rodeo my whole life, did mutton busting at our local rodeos every year until they wouldn't let me anymore. Got in trouble more than once at home for practicing during chores. Spent most of high school doing work outside of the classroom while I traveled for the amateur circuits. Went to the local community college to stay close to my base and keep competing, then wound up starting the rodeo team there with the guys." His jaw tightened visibly, and he threw the rock, only getting three skips from it. "I was at the top of my game when I got hurt. Roughies are used to getting hurt, way more than ropers. Happens all the time. We just come back when we the doctor clears us, and it's fine."

Talia could hear the bitterness seeping into his voice, and it hurt. This giving, funny, carefree man who was sweetly spending so much of his time with her was still suffering from his own loss, no matter how he tried to cover it with his good nature.

She wanted to cry for him, but she forced herself to throw her rock instead, getting one skip. "I'm so sorry," she said with a wince, "but what's a roughie?"

Ryan laughed softly. "Rough stock rider. The bull riders, bareback riders, and saddle bronc riders. We're called roughies on the inside. We're the crazy ones, ask anybody."

"I get that." She looked over at him, smiling. "I knew you were crazy a long time ago."

He shared her smile, his bright blue eyes crinkling. "Kinda hard to hide it, huh? And I try so hard."

Talia giggled and reached for another rock at the same time he did, their fingers brushing with an electric jolt that made her suck in her breath audibly.

If Ryan noticed, he gave no indication, though he had paused at the contact, too.

Swallowing, Talia plucked up a rock and pretended to focus on the water as she positioned herself. "How'd you deal with all that?" she asked quickly. "You don't seem like the wallowing type."

"Nah, there's no time to wallow on a ranch," he assured her. "But it wasn't easy. It took over my thoughts, even when I was working. I don't know if wallowing counts if it's only in your head, but that's what I did. I was obsessed with not being able to compete anymore, with losing what I'd worked my whole life for. Nobody wanted to talk to me, because the subject would always come up. So I buried it, forced myself to talk about other things, pretend I was fine."

The words could have been Talia's own, just on a different subject. She'd done the same thing after she'd lost Austin, and the pain of it had never gone away because of it. She'd kept everything inside her, lived in it during her most private times, over and over again, until it consumed her. The loss, the guilt, the misery . . . It had become less about Austin and more about the feelings she had because of his death.

Could one become addicted to thoughts and feelings? If so, she had.

"Are you still in that place?" she ventured to ask, watching as he tossed his rock and managed five skips.

"Sometimes," he admitted, wiping his hand on his jeans and reaching for another rock. "Not that often anymore. With Kells around all the time, it gets harder to go there. She's got a sixth sense or something, and knew when I was struggling. Even now, she checks in more than I'd like, but I love her for that."

Talia nodded, swallowing with some difficulty. "How'd you get out?"

He frowned in thought. "I had to come up with my own motivation to get moving. Not to move on, but to move at all, if that makes sense."

"Tell me," she pleaded. She turned to face him directly, rock skipping completely forgotten. "What was it?"

"Life is a bronc ride," Ryan said, smiling at her with a gentle, almost bemused expression. "Bucking you like crazy, and you just hang on for dear life. Sometimes, you're on top of the world, and it's good. Sometimes, you're not even on there long enough to count. You gotta decide for yourself. Are you gonna go again once you're thrown off? Or are you gonna lay on the ground and give up? And sometimes, you just need to find a better bronc to ride. And that's okay." He cocked his head a little, his smile spreading. "How's that?"

Talia bit her lip, letting the words seep into her, swirl around her, and toss over in her mind. "I think that makes sense," she told him, managing a small smile herself, "but I'm not sure. I don't speak rodeo yet."

His smile turned into a full grin. "*Yet* is my new favorite word, darlin'." He winked and gestured to the rocks. "Come on, let's go again."

CHAPTER 13

HE WAS IN TROUBLE. He was in a lot of trouble.

He'd never been so delighted to be in so much trouble.

Ryan smirked to himself as he walked the distance from his house to the fire pit they were using that night. He wasn't sure he'd ever enjoyed an afternoon more than the one he'd just had with Talia at the reservoir, and all they'd done was skip rocks and talk. That was it. Nothing more, nothing less.

Okay, so there had been some flirting, and he'd unnecessarily spent time holding her wrist and arm in a show of helping her form, but he was a red-blooded male, and she was a captivating, gorgeous female.

He wasn't going to apologize for taking advantage of such an opportunity, especially when it was such a little thing.

His feelings weren't little, though. And they were growing by the hour, it seemed. It had been just over two hours since he'd dropped Talia off at the homestead house, and he already was dying to see her again.

He'd finished up some ranch work, then gone back to his place for dinner and to wash up. His house was really more of a cabin on the land, just like the other ranch hands had, and he liked it that way. He didn't need much space, though his house had three bedrooms and a pull-out couch that had been his bed more often than he would ever tell his sister. He really was a simple guy, and for much of his rodeo career, he had lived in a trailer he'd pulled behind his truck all over the country.

Having an entire house was weird.

But today, he was grateful for the space. He had looked over the pathetic wardrobe he possessed to figure out what he should wear to the bonfire, and he'd never felt more stupid in his entire life, which was saying something. It was a bonfire. His clothing wouldn't be particularly noticed, and no one would care.

Monday, however, he would have to think about what he wore, and that was what led to his clothing being spread all over the place in his cabin-like house. If it stayed just as a date with just the two of them, he'd go with a button-down, but his sister would notice that a mile away. He needed to stay more casual.

Then he remembered that he had all the next day to worry about what to wear Monday, and if he didn't get to the bonfire early, he wouldn't be able to pick a spot next to Talia.

And if he wasn't careful, one of the guys would get that spot.

Which would make him agitated the whole night.

If not outright livid.

None of the guys should get an opportunity to know her tonight. Not one. That was his place, his honor, his chance. Sure, he wanted his friends to meet her, get their take on her, and eventually like her.

Just not right now.

He approached the fire pit, dressed in a flannel over a T-shirt, his hands in his pockets, his eyes darting all around the roaring fire to the logs set up, taking in each person and marking available spots.

There were no spots available for two people, and Talia wasn't here yet.

Drat.

He barely avoided making a face as he moved toward the log his sister sat on, the others now seeing him and calling greetings. He dipped the front of his hat, smiling. "Evening, all." He put a hand on his sister's shoulder as though he needed to use her for balance as he stepped over the log to sit beside her, pushing more than necessary.

Kellie whacked him hard in the stomach as he sat beside her. "Jerk."

"Hello to you, too." He nudged her side with his elbow before giving her some space and grinning. "How was your day?" he asked in a softer tone, concerned by the strain he saw in her face.

She shook her head. "I got a lot of applications today, and I want to take them all. Can't—a few of them have too much baggage still to be able to come—but reading through the stories..."

Ryan straightened and put his arm around her shoulder, pulling her closer. "You know people hurt, Kells. No one knows it like you. And just because they can't come now doesn't mean they can't come later. Can you send them a personal message? Tell them that?"

Again, she shook her head. "I can't afford to establish a personal connection before they're accepted. That makes me a resource for them, and professionally, I can't be that until they come here."

He got that, he did, but he didn't like the way such strict professional boundaries made his sister look and feel. Kellie had a big heart, and a warm one, which made her a fantastic person and therapist, but it also opened her up to a lot of complicated empathy she couldn't indulge in. She'd probably need to work hard on the ranch tomorrow to work through all of this, which was her usual habit, but he worried what else might be swirling beneath the surface.

She didn't talk about it much, but her own personal battles and heartbreak still ate at her from time to time. And times of emotional vulnerability managed to bring those things back to the surface.

"How was your day?" she asked, looking up at him, making no move to shrug his arm off, which told him just how much she was hurting despite her words. "Have fun?"

"The meeting wasn't fun," he told her with a firm shake of his head. "Tom Hauser needs a whole new committee, and with people who actually care about rodeo like him. The gig starts in ten days, and it's not even close to ready."

Kellie snorted softly. "I miss Bill Keeting. He and Tom didn't need a whole committee, they just got it done. I'll call Ginny Harland tomorrow. She'll get it hopping."

"Does she care about a small rodeo in Lost Creek?" Ryan pursed his lips, twisting them a little. "I know she'll sponsor, but real involvement..."

"She will," Kellie overrode. "She might even put herself on the committee."

"She'd *be* the committee."

"Who would?" Reid asked loudly, tuning in.

Ryan rolled his eyes. "Miz Harland."

Three of the guys shuddered at the mention of her name, making Ryan chuckle. "Come on," Kellie protested with a glare around the fire. "She's fantastic."

"That's one word," Westin conceded with a nod. "Got a few more I'd use first, but I won't deny that's on the list of 'em."

"Who's Miss Harland?" one of the ladies around the circle asked, her eyes wide. "Sounds scary."

"She's not," Kellie said at the same time most of the guys said the opposite.

Kellie ignored them. "She's the biggest name in the rodeo world, Jessica. She and her husband built an empire around the sport, and it's a big deal to have her input. She's actually one of the investors in Broken Hearts."

"I didn't know that," Lars broke in with some surprise. "Is she really?"

Ryan nodded at him.

Lars whistled low. "That's impressive, no denying."

"There's another word," Westin affirmed, this time smiling at Kellie with some teasing.

"Sorry I'm late," a new voice panted breathlessly from outside the circle. "I couldn't find my jacket."

Ryan was grinning before he saw her, his face erupting in raw delight. Talia's hair was down still, and somehow more wavy and attractive than it had been earlier, her majestic eyes reflecting the firelight with a brilliance he loved. She sat next to Jessica, tucking her hair behind her ears and rubbing her hands together before reaching out to the fire.

She was two logs down from him, and still it felt like an insurmountable distance.

"Guys, this is Talia," Kellie announced, gesturing a little. "Talia, that's Eric, Reid, Westin, Lars, and Ford."

Talia waved a little. "Hi. You're the rodeo guys?"

Eric barked a laugh and flashed a cocky, would-be charming smile that Ryan instantly wanted to punch off his face. "That's us, darlin'. You like rodeo?"

She stared at him with a completely blank expression, his attempt at charm falling flat. "I have no idea. I don't know a thing about it but what Ryan's told me in the last few days. Are you a roper or a roughie?"

Ryan could have kissed her for such a perfect response, and the other guys were snickering to each other. It was clear that Eric was in for it with her.

Eric's brow furrowed. "A roper. Why?"

Talia clicked sympathetically. "Sorry about that. I'm sure it's great, and you're probably good, but aren't you kind of the mall version of a rodeo guy, then?"

"What?" He looked at Ryan across the fire in horror. "What in tarnation have you told her, Ryan?"

Ryan held up his hands in surrender, laughing outright, no longer worried about Eric trying for her. "I didn't say a word against the ropers, hand over heart. I only said I was a roughie, and that we were crazy."

"True," Ford grunted, nodding. "Y'all are nuts."

"Says the steer wrestler," Westin scoffed with a loud snort. He leaned forward to look at Talia better. "It's the dumbest thing in the world, grown men tackling poor steers to the ground. I think it's a cry for help, myself. What do you think, Kellie?"

Kellie covered her face with a hand, laughing silently, her shoulders shaking under Ryan's arm.

Ryan grinned at the sight, then looked around. "Kellie's not available at the moment, please leave a message."

"No," Eric told Talia, coming back to the topic. "We are not the mall version of rodeo guys. We're the classic cowboys. You ever thrown a lasso?"

"I'm from Chicago," Talia deadpanned. "The only thing I throw is my opinion." She lifted a shoulder, glancing at Ryan. "And now some rocks."

Ryan smiled back, his chest tightening. She was even more beautiful by firelight than in broad daylight, and he was going to keep this vision of her in his mind for a long, long time.

"Would you care to tell me what exactly you're doing?" Kellie said through a tight smile, her low voice breaking Ryan's spell.

He glanced at her cautiously. "About what?"

Her eyes were hard despite her attempt at a relaxed appearance. She nudged her head toward Talia, who had returned her attention to Eric's attempt at explaining roping. "I think you know."

Ryan followed her nudge and allowed himself to keep smiling at Talia, though she wouldn't see it. "Helping a friend and enjoying every moment."

A strange sort of growling emerged from his sister. "What are you doing, Ry?"

"None of your business, Kells," he replied in a typical little brother singsong tone.

She gave him a disgusted, disbelieving look. "Actually . . . it *is* my business. It's never been more my business than right now."

She had a point, but he didn't like it. "It's fine, sis. I know the rules, and we're fine."

"Yeah, umm, that smile that exploded on your face the moment she started talking is definitely not fine." Kellie did shrug his arm off now, and she turned to him, glancing over at Talia and Jessica, who weren't paying any attention to them. "You can't take advantage of my guests, Ry. I know that's not what it looks like, but that's what it is. She's here, she's beautiful, and she's totally your type. But no."

"Nothing's happened, sis," Ryan assured her, feeling his defenses rising. "You said it was fine for me to teach her to ride."

"We teach guests to ride all the time!" Kellie protested in a hiss. "It's part of the ranch life!"

"And the rock skipping today?" he countered, raising a brow. "You said that was fine, too."

Kellie frowned at him, her frustration evident. "I didn't know it was a faux-date, Ryan."

He exhaled slowly. This was not the time or place for tempers to flare, and he did not want to attract attention to this particular conversation. "It wasn't. Am I attracted to her? Yes. Did I enjoy having one-on-one time with her away from ranch work? Yeah, I did. Do I want to date her? Without question. I invited her to go into Lost Creek with me on Monday, and I was gonna talk to you about this tomorrow. I'll happily escort any of the other guests out as well, it doesn't have to be a solo date. I love spending time with Talia. Doesn't mean I'm doing wrong."

His sister's sigh was heavy, and a little defeated. "Ryan, you know as well as I do that people deal with their grief in inexplicable ways. It's not always rational."

His ears buzzed at a few of his sister's keywords, and he reached out a hand on hers. "Talia isn't Brad, Kells. And that's not what we're doing."

She swallowed hard, nodding. "She needs to work through her grief about Austin, Ry . . ."

"We talk about Austin," Ryan told her, gently overriding her. "All the time. Today, we were skipping rocks because that's what she thought Austin would want to do if he were here. She suggested it after saying she needed to find joy."

His sister's eyes widened. "She did?" Kellie whispered.

He nodded. "She's listening to you, Kells. She's learning. I'm just the guy she's turning to while she does it."

"And you?" She swallowed, her expression softening into one more of concern that he recognized well. "Last time we talked about it, your head wasn't all the way straight yet."

Ryan wanted to joke her out of the serious moment, but sensed she needed her fears addressed in order to be comfortable. "I'm working through it. I can tell you that my days have been a lot brighter lately, that's for sure."

Kellie patted his leg, smiling fondly. "Just make sure you're not getting distracted by a new shiny toy instead of focusing on what you need."

"I'm not a cat, sis."

"I know. They have better hygiene."

He elbowed her hard, and she smacked his knee before they both tuned back into the conversation around them.

"So you ride the horse without a saddle at all?" Jessica asked, gaping at Reid as though he had sprouted two heads.

Reid was grinning without shame, like any insane bareback rider would when talking about his passion. "Yes, ma'am. I've got a cinch and some rigging, but no stirrups or saddle to speak of."

Jessica blinked at him, then looked at Talia. "I think the man used words, I'm just not sure what language those words are."

Talia snickered and gestured at Ryan. "Thanks to my riding lessons, I know what a saddle and stirrups are, but the rest is a mystery."

"Ohhh," Lars said quietly to Ryan from his left, the next log over. "So Talia is your riding student and your afternoon appointment?"

"Might be," Ryan replied cautiously, giving him a sidelong glance. "So?"

Lars shrugged easily. "So nothing. She's nice, and she's spunky. I like her."

"Thanks for the stamp of approval." Ryan paused, then allowed himself to smile. "Did Ford bring his guitar?"

"'Course. Did you think he wouldn't?"

It had been a dumb question, hands down. Ford's guitar was like the seventh member of the Original Six, which reminded Ryan of most of the guys in his middle school and high school who had used their mediocre guitar playing skills to get girls. But Ford was an artist on the guitar, and there was nothing better than having him bring that artistry out when around a fire.

"Y'all should come to the rodeo event the week after next," Westin suggested brightly to Jessica and Talia. "It's a smaller thing than the main events coming up, and you can see what we're talking about. Any of the ladies should come, we'll show y'all around."

Jessica smiled at the invitation. "I'm actually leaving the ranch tomorrow. Headed back home to Missouri and my kids. But if it's live streamed, I'll watch with popcorn!"

"I'll take it!" Eric nodded in approval. "Even if they don't have the live stream, I'll plug some videos from it on my YouTube channel for you guys to watch."

"Thanks!" Jessica narrowed her eyes at him then. "What's the YouTube channel's name?"

Reid laughed loudly and turned to Ryan in expectation. "Go ahead, Eric. Tell them where to find you."

"Rodeo King," Eric told them with a rueful grin. "Don't talk about my ego, that's not what it is. It helps with the keywords on the internet, okay? Plus, I've got a sponsorship with King Spurs, so it's a shoutout."

"I didn't say a word." Jessica shook her head, fighting a smile. "Talia?"

Talia held up her hands. "I got nothing. Maybe there are kings in rodeo. Maybe it's like prom."

Ryan busted up laughing, and he wasn't the only one to do so. He could hear laughter all around the fire at Talia's perfect quip, from Ford's deep rumble to his sister's throaty hoarseness. Even Talia was laughing—he could hear her musical laughter over anyone else, and it warmed him more than any fire in the world could hope to.

"That's my new favorite mental image," Westin told

Talia, wiping at the corner of one eye as he continued to laugh. "Eric in chaps with the prom king crown on his head. Thanks, Talls."

Talia hummed another laugh. "I haven't been called Talls in a long time. My cousins used it, but once I stopped growing, they stopped."

"Tell 'em who your cousins are," Ryan encouraged, suddenly eager for their reactions. When Kellie cleared her throat beside him, he backtracked. "I mean, if you want to. Privacy, and all."

Talia laughed again, this time her eyes on Ryan alone. "I don't have much to keep private anymore. And I don't mind." She leaned forward, rubbing her palms together as she stared into the fire. "I'm a cousin of Grizz and Clint McCarthy."

For a moment, the fire crackled in the silence, but then Reid coughed once. "Are you kidding me?"

Talia smiled and shook her head. "Not kidding. Their dad is my mom's brother. We all grew up running around together."

"Holy crap." Reid shook his head, eyes wide as he stared at her. "How . . . how? Just how?"

Westin smacked the back of Reid's head. "What kinda question is that? The same as your cousins are your cousins."

Reid rubbed his head, scowling at his friend. "My cousins are not pro-athletes."

"Technically, you are," Lars pointed out with a shrug. He looked over at Talia with a friendly smile. "Sounds like you're pretty proud of them."

She nodded, smiling herself. "I am. They're more like my brothers than cousins. I'm an only child, so they kind of adopted me as an honorary sister. My son . . ." She paused and swallowed, her eyes beginning to shimmer, but her smile remained. "My son thought they were his uncles, and that it was the coolest thing ever to watch them on TV."

Jessica reached over and laced her fingers through Talia's without a word, and Ryan had never been more grateful to anyone in his life. He wanted nothing more than to get up and go to Talia, wrap his arms around her, and rest his chin on her shoulder as she leaned back into him. He could see the scene so perfectly in his head, he could almost smell the scent of her shampoo over that of the smoke.

But he was over here, and she was there. Suddenly, it was colder.

"He wasn't wrong," Eric insisted with a grin. "I watch Clint on occasion myself, more because my sister's married to Rocco De Luca. He was on Clint's club hockey team back in the day."

Talia laughed a little, nodding. "I remember. Rocco was my very first crush, as it happens. Don't tell your sister."

"Mum's the word." Eric mimicked zipping his mouth shut and held his hand up in a sort of solemn vow.

"Can we keep him like that?" Lars asked of the whole group, making them laugh easily.

"Please," Kellie begged. She reached behind her and pulled out a platter. "S'mores, anyone? And Ford, would you please play something?"

Ford dipped his chin in a nod. "Happy to." He got up and moved behind the log to pull the trusty guitar out of its case.

"Hey." Lars flicked a couple of fingers in Ryan's direction, gesturing for him to lean in.

Ryan did so, raising a brow in question.

"Her son," Lars murmured, nudging his head toward Talia. "Did he . . . ?"

There was nothing to do but nod. "In November."

Lars whistled low, shaking his head. "Poor thing. That's beyond tough. She's in the right place, though."

"I think so, too."

Ryan smiled a little, straightening as Ford began to play, sitting back on the log and propping the guitar on his thigh. Kellie handed out supplies for s'mores, laughing at something Jessica said, seeming more relaxed now than Ryan had seen her in months. Even Talia was laughing and smiling, the thoughts of Austin not crushing her in any way he could see. Had she found joy in this moment? Had she thought about what Austin would love about this moment?

Was she pretending all of this for the benefit of those around her?

He watched her for a while, watched the fire play on her features, watched as she scorched her marshmallow beyond recognition in a sacrilege against all s'mores. Watched as she stared into the fire without speaking, her lips slightly curved in an expression of contemplation, if not contentment. Watched as her eyes lifted to his and held his gaze, neither surprised nor embarrassed to find him watching her.

Ryan swallowed, letting himself smile further as he watched her, and waited, hoping against hope...

His chest exploded in relief and delight when her smile grew as well, and she gave him a little wink before reaching for another marshmallow to torch.

"I can't, I just can't," Westin groaned, getting up to reach for a marshmallow himself. "Talls, for heaven's sake, don't make a tiki torch out of that. Look, I'll show you."

"I like the crunch!" Talia protested, laughing at his reaction. "And the char."

"You're a monster," Westin informed her without shame. "Ryan, c'mon, man, back me up."

Ryan inhaled, then released the breath in a rush, shaking his head. "Some things are worth waiting for. The perfectly golden marshmallow is one of them." He looked at Talia pointedly, wondering about her response.

"Prove it," she retorted, her smile sly. "Make me a perfect s'more, Ryan, and I'll test it out."

"What do I get if I win?" he demanded. "Not worth doin' somethin' for nothin'."

Talia's mouth curved further still. "A notch on your ego for proving me wrong. And bragging rights."

"Do it," Eric and Reid rumbled together in a perfect chorus.

"Well, I do love bragging," Ryan admitted, giving Talia a crooked grin. "You're on."

Chapter 14

"Now, I know we haven't been doing any kind of Sunday activities lately, but since we've got the rodeo coming up, I thought we could make pies today."

"To sell? Isn't the rodeo next week?"

"These pies freeze well," Kellie assured Kerri with a smile. "We'll only bake one or two today."

Talia gnawed the inside of her cheek. "I've never made a pie. I'm a disaster in the kitchen."

Some of the other guests echoed her sentiment, looking uncertain.

Kellie, however, was undeterred. She smiled around at the group and gestured for them to join her. "That's fine. I had a great teacher, and I brought reinforcements."

A woman Talia didn't recognize pushed off the counter, smiling with the same warmth Kellie possessed in spades, her face a little rounder, a little more freckled, and her hair more of a dirty strawberry blonde. "Hey, all y'all. I'm Mariah from Mariah's Bakery and Cafe in Lost Creek. Kellie and I go way back, and every spring, we go on a pie-making spree together."

Her smile somehow spread further, bringing out a faint dimple in her right cheek, and she laughed a little. "Who am I kidding? We do this at Thanksgiving, too. And any other time we can get away with a horde of pies!"

Her good humor was infectious, and soft laughter came from Talia and all the rest at her energy.

"I promise you," Mariah said with a more serious tone, though there was still a twinkle in her eye, "there are no pie disasters I can't save. The ugly ones just get eaten first, okay?"

Now Talia laughed in earnest, and her misgivings about creating something in the kitchen that would then be baked and, presumably, consumed, faded. It was still there, but between Kellie and Mariah, she felt like she was hanging out in the kitchen with old friends, which was much safer.

Oh, why not?

She glanced down the line of other guests, feeling a small twinge of pain that Jessica had left the ranch this morning, but still comfortable with those who remained. "Well, I guess we're in good hands, then."

Kerri, a copper-haired, blue-eyed nymph of a woman, grinned back at her. "Sounds like it! Let's do it!"

They divided up into two groups, one group doing a classic mixed-berry pie that Broken Hearts Ranch was known for, the other doing a classic Texas pecan pie. Talia had never even attempted either, but found herself drawn to the berry group just by her own personal tastes. Mariah was working with them, and it took about five minutes to discover that the woman was a baking genius.

She had them making their dough and rolling it out in no time flat, and explained her methods with more clarity than Talia had ever heard from a recipe or on a baking show. Suddenly, the prospect wasn't daunting at all, but a fun adventure. Mariah had them all laughing with stories about baking mishaps in her life, and what baking with her young kids was like, especially when the bakery was their family business.

It was impressive how friendly, warm, and open this woman was, almost in exactly the same way Kellie had been when Talia first met her. And as she was now, though on a much deeper level. These were women who Talia would want to cry with when things hurt, or laugh with when she could. Friends she hadn't known about, but now felt a kinship with that usually took her much, much longer.

Was everyone in Lost Creek exceptionally warmhearted? She had yet to meet a single person who was even remotely cranky, let alone cold. Granted, she hadn't actually gone out into Lost Creek itself yet, but that would happen tomorrow night with Ryan. The other ladies had been invited to come into town with them, and they'd all been excited to do so. That boded well, since the other guests had been before.

Talia didn't care too much about seeing the town or meeting more locals, though it would be nice. She really wanted to spend time with Ryan more than anything else. Something away from the ranch, away from her therapy, away from her grief.

It was a concept she had come to find herself considering in the last two days or so. She needed a vacation from her grief. A retreat from it, to use a word Kellie would approve of. It would never fully leave, she knew, but to not feel herself so surrounded by the fog of it all would be a blessed relief. She had begun to feel a lightening when she was with Ryan, riding or talking, and then when they skipped rocks . . .

Living made the fog lift.

She felt slight guilt for that, but it felt so good to simply live that she couldn't withdraw back into the gloom she had grown so comfortable in. She couldn't embrace the idea that

Austin would want her to be free from it quite yet, but she did know that he wanted her happiness. The image of his smiling face was coming to her mind more and more, and the last scenes of him less and less. His laughter was echoing in her ears more than the last artificial, ragged breaths.

That was her boy, she reminded herself. Alive, delightful, and mischievous.

Not the small, frail, fragile-looking figure hooked up to machines in the hospital bed.

This Austin was hers. Not that one.

The happy, loud, exasperating one. Not the silent one. Never that one.

"Kellie," Amanda suddenly asked over the sounds of conversation, looking at something out in the great room, "what's the horseshoe on the wall for?"

Talia looked, as did the others, and saw an aged iron horseshoe nailed to the wall above the front door, its ends pointed up. It was difficult to see any details from where she was, but it was clear that the piece had been there for ages.

Kellie laughed once, very softly, her smile fond. "When my grandfather finished the first house on the ranch lands, he wanted to make sure the family would have all the luck we would need. So he took a shoe from the horse that brought him here, carved his wife's name on it, and had it hung above the door. Said he needed angels and luck more than ever." She gestured up at it a little. "And it's hung there ever since."

Talia hummed pleasantly in thought, loving the significance and imagery of that. "And the ends of the horseshoe?" she asked, glancing over at Kellie. "Is that significant?"

"Well, I looked it up," Kellie told her, still smiling, "and it just depends which side you take. The ends can go up, or they can go down, either way should be lucky. Grandpa always said he wanted to catch blessings, not rain them down. So we go with the ends up."

Jill exhaled loudly, her voice touched with sentiment. "Well, I just love that so much! I wish we'd done that for my momma after she passed. I always felt that she was an angel guarding each of us as we left the house every day. Would have been nice to look up at the doorway and have that reminder of her, too."

"Yes," Talia murmured, suddenly feeling her throat tighten and a lump form. "I would love to see that for my boy. It would be . . . like getting a hug from him again."

Amanda wrapped an arm about Talia's shoulders, gently soothing without words. She rubbed a little, but the pressure of her hold was enough to steady Talia's heart.

And the fog of grief and despair never settled.

Maybe that was progress, then.

Finally.

"Right, who wants to learn how to make designs on the top layer for the berry pie?" Mariah asked, brightening the mood in a single stroke.

Talia raised her hand with the others, and Mariah was off again, teaching them all trade secrets, but with basic steps anyone could follow. Soon, all of them were creating fun, delicate designs for the top layer of pie crust without any of them making a disaster out of it. How could she make baking seem so easy when Talia had a lifetime of evidence that it was impossible?

"What about the filling?" Jill asked as she folded one of her design corners over. "We haven't done that yet."

"Correct," Mariah told them all, turning to the stove, where a saucepan and containers of berries sat. "I like to get my pie layers ready before my filling. Everybody got your bases in the pans and fluted to your taste?"

They murmured their assent, filing over.

Kellie's pecan pie group was mixing their fillings as well.

They didn't need the stove to do so, but a few watched the berry group with curiosity.

"Blueberries, sugar, cornstarch, and water," Mariah recited as she added each ingredient to the pot. "And how do we feel about cinnamon?"

"For it," they replied as one, giggling at the unison of it.

Mariah sighed happily as she added the spice to the mixture. "All y'all are my people. And a dash of salt. We're making a big batch, so like three dashes, right?" She took a hefty pinch of salt and sprinkled it over, laughing to herself.

Talia noticed Amanda fanning herself with a hand, looking exhausted in a rare moment without a cheery façade. "You okay?" she asked with a light nudge.

Amanda nodded, giving her a smile. "Just hot and sore. I spent the last few days helping with cleaning out all of the animal stalls—needed to clean something on a big scale, you know?"

Cleaning had never been one of Talia's therapeutic outlets, but she knew full well it could be for others, so she nodded as though she understood. After all, she understood the need to do something that proved she was functioning and capable of accomplishment.

Jill looked around Talia with a slight frown. "I thought you wanted to put yourself through the rock-strewn pastures of torture to work that gunk out. What happened there?"

Amanda snorted softly. "I was planning on it. Was actually looking forward to the drudgery. But Caleb told me I had to find something else to do, since Ryan spent so much time clearing the fields of rocks."

Talia's ears burned at the mention of Ryan, as though they had been waiting for this moment all day. Then her mind replayed the words, and her knees locked. "Rocks? Why would Ryan clear the fields? He's got so much else to do."

"No clue," Amanda told her, shrugging it off. "Caleb just said Ryan had gone through all the fields looking for rocks, and something about his wasting time looking through them all for some reason."

Heartbeat after heartbeat pounded within Talia's chest, rising up her throat and pulsing thunderously in her ears. Ryan had... *Ryan* had...

Ryan hated picking up rocks from the fields—he'd told her that straight off the bat. In the week she had been here, she knew that everyone under the sun, except Caleb's kids, thought it was the worst task ever. Yet he had taken the time to go through all of the fields that hadn't been done yet, look through them all for rocks of all kinds, then sorted through them all.

He had been finding their skipping rocks. Nothing of the sort had been said, but what else could it have been? The timing was right, and there was no other reason for him to look through the rocks when the day she had spent on that task, she had been told to just leave the rocks in their bucket in the barn to be hauled away.

Plus, Ryan was the sort to do that kind of thing. She didn't know why it hadn't occurred to her before. She'd never thought to ask where he'd gotten such perfect rocks for their outing, but of course, he would have found them himself. And of course, he would have taken his time to do so, making sure he had the best he needed. And of course, he would have sacrificed his time and his energy, when he had so much else to do, just to get as many rocks as possible.

She could barely breathe, her chest was tightening so much. It was agony and ecstasy in one motion, the need to fly mingling with the urge to burst into pathetic tears, and her face burned with the torrent of emotions and thought. No one had ever done something like that for her.

No one.

Mom, tell him thank you! Austin's voice rang in her ears over the sound of her own erratic heart, as clearly as if he stood by her side. She knew where the memory had come from, after a man with a sweet smile had helped her pick up groceries that had dropped, and she'd spent too much time apologizing and bumbling. Austin had cut to the chase and told her to say thanks, and it had taken her out of the mess she was making.

It seemed her boy was taking care of her still.

Talia swallowed hard. "Can you finish my pie for me, Jill? I need to . . . uh . . . I need some air." She didn't wait for an answer, couldn't think of a better explanation, and tore from the kitchen, bolting out of the screen door Ryan had come through that first night to get pie, when he had talked to her.

She needed to see him, and needed to see him now.

Running all out, like her life depended on it, Talia headed for the barn, not knowing if Ryan would be there, but not having any other options. Somehow, she still hadn't given him her number, or gotten his, and in the world of technology they lived in, that seemed strange. But she'd only known him a week, she reminded herself. One week, that was all.

That one week had been more than enough.

It was farther to the barn than she remembered, but that was her own fault. She'd never all-out run to the barn before, and doing so now when she had something important to say and do might not have been the brightest idea. It would be hard to have a conversation when she was being attacked by her own lungs.

Definitely not attractive.

But she couldn't stop. She needed to get there as fast as she could, needed to see him, thank him, hug him . . . Oh, who was she kidding? She needed to kiss the man until kingdom come.

Her stomach leapt within her until it hit her rib cage, and she almost hiccupped with the sensation. She hadn't felt like this in y*ears*, if ever. Even with Austin's dad, loser that he'd been, she'd never felt like this, and she'd thought that was the height of all feelings at the time. This was so much deeper, so much more sincere, so much more real.

She'd be terrified if she thought about it too much.

She rounded the corner of the barn and paused, looking up and down the length of it for a tall, lanky, ridiculously good-looking cowboy. "Ryan?" she called, her race from the house making her voice hoarse and almost frantic in pitch.

"Talia?" He suddenly appeared from one of the stalls, moving quickly and looking at her in concern. "What is it? Are you okay?"

Her eyes began to burn, touched by his immediate concern, knowing what he'd already done for her, and what else he might do. The air in her lungs vanished, replaced by heat that seemed to pop at odd intervals in her chest. She nodded, fighting to inhale enough to speak.

"Talia?" Ryan said again, stopping a few feet away, his face wreathed in uncertainty.

Swallowing, Talia managed a gasp for air. "You cleared the pastures of rocks for me? To find rocks to skip?"

His expression cleared, and he slowly slid his hands into his pockets. "Who told you that?"

She smiled at the evasive question. "Yes or no, Ryan?"

He pursed his lips a little in thought, his eyes narrowing. "Yes," he finally said.

Talia nodded once. "You said picking rocks from the fields is the worst."

"It is."

"Why would you do that?" she asked, unintentionally putting more emphasis into her words. "With all you have to do, all that you could be doing, why would you . . . ?"

"Because I wanted to," he overrode simply. He shrugged his shoulders, his cheeks coloring a little. "Because it was the obvious place to find rocks for us to use, and I needed lots of rocks. I didn't mind doing it. Not this time."

Talia stared at him for a long moment, her heart hammering against her ribs. Then, unable to resist one moment more, she closed the distance between them. She reached for his neck and pulled him down to her, arching up as she pressed her lips to his with no hesitation, sliding her fingers up into his hair just a little.

His arms reached around her, one hand going to her face and tilting her chin up for the most perfect angle known to man. His lips moved against hers, a ticklish friction that shot down her sides and wrapped around her stomach. Her lips parted under his attentions, and he ventured further, the arm around her back pulling her closer.

Talia clung to him, giving and taking, taking and giving, molding into him, against him, with him, as their lips moved and danced together. Ryan's thumb stroked against her cheek, curling her toes with the gentle caresses, and she sighed into his kiss.

He chuckled, shifting his mouth to kiss the corner of hers and at her jaw before settling back on her lips tenderly.

"Thank you," Talia whispered, cupping his jaw and swallowing.

"For that? You're very welcome, anytime." Ryan hummed another laugh and pressed a kiss to her brow.

Talia gently slapped the back of his neck, grinning at his teasing response. "You know what I mean."

"I know what *I* mean," he told her, stroking her cheek again. "I can't really remember what happened before you kissed me, so give me a minute."

She blushed, leaning into his touch a little. "Take your time. I'm in no hurry."

"Yeah, I'm kinda loving the moment right now myself." He kissed her brow again, letting his lips linger there while he simply breathed.

Talia tightened her hold on him, leaning her head against his chest and loving how he pulled her just as close as she wanted to be. There was comfort in his arms that she hadn't known anywhere else. Something deep and soothing settled her soul and quieted her mind. It was the closest thing to home she'd known since Austin had died, and that both delighted and terrified her.

Was she fishing for something to anchor her? Was she feeling this way because she had started to feel again? Was this some sort of grief rebound? Or was this as real as it felt, inexplicable a connection as it was?

She wasn't about to let go of it, didn't have the slightest intention of heading for the hills or making up excuses. She just wanted to make sure all of this was fair for Ryan. He was giving so much, and deserved to have much in return.

What he was getting right now was a broken woman trying to find the right kind of glue to put herself back together.

Was she even ready for this?

"You don't need to thank me," Ryan murmured against her hair, one hand sweeping up and down her back. "I'll do anything to help you without question. You know that, right?"

"If I didn't before, I do now," she assured him, loving the feel of his heart pounding beneath her cheek. "Why me? I'm as broken as they come. No doubt, you've seen a few guests come through here, and I doubt you were going to these lengths for them."

"Nope, you're the first." He paused, then exhaled heavily. "Who am I kidding? You're the only. I'd made up my mind to keep a professional, respectful distance to all of Kellie's guests.

Our guests, I guess, since I'm ranch manager. Thought it would be best, and I'd been doing fine. But from the moment I saw you, I wanted to know everything. I wanted to know anything. Distance didn't fly for you."

Talia smiled against the flannel of his shirt, one hand sliding down from his neck to play with the buttons curiously. "I hope that doesn't change. I like the lack of distance."

He chuckled, and the sound rippled along her entire frame. "Oh, don't worry. There's no way we're going back after this. I've wanted to kiss you from the moment your golden eyes met mine, and now that I have, I find I've taken a liking to it."

She peered up at him, resting her chin on his chest and giving him a dreamy smile. "You don't taste so bad yourself, cowboy."

Ryan leaned down and softly but thoroughly kissed her. "Thank you, Princess. Feel free to sample anytime you like."

Talia snickered at the thought, then sighed, her hand at his neck now stroking softly. "What are we going to tell Kellie? I don't want to get kicked off the ranch."

"She'd have to cross my dead body to do that," he promised, giving her a crooked smile. "Don't worry about Kells. She kinda already knows, and as long as we don't draw attention or make trouble, and you're still making progress, we should be fine."

"Good."

They held each other without speaking for a few minutes, Talia just breathing in the scent of him until she would never be able to forget it. She wanted to remember how his arms felt around her, the exact sensation of his heart against her face, the sound of his breathing...

She knew now only too well how fast those little details could leave a mind. Ryan wasn't Austin, and the feelings were so different, but he was growing more important to her as the days went by, and she needed to commit him to memory.

Just in case.

"Tell me what you're thinking," Ryan murmured, nuzzling gently against her hair. "You're quiet."

Talia smiled to herself, turning her face to kiss his chest before looking up at him. "Austin would have loved you. He'd have been your little shadow, following you around as you did everything on the ranch, peppering you with questions about every little detail. I think you'd have been his hero."

Ryan gave her a soft smile. "Maybe before my injury, but I'm not really a hero now."

"Not true." She shook her head emphatically. "I didn't know you before the rodeo, and you're pretty much my favorite person now. I think you're more of a hero now because of your injury. And Austin would have loved you."

His bright blue eyes searched hers for a minute, then he bent to kiss her again, the fervency unmistakable even if the urgency wasn't there. She whimpered against the emotion behind his lips, embracing the change and reaching for more.

Ryan broke away softly, touching his brow to hers. "I'd have loved that kid back. I can tell you that for sure."

"I know," Talia whispered, tearing up, but smiling through it. "You'd have been the best of friends."

He exhaled slowly, his nose brushing hers. "When I first met you, you said you have trouble letting things go, and I said I'd help."

Talia nodded against him. "You have. In so many ways."

"Well, I've got one exception."

She pulled back a little, raising a brow. "Which is?"

Ryan's expression was serious, but there was a light in his eyes that lit a fire in the pit of her stomach. "I'm not doing a damn thing to help you let go of me. I aim to make it impossible. So if you have any plans for that, woman, I wouldn't advise you to act on 'em."

Grinning, Talia locked both hands behind his neck again, going to her toes and still not matching his height. "Well, that's good, cause if I'm ever dumb enough to try, I'm gonna need you to stop me."

"Yes, ma'am." His smile turned crooked, teasing, and achingly attractive. "It would be my pleasure."

CHAPTER 15

IT WASN'T THE TURNOUT they'd had in years past, but it wasn't half-bad considering where they'd started.

The stands were maybe half-full, and for the first day of the rodeo, that was about right. Each of the riders had gone through their own workouts, and everything seemed to be working out okay. Ryan wasn't too pleased about the chute staff and their carefree attitude about the whole thing, but he was sure the riders themselves would be able to keep tabs on things. That was one of the beautiful things about rodeo—the competitors were probably the most self-sufficient athletes in the world.

He scanned the crowd silently, mounted on his horse as a designated pickup man, waiting for the events to get underway. So far, he hadn't seen any sign of Talia, Kellie, or any of the guests from the ranch, though he had been assured that they would be coming.

He wasn't sure why he'd been so insistent on Talia showing up. After all, he wasn't competing, and there was nothing exciting about being a pickup man, considering all the other action that would be going on. But it would be hard to find private moments for them over the next few days, and after a week-and-a-half of getting really good at finding private time, that would be tough.

And pretty painful.

So much had changed for them since that day she'd kissed him senseless in the barn. Without anyone actually giving them titles, they were in a relationship. They could hold hands without anyone staring, though his friends were still teasing them mercilessly every time they caught the slightest whiff of PDA. They walked and talked together every night, each outing ending in a kiss, though the nature of those kisses varied with the tone of the day. When Talia had endured a difficult therapy session, she preferred a short kiss and being held. When the day had been a lighter one, the kissing became the focus.

Ryan was perfectly content in taking what she was willing to give, and gave her as much as he could without overwhelming her. The truth was, he'd be happy to settle down with her this second, which would terrify his sister for a number of reasons. He had his issues, for sure, but he'd rather figure them out with Talia by his side than on his own.

Kellie had accepted the unique relationship between Ryan and Talia, though she gave him enough warning looks for a lifetime. He'd pulled her aside and assured her that if any warning signs came up in sessions with Talia, she could tell him with all professional courtesy to back off, which seemed to settle her ruffled feathers on the subject.

She hadn't done anything of the sort yet, so he had hope.

They were being careful, after all. Talia knew full well that jumping into something while she was grieving was a bad idea, and Ryan knew he wasn't exactly a stellar candidate for healthy life adaptation, though he could certainly have been worse. Part of their nightly discussions had begun to turn toward dealing with their particular issues and trying to help each other out. Wasn't it a sign of a healthy relationship when you could be equal partners in things? When you could communicate with real honesty and depth without getting worked up about any of it? Kellie had helped Ryan become more self-aware in his darker times, and private sessions with her seemed to be doing the same for Talia. What could be better than for two self-aware people to find each other and work together in improving their awareness?

Why was he defending them to himself at this moment?

No one had been asking him to explain himself in the last few days, and yet he had a defense ready. Almost like he needed to remind himself that this was okay.

He felt great being with her, felt confident being in this relationship without definition. It was just that their situation was one that could raise some eyebrows.

He was head over heels for Talia, though. No question there. The more time he spent with her, the more time he wanted to spend with her, and he already thought about her pretty consistently when they were apart. At this rate, he was going to need to have a serious conversation with her cousins in the next few days, just to make sure they weren't sending out a hit squad for him.

They'd talked about her family a lot, so he felt pretty familiar with them. Grizz would be overprotective and defensive, which Ryan could understand, as he was the same way. Clint would be fair and open to listening, but reluctant to actually give the go ahead. The other cousins, as many as there were, would go along with what Grizz and Clint agreed to with minimal reservations, so he would really only need to talk with those two.

It would probably be enough.

They'd talked about Ryan's family, and how his parents

were enjoying retirement in San Antonio. She'd even talked to his mom the other night when she'd called during their walk. He wasn't positive, but he thought his mom might even have Talia's number now so the two of them could chat when he wasn't around, since they'd gotten on so well. Ryan had barely participated in the conversation once those two got connected.

If that wasn't a sign of something, nothing was.

His dad, on the other hand, was more like Kellie, and had texted Ryan the next morning just reminding him to be careful and take his time. Talia had a fragile heart right now, he'd said, and Ryan needed to make sure he was taking the best possible care of it.

Good ol' Dad.

The one thing they hadn't really talked about was the rodeo. It was strange, but Talia seemed hesitant about the whole thing despite loving the ranch, riding with him, and being able to joke with his friends like she'd known them for ages. But during their nightly walks and talks, her conversations on his struggles were more about his dealing with the situation than his past with the rodeo itself. She didn't ask any questions about the sport or the events, and her terminology hadn't improved even with all the time they'd spent together.

He'd managed to snag an opportunity to chat with her this morning before he headed out to the rodeo grounds, and asked if she'd watched any of Eric's previous rodeo videos on YouTube, figuring that was a safer question than asking if she'd watched any of his highlights. She'd shaken her head and said something about not being sure she could scare herself intentionally, now that she knew them all.

Maybe he'd overestimated her intentions to come, and underestimated her nerves for something like this.

Austin had been killed by a car, for heaven's sake. She

probably hated anything with a certain risk of injury. It wasn't as though Ryan was in danger now, given his designation as staff, but was anybody ready for the insanity of rodeo events when they hadn't grown up with it?

He shook his head now, mentally kicking himself for not paying more attention to that. He should have fully prepped her, not just assumed that she'd be fine. Just because he loved the thrill of daring events didn't mean she would.

Please let today be an injury-free day, he silently prayed, exhaling slowly. He didn't want to have to make a decision between the sport he loved and the woman he . . .

Well, it wouldn't be an easy decision, he could safely say that.

Even without competing, he still loved the thing. Getting involved with the rodeo in Lost Creek from this side of things wasn't the same, but it did keep him connected. Avoiding it had been the worst thing he'd done, and he wouldn't have realized it had he not joined in this circus. Maybe he ought to consider joining Tom Hauser's board for future events in Lost Creek.

A whistle lit the air, and he jerked his attention to his left, scanning the seats. He knew that whistle—he'd taught it to her, inflection and all. She'd put her own spin on it, but there was no mistaking the identity.

He grinned as he saw them all together, a group of six women in a row, mostly looking out of place, aside from Kellie, who was eyeing the entire arena as though the events had already started.

She could have run this whole show with her eyes closed, no question.

Talia was watching Ryan, smiling openly. He stared at her for a long moment, then tipped the front of his hat to her. Her smile grew, and she waved a little, which made his heart do a little flip in his chest.

It was the stupidest thing, but he felt kinda stupid these days. There wasn't much to do about that. He was pretty sure it came with the territory of falling for a beautiful woman.

The guys made him feel like the first man in the world to feel this way, or like a new exhibit at a zoo. Dumbfounded looks, stupid questions, and all around confusion were common, and a few of them were a little whiny about Ryan wanting to spend more time with Talia than with them. They'd have to get over that, since Ryan had no intention of changing that anytime soon.

He'd actually spent more time with them today than he had in the last three days combined, and the events hadn't started yet.

Part of the events today had included the Original Six doing roping tutorials for the community, and the turnout had been more than they'd hoped. The signups that Tom and the committee had given them had been less than impressive, but when more people had shown up for the clinic at the scheduled time, they'd just taken them all. A few of the local teenagers had wanted tips, and they had been more than happy to do so. Eric had loved showing off his skills, and had received his share of praise for his talents.

Ryan was plenty skilled in roping from living on a ranch, but he'd never cared to compete seriously in a rodeo. Sure, he could probably compete in it, and maybe some exhibition roping events now and then would be in the cards, but he wasn't about to turn full roper. He was a roughie at heart, and that wasn't going to change.

Sitting here on the horse, though, he felt the same sort of thrill he'd always felt before a rodeo. He wouldn't be competing, so there were no nerves to go with it, but the excitement and energy was humming through the arena. He soaked it in, felt almost renewed by it, and now having Talia here in the stands made everything complete.

"Ladies and gentlemen," the voice of Sal Hendricks boomed from every speaker. "Welcome to the Lost Creek Rodeo showdown!"

Applause scattered about the place, and Ryan's horse snuffled with the energy of it.

"Easy," Ryan murmured, patting his neck. "Easy, boy."

"We thank you for comin' out as we kick off this year's rodeo, and remind you that the rules and regulations of the Lost Creek Rodeo Arena still stand. Any breaking of these guidelines will result in your being escorted from the facility. We'd like to thank our sponsors: Harland Ranches, Incorporated; Big Heartland Stock and Feed; Showdown at Sundown Apparel; and Jim Joray's Auto Parts. The concessions tonight are provided by Down Home Barbecue, so make sure you get up there before the brisket is gone!"

Ryan smiled to himself, wondering how much work had gone into getting those sponsors to kick in enough for the show, considering only Big Heartland had been on the list at the last meeting he attended. Still, Sal would never be anything less than gracious over the intercom, and his voice was the heart of the Lost Creek Rodeo. Had been for decades.

How much had they offered him to do a gig at the last minute?

"As always," Sal went on, "we'd like to take a moment to honor this great nation of ours, and the men and women giving their lives to maintain our freedoms. We ask you to please rise, remove your hats, and join last year's Miss Harville County, Alyssa Jean Marley, in the singing of our national anthem."

Ryan removed his hat, as did everyone else, and held it over his heart as the Stars and Stripes were carried by a rider on horseback into the middle of the arena, spotlights fixed on its waving fabric. This had always been his favorite part of the rodeo, aside from his ride itself. This pause while the flag waved, the stirring strains of the song rippling around them, and realizing, time and again, that he was fortunate to be able to compete, that when all else failed, he had this great nation in his life, and that the results of the rodeo were small when compared with what so many others had given.

He didn't compete now, obviously, but the pause was still moving for him, and the realizations were still hitting him. No matter what happened next in his life, no matter what he chose to do in the future as far as rodeo was concerned, no matter how the ranch panned out, he'd be all right.

He'd get by.

Cheers and whistles hit him like a wall of sound as the song finished, and he replaced his hat, soothing his horse a little more.

"All right, all right, all right," Sal drawled in an overdone twang that was perfectly suited for the evening. "Let's meet your pickup men for the night! Take a lap, boys! Local grown-and-fed favorite neighbor, Jed Oscar! A familiar face around here, Mikey Jessop! And newcomer to the title, but certainly not to the crowd or this arena, ladies and gents, welcome back Ryan Prosper!"

Ryan lifted a hand in the air in acknowledgement as he galloped a lap, but the roar of the crowd took him by surprise. He joined Jed and Mikey shortly, shaking his head, eyes wide with disbelief.

Jed chomped on his gum, grinning. "Well, get on back out there, son, and give the people a proper salute!"

Nodding, Ryan turned his horse and rode back out a little, sweeping his hat from his head and holding it aloft, bringing people to their feet with louder cheers and more whistles. He laughed at the sight, the sound, and put a hand to his heart, patting softly in a gesture of thanks.

No ride in the world had ever given him a moment like this.

He'd never forget it as long as he lived.

He put his hat back on his head and rode back to join the other pickup men again, trying to hide how choked up he was getting. This was all about business—he couldn't be a weeping mess of emotions.

To his surprise, Mikey was red around his eyes and swallowing hard.

"Y'all right there?" Ryan asked around the rough patch in his throat.

"Yup." Jed grinned again, nudging his head toward Mikey. "He swallowed down the wrong tube. No worries. Ready for this?"

Ryan nodded once. "Ready."

"You ever ride pickup before?" Jed asked, narrowing his eyes. "I know you can ride like the devil, but you ever done this?"

Ryan shook his head. "Nope. Think I got the general idea, though."

Mikey barked a laugh. "I'd hope so, after the years you spent around here. Normally, we work in pairs, but Lost Creek likes three. One for the rider, one for the animal, and a utility to help the others if needed. Got a preference?"

"I'd prefer the rider, if you don't mind," Ryan told them both, almost apologetic. "It'll keep my sister from getting a heart attack."

"Fair enough. I got animal." Jed nodded once and whistled at his horse, who immediately turned to the right and galloped toward the chutes.

"I don't mind being utility," Mikey said with a laugh. "Keep an eye on the flankmen, will ya? I heard someone say they're new. Not gonna like that if it's true." He dipped his chin and rode off to another side of the arena.

Ryan nudged his horse into a quick trot, moving over to a better vantage point to see both the chute and the rider as they set up for the bareback event. Coincidentally, the best position also provided a decent view of Talia and his sister. He caught their eyes and slowly grinned, letting his true emotions from his intro shine through.

Talia had her arm around Kellie's waist, beaming with pride that shone like the sun. Kellie was wiping her eyes, smiling a watery smile that would have embarrassed him had he not felt the same thing swirling within him. He wasn't a man prone to tears, but even he was struggling at the moment.

He'd missed this. It was different now, but the spirit and energy were the same. Maybe that was enough for him now.

Maybe.

Ryan tapped the front of his hat with a quick grin for his sister, saw her wave in response, and turned his attention to the chute as the first rider prepared to start.

Reid was seventh in the lineup tonight, so there was plenty of time for him to prep for his ride. As a matter of habit, Ryan glanced over to the chute Reid would be launching from, and sure enough, there he was. It was his prized superstition, hanging out by his chute way before he was on deck. He insisted it got him in the proper mindset and was better than visualization.

Considering Reid rode out of his mind every time he did so, no one said anything to him about it.

He wouldn't meet Ryan's eyes, though he would see him looking if he paid any attention. Reid was in the zone from the moment he set foot near the chute, and there would be no breaking his concentration until he'd finished his ride, be it the required eight seconds or only two.

Sal came over the sound system again, this time announcing the first event of the night and the first rider in it.

The bareback event was always a hot one to watch, which was probably why it happened first in the lineup. Everybody wanted to see the crazy people ride.

Everything looked good in the chute, which really wasn't Ryan's business, but he knew the ins and outs of the participant side of things, so he saw a lot more than the average pickup man. Ryan sat up straighter in his saddle as the first rider signaled he was ready, watching carefully.

Then the rider burst from the chute, the horse bucking wildly and tossing him about in a classic representation of this event. Ryan found himself counting along with the clock, holding his breath in anticipation of the eight-second mark.

Four ... five ... six ...

"Come on," Ryan hissed, his eyes flicking from rider to clock and back again.

At seven seconds, Ryan dug his heels into his horse, riding hard. When eight seconds hit the clock, he came alongside the still-bucking animal Jed was now approaching.

"Hup," Ryan called to the rider.

He jumped from his horse to Ryan's, exhaling in a huge gust before sliding off his much calmer animal. He whooped and waved Ryan on, giving him a thumbs-up as he hustled away, grinning like a madman.

Ryan nodded in acknowledgement, turning his horse to survey the others and the calming efforts for the bucking horse. Everything was under control there, which meant the first ride of the Lost Creek rodeo had gone off without a hitch.

Now they just needed the rest of them to do the same.

Ryan sputtered noisily to himself as he rode back to his first position, settling in for what could be a long night.

As it happened, the bareback event moved along at a pretty good clip. The fourth guy didn't make eight seconds, and the sixth barely did, but no one had major injuries or penalties, which meant Ryan's job was decently simple.

Now it was Reid's turn, and from the looks of things in the chute, it was going to be a doozy.

The animal was not cooperating, and the flankman wasn't helping matters. Reid struggled to get his left foot down into position, with the horse leaning to the left once he'd sat down. He had a decent hold on his rigging, and the cinch seemed to be in place, but there was something off about the way it sat. It was tough to tell from here, but Ryan was shaking his head as he watched. Something was definitely off, and he couldn't put his finger on it. Reid was focused on trying to get his foot free, understandably, and the flankman was doing a weak job of controlling the situation.

He could not let his friend go into a ride when something was off. He couldn't let any rider do it, friend or otherwise.

Before he could think of proper procedure, he clicked his tongue and was riding toward the chute, hand in the air.

A murmur of voices rippled across the stands as he rode, but he ignored them. No one noticed when he reached the chute, and he saw the problem at once when he looked closely. He whistled loudly, bringing heads around, including Reid's, who was in full action mode.

"What?" he barked, wrenching his foot free finally as the horse listed right.

Ryan didn't look at him as he glowered at the team working the chute. "Was anyone planning on actually tightening the flank strap on this horse? Or were you planning on having Reid here break his neck on the first second out when he goes somersaulting over the back end and gets kicked in the head once he's landed?"

Reid's eyes widened as he looked down at the team tasked with assisting the rider and prepping any animal in chute seven. The way his jaw tightened, Ryan knew there were at least a dozen curses running through his head, but his decency prevented him from lashing out.

Which meant Ryan would.

"If you can't work the chute," he ordered without sympathy, "get out of it. Give the man a stable base for his grip, or you'll be the one we send the hospital bills to. Got it?"

"What's the problem, folks?" the paunchy chute boss asked as he sauntered over. "Holding us up."

Ryan looked at him coldly. "The problem is your inability to keep a firm grip on your people, bucko. I wouldn't let my worst enemy ride out with a crap job like this, but you go ahead and let the damn rodeo all-stars of America get killed by your own ignorant teams on your watch. That'd shape up real nice for you, wouldn't it?"

Ryan looked back at the team, now looking sour but chagrined. "Strap him in right, or so help me, I'll get in there and do it myself." He nodded without waiting for a response, and looked at the blustering chute boss again. "Get yourself people who aren't distracted by the high-strung ones, all right? This isn't a job for greenhorns."

"I know how to do my job," the man grumbled, scratching at his neck.

"If that were true," Ryan snapped, "we wouldn't be having this conversation, and I would be happily minding my own business. Figure it out."

He looked up at Reid, who was steaming, but silent. He gave Ryan a firm nod of thanks, then turned his attention to the team now actually doing their job.

Only when all was set according to Ryan's standards did he leave the chute, riding back to his position. He nodded at Jed and Mikey, but did not answer their questioning looks. If he had done his job right, Reid should have the most perfect conditions to ride ever.

Whether he rode to perfection in them remained to be seen.

Reid's hand went into the air in the ready position, and all went silent. The chute gate opened, and the horse dashed out, bucking madly and with impressive heights. Reid was in full control, battered back and forth like a rag doll, but with the perfect form only a rodeo rider could appreciate. The horse would get a high score for sure, and if Reid could hold on, keep himself steady . . .

The crowd was wrapped up in this one, cheering hard as the time ticked on.

Ryan watched Reid with a hint of a smile, knowing only too well the thrill of such a wild, perfect, beautiful ride. He would be flying high the rest of the night.

"Seven," Ryan muttered as he rode toward him. "Eight." He matched the horse's speed, coming alongside. "Hup."

Reid straightened as best as he could and flung himself onto Ryan's horse, lying on his stomach across the back, one arm gripping Ryan's side.

"Whew!" he hollered as Ryan peeled off from Jed and the other horse. "That was a beauty! Thanks for saving my neck, Ry."

"Glad to see it was worth the effort." Ryan slowed his horse so Reid could easily hop down, then turned to check on Jed and Mikey before taking his position again.

The next rides were fairly standard, though there was a terrifying near-miss moment with one of the bareback riders. The crowd held its breath, then exhaled together.

Since the next event was steer wrestling, Ryan wasn't needed for pickup duty. He debated between checking in with his friends or going up to the stands to see Talia and his sister, but the debate didn't last very long.

His friends should be getting ready for their events, anyway. They didn't need him as a distraction.

He saw the women before they saw him, and he watched

for a second as Kellie explained the fine art of steer wrestling to the group, gesturing to the event a time or two as contestants came out. Not a single lady looked intrigued by the event.

Poor Ford would be so disappointed.

Ryan ambled down the remaining distance between them and sat behind his sister roughly. "Evening, all."

Kellie and Talia whirled, looking up at him, then grinned, Talia more than Kellie. "Hi!" she squealed, putting a hand on his knee. "You looked great out there!"

"Why, thank you, ma'am," he said playfully, dipping the brim of his hat. "I rode just for you."

She rolled her eyes and wrapped an arm around his lower leg, which was about the cutest sort of bleacher embrace he'd ever had.

"What was the deal with Reid's first ride?" Kellie demanded without any greeting. "I saw you ride over, but I didn't . . ."

"Idiot chute team," he muttered, shaking his head darkly. "They didn't tighten the flank strap. Dang animal was fidgety and leaned left, so he had his foot caught, and the flankman didn't know the horse's nose from his nether regions, so he just stood there, and no one tightened the darn thing."

Kellie's eyes were round when he finished. "Are you serious?" she half-whispered. "Ryan, that could have been disastrous!"

He nodded soberly. "Definitely could have. And the chute boss is more upset that I caught it than that it happened."

"I'm texting Tom Hauser." Kellie yanked out her phone, shaking her head. "Unbelievable."

"I have no idea what exactly you said," Talia said as she looked up at him, her fingers tracing absently against the denim of his jeans. "But it sounds serious."

Ryan managed a rueful smile. "Sorry, Princess Rookie. I'll try again." He wet his lips, thinking quickly. "Reid rides bareback. Means no saddle. But he does have a kind of handle called rigging. It hooks into what we call a cinch, which is a band that goes tight around the horse right about where you would consider the shoulder, what's called the withers of the horse. Just behind the front legs, okay?"

Talia nodded, listening attentively, as were a few of the other guests.

"Now," he went on, his right hand gripping at air like Reid would have grabbed his rigging, "if everything is tight like it should be, Reid still has something taut attaching him to the horse. Keeps him from actually flying off the horse, if he can hang onto it. If the flank strap isn't tight, that rigging wiggles around like he's flying a kite in a twister, and he's got nothing anchoring him to the horse. Nice way to break your arm, if not send you end-over-end off the animal."

"Holy crap," Talia breathed, fully comprehending now, her hold on Ryan's leg tightening. "Reid could have died."

He hadn't gone to that extreme in his mind, but he couldn't deny there was a possibility, given the risks. "Potentially," he evaded without conceding. "Definitely could have ended his career, no doubt."

Talia shook her head slowly, then the corner of her mouth curved a little. "And y'all call this fun."

"It *is* fun," he insisted. "When it's done right." He cocked his head at her, grinning fondly. "Did you just say 'y'all'?"

She shrugged. "It's rubbing off."

He leaned forward, wanting to kiss her like crazy, but knowing better than to do so here. "I've never found you more attractive than right now."

As he'd hoped, she blushed furiously, her free hand slapping at his leg. "Shut up."

One of the new guests rose at the end of the line and started toward them. "I'm gonna go up for concessions," she told the rest. "Anybody want something?"

Ryan rose at once and stepped out into the aisle. "I'll come with you, June."

She seemed surprised by that. "You don't have to, Ryan. Take a break."

He shook his head very firmly. "No, ma'am. At an event like this, I'd not let any of you go by yourself, except maybe my sister, and that's only because everybody knows not to mess with her." He smiled as kindly as he could while still being firm. "I don't anticipate trouble, but I'm overprotective."

"You can say that again," Talia laughed, rising as well. "Just the other day, he wouldn't let Jill go up to pay for her own tab since there was a guy at the bar eyeing her."

"I stand by that," he protested without shame. "Jill even thanked me before she left for the airport."

"My hero," Talia said in a perfectly flat tone.

June seemed fine with the escort, however, so the three of them started up the stairs together.

"Is it terrible to admit that I'm kind of glad you're not competing?" Talia asked Ryan softly as they reached the top.

He gave her a bewildered look. "Why's that?"

She shook her head, swallowing. "I finally looked you up on YouTube, and I saw a couple of the videos where you got injured. Scared me to death, babe. I don't know how you ever did it, or how your mother slept at night."

He draped an arm around her shoulder and pulled her tight into his side. "It's safer than you think."

"Oh, really?" she retorted, sarcasm dripping. "Tell that to your left kidney." She shuddered and rubbed at her arms. "I have no idea why you would love something that could get you killed, and almost did. And then you tell me how Reid could have been injured today . . ."

"Talia." He traced his fingers along her upper arm as they walked, glancing briefly to check on June where she was on his other side, staying close. "Did you watch any of the videos where I didn't get hurt?"

She shook her head stubbornly. "I couldn't watch any more."

"Hmm." He did his best to hide his smile, but couldn't quite manage. "I love that you were worried about me. It's cute."

She punched him in the side softly. "It's not funny."

"Didn't say funny. I said cute." But he chuckled and pressed a quick kiss to her cheek. "I'm fine, Talia. Alive, well, walking next to you, and riding a horse without any pain or hesitation down there. It's fine. Next time you're curious, though, watch the ones where I don't get hurt. I was really something."

Talia laughed once and looked up at him slyly. "Still are, Ryan Prosper. Still are."

CHAPTER 16

TODAY WAS THE DAY. Her journal said so, her morning session with Kellie said so, and her mind said so.

Her heart, on the other hand, wished she'd stayed in bed.

She hadn't told anybody what she'd discovered was at the root of her grief over Austin, not even Kellie, though she suspected her friend and therapist had more than a hunch. She hadn't even told Ryan what it was, though he knew she would be sharing her breakthrough in group therapy today.

He easily accepted her wish to be alone today leading up to the group therapy session, and supported it wholeheartedly. He had the rodeo again tonight, and she had promised to swing by his place before he left, if for no other reason than to give him a kiss for luck.

Or for anything.

Kissing Ryan was on the list of greatest things she'd experienced in her life.

He was, without a doubt, the sweetest man she had ever met. He went out of his way to do things for her, to spend time with her, to listen to her, and read each and every one of her signals perfectly. He held her when she needed to be held, made her laugh when she wanted to laugh, let her cry in those moments when her reality overwhelmed her or her longing for her son was too much. It was like he couldn't decide on her love language, so he made sure to excel in all of them just in case.

It made falling for him a challenge. Not the actual falling part—she was joyfully drowning in loving him—but what could she offer the best man she'd ever met when he constantly gave? She was a broken woman caught in a whirlpool of grief, though she was on her way to healing and finding a way out. How could that be in any way appealing to him?

And if she told him her breakthrough . . .

Would he think she was as selfish as she thought she was?

She'd be willing to risk it, if the group session went well. She was counting on it to bolster her courage so she could share with him what she shared with them. It was a sign of progress, she decided, that she trusted this information to her group first and to Ryan second. These women were broken themselves, some further along in their journey than Talia, others at the very beginning, but they all understood the pain of being stuck. Of feeling shattered. Of not being understood.

Before her arrival, Talia had been confused as to how women from different walks of life and different trials could be united by their grief, but now she understood. It didn't matter what had caused the breaking of their hearts; what mattered was that they were broken, and broken hearts understood other broken hearts.

She could tell them this thing.

And as for Ryan . . . She would say he had a broken heart, too, though he seemed to have found his peace with it. His openness with her had allowed them to share more than she might have done with anybody else, and in a way, he had come on this healing journey with her. Had they not developed their relationship into a romance, she might have shared her feelings on her grief with him the moment she'd realized them. As it was, she was afraid to. Ryan was a rock to her now, and if he found her revelation horrible, she could break all over again.

She'd risk it, given the need to continue moving forward in her healing, but she desperately needed him to be with her in this massive step.

Time would tell.

She glanced up at the clock from her seat on the bed, her leg bouncing up and down anxiously. It was time, and unless she wanted to take one large step back, she needed to head out to the great room.

You've got this, Mom, Austin's voice said in her mind, making her heart swell and her eyes burn.

He'd tell her that whenever she was reluctant to do something, be it a bake sale, grocery shopping, or a job interview. He'd once said it before the first day of school, when she was making a big deal about his being older and being gone all day after a perfect summer of great adventures together. No matter what she was doing, Austin had always encouraged her with wisdom beyond his years. Sometimes, it was unclear who was the parent and who was the child.

She missed that daily, but every now and then, her memories brought him back to her.

"Thanks, baby," she whispered to the memory, pushing up from her bed.

Rubbing her fingers together, she left her bedroom and started down the hall for the great room. Someone had started a fire in the great stone fireplace, and Talia changed direction to sit beside it, wanting the heat to seep into her as much as anything else. The comfort that she usually felt around a campfire could work in her favor here.

June and Amanda were in the room already, and Kellie approached from her office, notebook in hand. Tracy, another recent arrival, soon arrived with an eager smile, followed by her fellow newbie, Megan. The last to arrive was Cassie, and her perfect white-blonde curls bounced with the same energy she always carried.

"Sorry," she panted breathlessly as she slid into a seat. "My sister would not shut up. She just yaks, yaks, yaks. My gosh. Okay. Hi, I'm here."

Talia giggled, as did a few others.

Kellie smiled, shaking her head. "It's fine, I'm not that strict, you know that. How's everybody doing? Feeling okay?"

Nods bobbed all around, a faint murmur of acknowledgements without many specifics.

"You all know each other well enough now, right?" Kellie asked as she looked around the group.

Again, everyone nodded.

"I hope you're going to be more talkative than this in our session," Kellie told them all with a laugh. "Otherwise, it's going to be a long one."

Now they all managed to look a little sheepish, but comfortably so, if that was a thing. It was impossible to be anything less with Kellie.

Kellie crossed one leg over the other, which was sort of her trademark for beginning the session in earnest. "Okay, for those of you who are new, we have just a few rules. No cross-talking during shares. There is a discussion section after shares, so any questions or suggestions are welcome at that time. Anything personal shared in here stays in here. No outside discussion, okay?" She glanced around for the nods of understanding, then nodded herself. "Anyone want to share first?"

Talia swallowed hard and raised her hand. "I do."

There was no hint of surprise on Kellie's face as she looked at Talia, smiling in encouragement. "Go ahead, then."

Exhaling slowly, Talia looked down at the ground for a moment. "My son died in November. It was the first snowfall of the year, and he and his best friend were walking home from school. They paused to have a snowball fight. I didn't know any of this—I had stayed late at work and was racing home on a later train than usual. If I hadn't done that, I'd have gone looking for him when he wasn't home at his normal time. I was a worrier mom."

She heard a few hums of understanding and looked up, seeing the eyes of all the guests on her, many showing a strong solidarity with that particular mom vibe.

"A car was going too fast in the neighborhood," Talia went on, keeping her connection with the others. "The roads were slick. The car skidded on a turn and hit Austin head-on. He was unresponsive at the scene, but still breathing. The driver was hysterical; she called 911 and stayed with Austin until I could get there. I forgave her, of course. She sends me a card every month."

She paused, swallowing hard. "I've never been able to tell the whole story without breaking down. It still hurts, but I don't feel like I'm dying when I tell it. I realized that it's not the grief of losing my son that has made me stuck in this cycle. It's guilt."

The word hung in the air, and Talia let it hang, her chest buzzing with anxiety as she reached the point of her sharing today. "Not guilt about staying late," she clarified in a rough voice. "It wasn't intentional on my part, and that happens. It was guilt about what I did at the hospital."

Her jaw began to quiver, and she clamped her teeth together to steady it. "Austin was hooked up to all kinds of machines. Lying there in his hospital bed, all the tests in the world being run on him. He could breathe on his own, but barely. Pulse was weak, but there. They told me that he was brain-dead, and there was no coming back from that. I sat there for an hour, staring at my baby, listening to the machines that kept him alive. I had the paperwork in my hands to end it all. But how could I do that?"

She heard a sniffle in the room, though she couldn't stare at anyone directly, so she wasn't sure who it was.

"But that boy in the bed," Talia told them, trying to be firm, "the one who looked so small and fragile with everything he was hooked up to, wasn't my Austin. I didn't want to keep him here like that. He'd have hated it. So I signed the papers, then climbed into the bed and lay down beside him. I held him in my arms, and I told him that it was okay to let go. I told him he didn't have to hold on anymore. I told my baby boy to let go." Tears filled her eyes and spilled out onto her cheeks, the memories as clear as her vision. "And he let go. Within minutes, he was gone. And the moment he was, I hated myself. I told him it was okay to go, but it wasn't okay. I wasn't okay with him going."

She shook her head, her throat constricting for a long moment. "My baby boy left because I told him to go. What if I could have fought for him? What if there were other options? What if . . .? I've asked myself all of the questions, and even though I know the likelihood of all that, I know the logic isn't there, I still have this crippling guilt. I told him he could go when I didn't mean it, and because of that, I feel like the world's worst excuse for a mother. I did what I thought was best for my son, and I hate myself for doing it."

There was silence in the room but for another sniffle, and Talia inhaled, then exhaled slowly. "Guilt, not grief, is what's trapping me. Now I know that, but I'm not sure it changes my process." She managed a very weak smile as she looked across the circle at Amanda. "And then there's the guilt that I feel more guilt than grief, but let's not complicate things further."

The group laughed gently with her, and smiles were on every face, along with a few tears.

What was more, Talia felt as though she had unlocked something within her, some room she had forgotten or ignored that was now open and acknowledged, aired out for the world. And for herself, most of all. She had shared something that she had been passing over for months and months, something that she had been too ashamed to admit to herself.

One step. She had taken one step, though it felt like she had done a hundred-meter hurdle race by the way her heart was pounding and her head was swimming.

But it was exhilarating, she wouldn't deny that.

She looked at Kellie, unsure if she was looking for approval or permission or something less easily defined. Kellie was smiling at her with pride, her warmth somehow magnified and enhanced in this moment. Like receiving a hug without either of them moving, and the comfort in that was profound.

"Thank you," Kellie told her, the tone of her voice soft and clear. She looked around at the others. "Who would like to go next?"

That feeling of exhilaration didn't fade when the session came to an end, even after four others shared—June had taken the session to just listen to the others. The discussion had varied for them all, and Talia had been told repeatedly that her feelings were absolutely justifiable, and she did not need to feel like she was somehow less of a suitable mother because of it. She'd offered some advice for the others and asked a few questions to add to the conversation, then Kellie had led them in a discussion about action when they lack motivation.

It had been useful and thought provoking, but Talia had been waiting for the end of the session to get out to Ryan's place. The response of her fellow guests had been encouraging, and the follow-up questions and affirmations had given her confidence. She had to keep going in this vein, had to find other breakthroughs to keep her skipping along like a rock on the water, had to share this incredible feeling with Ryan . . .

She might even have to tell him that she was in love with him, but she might lose that bit of bravery on the walk over.

"Kellie?" Talia called as she passed the kitchen on her way to the door. "I'm just heading over to see Ryan. I'll be back to help with dinner ASAP."

"Take your time, sweetie," Kellie called back brightly. "I got this. Tell him to keep a sharp eye out from me, okay?"

Talia grinned at the sisterly suggestion. "You got it!" She pushed the door open and jogged down the porch stairs, inhaling the fresh ranch air that she had come to love so much. It had a saltiness to it that added a nice spice to things, not like a sea salt, but more like a raw, natural salt that came with the smell of grass, straw, earth, and hard work. It was a special fragrance she had never experienced anywhere else.

It reminded her of Ryan, since the same scent lingered on him with every kiss, every hug, and every whiff of his ridiculously good-smelling self.

Walking to his house was a bit of a hike, but she loved doing it, and the ATVs intimidated her too much to cut the time of her journey. Besides, she needed the exercise. She texted Ryan, though, just to see if he could meet her in the middle.

His response came back at once.

"Already coming out, my princess. Kells told me you were headed over."

Talia grinned at her phone, shoving it back in her pocket,

wondering why in the world Kellie would have given Ryan advance notice, but not particularly bothered by it. The siblings were close, and she envied that, being an only child. Her cousins were close to each other, and she was close to them, but that was different.

She squinted at something in the distance, then felt her heart dance as the familiar figure of Ryan came toward her. She hadn't seen him all day, and it was a painful amount of time that was only hitting her now.

How had he become so important to her so fast?

She whistled suggestively as they neared each other. "Who's that gorgeous cowboy striding toward me?" she drawled with as much of a twang as she could drum up. "He looks like a guy I wanna know."

"He's all right," Ryan called back. "Totally into the princess of his dreams heading in his particular direction right now. Hope that's not a problem."

"Oh, babe, you have no idea how good that sounds." She bit her lip and picked up her pace. "Get here now. Right now."

His smile would have set her on fire if she let herself dwell on it, but instead, she launched herself into his arms, her mouth finding his with an easy familiarity that was second nature now. Her lips tangled with his, a sudden longing and urgency rising to a fever pitch within her, curling her toes and tightening her hold on him until it was almost painfully close. She wanted to lose herself in him, find the root of this feeling he instilled in her, breathe in the flavor and fragrance of him until nothing else existed. Whatever she'd unlocked today, he was reaping the rewards.

One of his hands slid to her face, and he gently pried her away from him, though he kept her close with his arm around her back. "Not that I'm complaining," he told her with an unsteady voice, "but I gotta work tonight, and you're about to make me lose my mind and my manners. What brought this on?"

Talia hummed as his thumb traced a line down her jaw, then dipped beneath her bottom lip. She blinked almost dreamily, sighing. "I had a breakthrough. A freeing, brilliant breakthrough that might change everything. It might change nothing. I don't know, I was scared to death, and still am."

"Why?" Ryan asked with concern, his bright eyes searching hers. "What's wrong, darlin'?"

Her overwhelming emotions returned, and she encircled his wrist with one hand, holding on for dear life. "I'm afraid you'll hate me when I tell you. That it will disappoint you. That you won't . . . feel this way anymore."

"You serious, Talia?" His brow creased, and he kissed her hard before touching his brow to hers. "What part of not letting go of me wasn't clear enough? You say you killed a man, I'll get a shovel. You say you're on the run, I'll get my truck. There's not a darn thing that would change the way I feel. Okay?"

"I love you," she whispered before she could stop herself, shaking in his hold. Blushing, she added, "And I really hope that's not my breakthrough talking."

Ryan chuckled softly. "I don't care if it is, I'm taking that as truth. And I love you back, so I think we're square." He pressed his lips to her brow, then pulled her against his chest, holding tightly. "If you wanna tell me, tell me. Otherwise, I'll just hold you until I have to go."

Talia inhaled the glorious scent of him, relishing in the feeling of perfect rightness that being here gave her. She'd never felt this before, never known it existed before, and she never wanted to be without it.

She could trust him with this.

"I told Austin he could go," she said as she laid her cheek against him. "When we were in the hospital, and he was all hooked up. I signed the papers to take him off the machines and told my baby he didn't have to hold on anymore. That it was okay if he let go."

Ryan didn't say a word, but his hold on her tightened further still.

Talia shook her head. "But it wasn't okay. I wasn't. I didn't want him to go, and as soon as he did, I hated myself for letting him go. I've been carrying around that guilt ever since. And that hate. More than my grief, a lot of the time. I miss my baby, I miss him with all my heart. But I feel so guilty, Ryan, that I said he could go when I didn't mean it."

"I don't think it's that simple, love," he murmured, kissing her hair gently. "You meant it, just not for your own heart. You meant it for Austin, since he wasn't really living on those machines. But telling him he could let go of life doesn't mean you let go of him. Doesn't mean he let go of you. And I don't think he'd have gone so quick if he didn't think his mama would be okay."

She looked up at Ryan, resting her chin against him. "You think so?"

He nodded slowly. "Mm-hmm. I do. That boy took care of you, as much as his age would let him, and I think he knew your heart. He knew you have trouble letting go of things, and he knew you'd never let him go for good. And I don't think any mother in the world would feel differently than you on this one. Give yourself some grace, Talia. Don't let go of Austin. Let go of the guilt."

"I'll try," she whispered, smiling a little. "Now that I've realized this, I can try. You don't think less of me?"

Ryan raised a brow at her. "I'd cart you off into the sunset now if I didn't have a prior engagement and a very protective sister who would have my hide for taking you away from here before she signed your completion."

Talia pursed her lips, eyes narrowing. "I think that's a no to my question, but I'm not sure."

He kissed her softly and thoroughly, making her ears ring with the deliciousness of the feeling. "Sure now?"

"Uh-huh," she slurred, nodding. "Got it."

"Good." He cleared his throat and pulled back just a little. "Now, I got to looking at my calendar, and I realized that Austin's birthday is just after you're scheduled to be back home. I didn't like the idea that I wouldn't be there to help you that day, so I made you something. Kellie gave me the idea . . ." He dropped the arm around her back, and she saw, for the first time, that there was a small, flat box in his hand.

"What's this?" Her heart pounded as she took the box from him, all nerves on end.

He nudged his head at it. "You'll see."

Talia swallowed, tugged the string ribbon off, and lifted the lid.

Inside sat an iron horseshoe, a piece of thin rope hanging between the two ends, and along the center was inscribed the name "Austin."

"I thought you might like to have that in your house for luck," Ryan told her, his voice sounding almost hesitant. "Bit of heaven on earth, maybe. And if you'll lift it . . ."

She did so, tearing up when she saw a thin, silver band of a bracelet, a pattern of horse shoes along its surface. She lifted it up and turned it over, gasping that on the inside, where it would be against her skin, was Austin's name as well.

"Oh, Ryan . . ." She shook her head, setting both things back in the box and closing the lid. She went to him, folding her arms around his neck and pulling him down to her. "Thank you. Thank you, thank you."

"I meant what I said," he told her, his lips brushing her ear. "I love you, Talia James. I know it's not been that long, and I know you're here for Austin, but that doesn't make it any less true."

"I know," she assured him. She kissed his neck, then pressed her brow to it. "I know." She exhaled roughly, sliding back down to the ground and giving him a disgruntled look. "Could you be less perfect sometimes, please?"

Ryan laughed once, one hand going to his hips in a perfect cowboy stance as his cheeks turned red. "Aw, I'm just a run-of-the-mill cowboy, Princess Angel."

"Run-of-the-mill?" Talia repeated in disbelief. She coughed a laugh. "Okay, Ryan, there are good guys, and then there's you. It's like dating Santa Claus, only way sexier."

"I'll take sexier, that sounds good," he quipped with a quick flash of a smile.

Talia widened her eyes and gestured an obvious "duh" to his statement. "Yeah, it *sounds* good. But regular human beings who love such a person kinda struggle because it feels like . . . I feel like I have nothing to give you, and you give so much."

"Nothing to give?" It was Ryan's turn to be shocked, and he seemed almost mad about her statement. "Honey, you give me the sun when I've been living in a constant state of rain. You make my heart beat when it hasn't done that in years. You give . . . Hell, you give me a reason to get out of bed every morning."

"You've got the ranch to get up for."

He gave her a pointed look. "You can be awake and moving around without actually leaving your bed. I know you know what I mean."

Her lungs constricted with the truth of the statement. It had been her life since November; she knew exactly what he was saying. "Yes."

He lowered his chin a little, meeting her eyes more intently. "I would still be in that place if it wasn't for you."

Something about his statement made her ache, and not in the way she wanted to. She shook her head sadly. "I can't build a relationship on being your happy pill, sweetheart. It needs more."

"Yeah, I know. Remember who my sister is? I'm sure, as sure as I know I'm standing here, that you have changed me." He smiled and held out a hand to her. "I may not have the right words yet, Talia, but I know I love you, and I know that's not a happy pill. Can I walk you back?"

She nodded, taking his hand and squeezing hard. "I would love that. And I can't wait for you to get those right words, because I sure love the heart that will be saying them."

He tugged her hand to his lips, kissing it softly and winking. Then they started back to the house, the box tight in her hold, her heart tugging in two directions where he, and they, were concerned. She loved him, he loved her, but could either of them trust a relationship that started at a ranch meant for healing broken hearts? She wanted to, she wanted to badly, but if there wasn't more than what he'd said . . .

He needed those right words if they were going to make this work when she left.

She didn't even know what those words were herself.

"I watched more videos of you," she told him, desperate to lighten the mood. "The non-injury ones."

"Did you? And?"

She made a show of fanning herself. "It was about the sexiest thing I have ever seen. I can't wait to go to the rodeo tonight to get more."

"Huh-uh, no, ma'am," he said at once, his hold on her hand tightening playfully. "You are excused from attending if you're finding yourself hot and bothered by any roughie with skills. I may be a has-been, Princess, but I do have my pride."

Talia nodded in thought as he blustered, fighting the urge

to laugh. "And if I wanted to go so I could see how these wannabes match up with your gloriousness? What then?"

"In *that* case . . ." He tipped his hat back and gave her the most dashing crooked smile known to cowboys anywhere. "Front row seats, ma'am. And a free rodeo T-shirt for your troubles. My treat."

Laughter bubbled up within her and erupted without restraint, echoing out across the land of the ranch.

CHAPTER 17

HE'D HAVE KICKED HIMSELF if he had the flexibility and the spurs to make it worth his while.

Talia thought she was his happy pill? That was the impression he had given her?

She was so much more than that. She was the brightest part of his life, not the only bright spot in his life, and that he'd made her think anything less was a crime.

The fact that she was still talking to him, when he'd clearly done a lousy job of making his feelings and intentions known, was a miracle. She should have stormed away from him, or walked back to the house alone to let him stew in his stupidity. She should have told him not to see her again until he got his priorities straight, or his head on right, or something equally as paralyzing.

But Talia was gracious, forgiving, and patient, and she'd not brought the subject up again, despite the few days that had lapsed since then.

The rodeo had wrapped up, which had occupied Ryan decently after getting that miserable revelation, and the actively competing members of the Six had impressed the locals suitably. Plenty of requests for autographs and questions as to their intentions for the upcoming circuit, which had made a few of them happy. Ford and Lars didn't really care, which was typical for them, but they had delighted a few people by promising they'd come back for future rodeos.

Ryan had surprised himself by how much he'd enjoyed his participation in the rodeo, given he never got on a bull or competed in any way. In fact, he'd enjoyed it so much that he'd already gotten in touch with Tom Hauser about working on future rodeos. They were going to meet up next week to iron out the details, and he planned on lodging a formal complaint about the lousy flankmen and chute boss, but the prospect of taking on a bigger, more involved role in future events was exciting.

Provided, of course, that this next conversation went the way he hoped.

Kellie could be a tyrant when it came to matters of the ranch. He loved her to death, but she knew just how to get under his skin, and prided herself on doing so.

"Kells?" Ryan called as he entered the house, timing his visit during the morning hours, when the guests would be working on their chores for the day, to give them privacy.

"In here," came the muffled reply from the direction of her office.

Ryan changed direction and headed over there, knocking on the slightly ajar door. "Is here the here in 'in here?'"

"You're an idiot," she said in the same tone as her first response.

Laughing to himself, he pushed open the door and grinned at his dour-faced sister. "Come on, that was funny."

Kellie shook her head firmly. "No. It wasn't."

He shrugged and dropped himself into the easy chair usually reserved for her clients. "Got a question for you."

"Professional or personal?"

He winced slightly. "Both."

Her eyes widened, and she set her pen down and folded her arms across her desk. "Okay... What's up?"

Ryan exhaled carefully, weighing his words, given his recent history with screwing them up. "How would you feel about my taking on a more active role in the Lost Creek Rodeo?"

Kellie blinked at the question. "Are you serious?"

"It wouldn't take up all of my time," he assured her quickly, sitting forward. "Probably wouldn't even take most of my time, but I haven't met with Tom yet. I'm looking to do more than just be pickup, maybe even be chute boss a time or two. Next year, though, I'd want to get more hands-on in the whole thing, see if we can avoid the fiasco that almost happened this year. But the ranch would always come first. My priorities are here, I just want to see about keeping in touch with that part of my life."

"You *are* serious," Kellie said in disbelief, a little slack jawed as she stared at him. "Ryan..."

He screwed up his face in apprehension. "Go ahead, let me have it."

"This is the best thing I've heard you say since you came home from the hospital."

His eyes snapped open, and he jerked in surprise. "What?"

Kellie grinned so wide, her eyes crinkled almost to slits, and she started to laugh, clapping her hands together. "Ryan, of *course* you need to stay involved in rodeo! I'm thrilled! This is fantastic. I was so afraid you'd avoid it forever! It broke my heart to see you keeping your distance, but I knew you needed to find your own way, and you asked me to stop pestering, so I did..."

"Was that what that was?" Ryan teased as relief rolled over him in continuous waves, sinking him into the chair more fully. "I thought stopping meant, you know, leaving me alone."

She ignored him—probably for the best. "But you looked so good out there, bud. An absolute natural, and you know rodeo so well. I'm not worried at all about the ranch, I know you'll do fine at balancing. And I can always step in while you're finding your footing, you know that. Whatever you and Tom want to plan for future rodeos, do it. Just do it, Ryan."

Ryan smiled at his sister with all the affection in the world. "Sometimes, you're the greatest, you know that?"

"I've been trying to tell you, but would you listen to me?" She laughed again and looked up at the ceiling, shaking her head. "Amazing. I can't wait to see what you figure out."

"Me, too." He sighed, leaning his head back on the chair. "At least it's one thing I've figured out, despite everything."

Kellie's eyes lowered to his with perfect accuracy. "Talia?"

He nodded, for once grateful his sister had a sixth sense about him at times. "I tried to tell her how I feel, what she does for me, and it came out sounding like I think she's my happy pill."

The wince that crossed her face gave him more of a sinking feeling than he expected. "Yeah, that's not a healthy relationship. I know that's not what you mean, but it would definitely throw up some red flags with the work she and I have been doing. I'm assuming you're in this for the long haul?"

Again, he nodded. "Oh, yeah. This is one-and-only material here. But it's come at a time when we're both trying to embrace a new way of life, not just adjust to it, so the lines are blurry at best. I didn't think it was a complicated situation until we started throwing the word 'love' around, and then it just exploded into chaos."

His sister said nothing, which made him smile without humor. "What? Not going to say 'I told you so' right now?"

"I'm biting my tongue so I don't say that, yeah." Her smile was far more kind, and actually made him feel a little better, for some reason. "Happy to hear you're trying to embrace your life, though. You've been so private about it . . ."

"It's actually something Talia said," he told her, looking over at the quote on the wall he'd never really thought about. "She said she wanted to find joy instead of walk in her loss. I realized I'd been holding onto the loss of my life in the rodeo like it was some badge of honor, or a sign to wear around my neck. I didn't even look for other ways to be."

"I told you that!" Kellie protested, sitting up and jabbing a finger in his direction. "I've told you that like a hundred times!"

Ryan shrugged without concern, smiling mischievously. "Yeah, but it sounds better when she says it." He turned serious for a second. "In all honesty, Kells, you helping her has helped me probably just as much, and not because it brought her here. When she shared her insights with me, I found myself learning with her. Maybe I'm just a slow learner."

"Or you needed to hear it from someone you aren't related to," Kellie suggested easily. "It happens all the time. So you're doing okay? Better, at least?"

"Much better." He glanced out of the window, regret twisting in his stomach. "Or I would be, if I could figure out how to say the right things."

Kellie hummed a laugh. "I think you'll find Talia is a fantastic listener, and she reads between the lines, too. Get out of here and try out the conversation again. She's rubbing down the horses."

Ryan narrowed his eyes at her. "Why do I feel like you're setting me up?"

"Because I'm your sister, and setting you up is what I live for." She batted her lashes, giving him a cheesy smile to end all cheesy smiles.

Pushing out of the seat, Ryan moved toward the desk rather than the door. He leaned over and kissed his sister's head quickly. "Watch out, sis. What goes around comes around."

She tried to swat him, but he dodged and scooted out the door at a fast clip.

The barn had never seemed farther away than at this moment, but he did his best to hurry toward it, wondering if this feeling of dread as he jogged was what Talia'd dealt with on the occasions she had sought him out. There was no way he'd have been able to do it with as much determination as she had. He'd have given up halfway through the first attempt, feeling like this.

But then, with Talia at the end of it, maybe he'd have pushed through. Was that what all of this boiled down to? The uncomfortable moments in life were more bearable because what lay at the end of them was a reward beyond imagining?

He could only imagine how much better those uncomfortable moments would be with someone beside him. Especially when that someone was Talia.

That was everything.

She was everything.

And that was it. That was what she needed to understand, and what he needed to express.

If only he could manage that.

He was to the barn in a few more minutes, and he strode in with a confidence he had been looking for since their last conversation. "Talia?"

"Right here!" Her head peeked out from around a stall, her hair pulled back in a long braid, her eyes bright. She grinned as soon as she saw him. "Hey, hot stuff."

He bowed playfully. "Princess." He moved toward her, loving how right it felt to have her here in the barn, to have her working here with him, to see her so comfortable on his land . . .

Everything was right.

"I think I found some good words for you," he told her as he neared. "Care to hear them?"

Talia's eyes took on a more golden sheen as she smiled up at him. "I'd love to." She turned and walked with him to the other end of the barn, the doors open to the bright, blue sky and the warm sunshine.

"Let's sit," he suggested, gesturing to the step.

She did so, and turned toward him as he sat.

He picked up her hand and laced their fingers, taking a moment to appreciate how her skin felt against his, and to feel the soft abrasion of her newly formed calluses against his hardened ones. "I told you that you give me a reason to get out of bed in the morning. And you were worried that I saw you as my happy pill."

"Not worried, per se," Talia corrected gently, setting her other hand around his. "Only cautious."

"You had a right to be so. You *do* have a right to be so." He looked down at their joined hands, taking a moment to be cautious himself. "It wasn't fair for me to say that. The truth is that I've had a reason to get out of bed for a long time. I didn't always choose to see it that way, but I had started to when you came along."

"I get that," Talia murmured. She nodded, smiling at him. "Choosing is so important. I'm learning that, too."

Ryan swallowed, meeting her eyes again, taking strength

from the love and goodness he saw shining back at him. "I get up now because I have a purpose. And I have hope. But you gave me a new reason to *want* to get out of bed. To look forward to it. I'd be lying if I said you weren't right there at the very top of things that bring me joy. Your journey helped my journey, and I fell in love with you on the way. You're not my happy pill. You're the world I want to be part of."

The brilliance that filled Talia's face as her smile spread would have eclipsed any brightness known to man, and it enveloped him in its warmth. "Oh, Ryan . . ."

"I don't even hate that I can't compete in rodeo anymore. If it weren't for my injury, my career ending, I'd have never met you. And now that seems like a pretty great trade-off. I come out way on top with you." He brought her hands to his lips, kissing them softly. "I love you, Talia, not for making me happy, though you've done that. Not for helping me to see more clearly, but you've done that, too. I love you for the way you've tackled life since you've been here. For the fierceness in the way you love Austin. For the spitfire you are, and the way you've learned to whistle. For every little thing, and every big thing. I'm better with you, Talia James, and I'm not sure I could ever let go of you. Please don't ask me to."

"I'm not," Talia whispered, her voice seeming to rasp in her throat. "I don't want to ask you to. Ryan, I'm not going to. Come here." She pulled him in, wrapping her arms around his neck.

He kissed her then, slowly and surely, and she was just as intent in her actions and attention. There was no frenzy here, no frantic rush of passion, no clashing of desire and eagerness—only the steady, certain, perfect depth of feeling that blew everything else away.

This was perfection.

Eventually, they faded into simply holding each other, the moment too significant to lighten right away.

Then Talia sighed as though releasing a huge weight. "Those were some really great words, Ry. Big fan of them."

He chuckled, moving her braid to the side to kiss her neck lightly. "Thanks. I worked real hard on them."

"I could tell." She pulled back, smiling brightly. "I've got some words, too. And a potential plan, actually."

"Plans are good," he told her with an approving nod. "Care to share?"

Her shoulders lifted in a pose of little-girl excitement that made him laugh. "I think I'm going to go to school. I never did after high school, and I think it's time I look at my life through a new lens: what could be. I would have loved going to college, if I'd been smarter about how I lived my life. A single step is enough, and this is the step I want to take."

He couldn't believe what he was hearing, and excitement hit the center of his chest with a swiftness that stole his breath. "That's fantastic!" he managed, squeezing her hands. "I'm so proud of you! Have you thought about what you'd like to study? Where you'd want to go? My gosh, there's gotta be dozens of options for you out in Chicago. You could go anywhere!"

Talia smiled at that, biting her lip. "Exactly. And I've . . . I've been looking at SHCC, and I think I'd like to go there. If there's a reason for me to go to school there instead of Chicago . . ."

Ryan blinked, breathless for an entirely different reason as he stared at her in shock. "SHCC? But . . . that's out here."

"Yeah, I know." She grinned outright, clearly loving this.

He couldn't laugh so easily. "Honey, you can't . . . You can't be that far from Austin. It would kill you. I'd love having you here, beyond anything, but I can't see you breaking your heart just to stick around."

"I wouldn't be," she insisted with a quiet firmness he had

no choice but to believe. "It would be hard, sure, but that's why we have planes. My family is in Chicago for life, I'll be there often enough to visit. Austin is buried next to my dad, and I've always thought the two of them would look out for each other. Besides, I have this now." She showed him her wrist, where the cuff bracelet proudly sat. "And a beautiful good luck charm that will go with me wherever I live. After being here, I know that Austin goes with me, too. He'll always be with me, and he would want me to go to school where I would be happiest."

Ryan stilled as she reached up and put a hand to his cheek, stroking very softly.

"And I would be happiest here." She smiled with a tenderness that tied his stomach in knots and sent a scorching heat through his chest. "With you."

He turned his face to kiss the palm of her hand, giving her a solemn look. "If you're sure, I'd love nothing more than having you close. But I don't mind flying out to Chicago, either. We can make this work anywhere, hon."

"We've got time," Talia said, shaking her head a little. "We can figure all of this out, the semester doesn't start until August. I go home in a week and change, and I don't want to be away from you for very long. Depending on how everything lines up, I could even start a couple of summer classes. Still a big gap, though."

"I'll book a plane ticket tonight," he told her without hesitation. "Every other week for three days at a time, whatever it takes."

Talia had opened her mouth to reply when her phone rang, the tinny ringtone blaring from her back pocket. She pulled it out and glanced at it, then looked up at him. "I should take this. Do you mind?"

"Nope." He started to get up, but she put a hand on his leg, holding him still.

"Where do you think you're going?" She raised a brow as she hit the answer button, turning her attention to the screen as he got comfortable again. "Hi there!"

"Hey, yourself!" boomed a deep, masculine voice that set Ryan on edge immediately, the screen showing a dark and well-groomed start of a beard. "How's the ranch?"

"Perfect," Talia gushed with feeling, soothing Ryan's nerves. "I've been brushing the horses today."

A rough and rumbling chuckle echoed in the barn. "Did you swap stories, too? Put in braids? Talk about boys?"

Talia made a snarky face. "Ha ha, Grizz. I see you're all ready for when Chloe goes to junior high."

"Not funny," he grumbled. "My baby girl is never growing up."

"Nice try." She glanced at Ryan. "Grizzy, there's someone I want you to meet." She scooted over and included Ryan in the video. "This is Ryan Prosper. Say hi."

Grizz grunted as he looked at Ryan. "So this is the cowboy you keep talking about, huh?"

"I hope so," Ryan quipped without hesitation. "I'd hate to think there was another one."

Grizz snorted, which Ryan hoped was encouraging. "Lemme ask you something, Mr. Prosper: What is the best thing about my baby cousin there?"

"There has to be one best thing?" Ryan asked him. "Can I do a list?"

"Correct answer," Grizz praised, nodding sagely. "What was the physical feature you noticed first? Take note, I have access to a private plane and could pound you less than five hours from now."

"Her eyes." Ryan ignored the blatant threat, knowing he would have made the same one for Kellie.

Grizz made a sound of acknowledgement, if not consideration. "Granted. Last question: What's one thing you would change about her? Be honest."

In truth, Ryan wouldn't change a thing about the glorious woman leaning against him, but he sensed Grizz was testing him, and he liked a challenge. "Well," he drawled, tipping his hat back a bit, "I really wish she would let me treat her like a princess, but every time I call her Princess, she kinda twitches. I think she should get used to hearing that, I don't know. What do you think?"

The smile amid the scruff was better than any blue ribbon Ryan had ever won. "I think, Mr. Prosper, you might be just what I've been hoping for here. Let's start this again. Hi. Grizz McCarthy. Pro catcher. Overprotective cousin and adoptive brother."

Ryan smiled back, flicking the brim of his hat in greeting. "Howdy. Ryan Prosper, rodeo has-been. Overprotective boyfriend and hopefully, someday, more."

Talia coughed a surprised laugh, and Grizz howled with laughter. "Atta kid, Ryan! That's it, next game I've got in Texas, I'm swinging by. We gotta hang out."

"Come on down," Ryan insisted with a crooked grin. "I'm not goin' anywhere."

"Thank goodness for that," Talia murmured, leaning against him more fully.

Ryan grinned down at her, then kissed the side of her head quickly before returning to the conversation at hand. "So who's gonna be your biggest challenge this year, Grizz? I heard Texas might be hot this season."

EPILOGUE

THERE WAS NOTHING WORSE than living in a constant state of secrets and nerves when you were in a relationship with an intuitive person.

Ryan didn't have another choice right now, but it was definitely getting old.

He'd been thinking about this seriously for two months now, and with the next Lost Creek Rodeo approaching, he did not have much time left.

So he'd done what he had never thought he would do.

He'd called in reinforcements.

Reid thought he'd lost his mind, Eric thought he was a genius, Westin gave him two thumbs-up, Ford didn't care, and Lars . . .

Well, Lars just shook his head.

Figures.

It would be the fastest recon rendezvous known to man, but desperate times called for desperate measures, and Ryan was definitely desperate.

He paced the floor of Roosters anxiously, wishing the bar

in Lost Creek had a more private room that this meeting could take place in, but satisfied that it would do the trick well enough.

He hoped.

"Alrighty, buck, what's the issue? I already told you yes, what more do you need?"

Ryan turned on his heel, exhaling roughly with abject relief as Grizz McCarthy strode into the bar, gesturing for him to join him at the counter, sliding onto a stool. "Thanks for coming, man. I know it's not convenient."

"No, but it would be worse in three months when Rach is massively pregnant," Grizz assured him, rubbing absently at his oddly bare face. "And Cole wasn't using the jet. So what's up?"

Ryan buried his face in his hands, groaning. "I don't know what to do."

"Uh, about what?"

"Proposing." He turned his head to look at Grizz, ashamed to have admitted something so pathetic.

Grizz's face held no sympathy. "You're still going to do it, though, right? I mean, I don't want to pressure you, but I already told my wife, and she's started planning with my sister-in-law, Bree, and I've made it a point to never disappoint either of them."

Ryan scowled at the completely unhelpful statement. "Thanks, Grizz. Really. Glad you're with me on this."

"Hey, I know you're the right guy for her," Grizz said simply, holding up his hands in surrender. "I've got no qualms there, unless you'd changed your mind, and then we'd be having a different kind of conversation."

"I'm not changing my mind," Ryan ground out, a little rankled that it would ever be suggested. "I adore Talia. I'd have married her last fall, if I thought it was the right time."

Grizz considered that, then nodded. "Yeah, it's better you gave her more time. Might get a more enthusiastic response."

"Because that's my main concern." Ryan shook his head and folded his arms on the bar. "I just don't know how to do it. Everything I think of just sounds stupid or like something she would hate. It should be perfect for her, but I don't know what she would think is perfect for her in this kind of thing. It's a big deal, and women talk about this." He gave Grizz a serious look. "I know they do. Women rotate through the ranch like clockwork, and the happily married ones *always* tell their proposal stories."

"Well, no pressure, or anything." Grizz flagged down the bartender. "Two beers, whatever you've got on tap."

Ryan raised his brows. "You're drinking?"

"Just until spring ball starts," Grizz assured him. "Then I go dry." He shrugged his broad shoulders, and snapped his fingers, pulling out his phone. "Sorry, I forgot Clint wanted in, too. He's in Detroit for a game. Hang on."

Oh, good. Both members of the peanut gallery for his moment of embarrassing pleading. How perfect.

The phone rang once, then Clint picked up. "Talk to me."

"You're a moron," Grizz said at once.

"Better athlete, though," Clint shot back. "Ryan there?"

"Hey, Clint," Ryan greeted lamely.

Clint hissed. "Ooh, that sounds promising. What's the problem?"

"Proposal blues," Grizz answered before Ryan could. "Poor guy doesn't know what Talia would want."

"To say yes," Clint told them both, his voice drier than Texas. "No bells or whistles, just ask her."

"Because that's romantic," Ryan snapped. He rubbed his brow, taking the glass of beer when it arrived. "I don't need bells or whistles or frills or a damn parade. I just need something that isn't stupid or embarrassing."

Clint laughed once. "Proposing is embarrassing, dude. And hard. And terrifying even if you know she's crazy about you. Sucks to be you right now, not gonna lie."

Ryan scowled and looked up at Grizz. "Can we hang up on him?"

Grizz shrugged, nodding at the idea. "We could."

"Don't you dare," Clint warned. "Ryan, listen: It doesn't have to be epic. What has time with Talia told you about her taste and style?"

Ryan thought about that, sipping his drink slowly. "Understated, simple, and meaningful. She'd rather have breakfast at home if we've made it together than go out to a diner."

"And with her being in school full-time at SHCC," Grizz said, thinking out loud, "she probably doesn't get a ton of time away to enjoy herself during the semester."

"Nope, and she hates that." Ryan twisted his lips in thought. "Okay, so . . . maybe we go riding on the ranch and I just ask her while we're out?"

Clint made a thoughtful sound through the phone. "Can you have a picnic set up somewhere or some such? A pop-up romantic meal never hurts."

"Totally." Ryan grinned as the ideas began to flow. "My sister would get a food truck on our land if she thought it would help Talia say yes."

"Remind me to get on your sister's good side," Grizz said in appreciation.

Ryan glanced at him slyly. "Let Texas win a game this season."

Grizz narrowed his eyes. "What kind of food trucks are we talking about?"

"Ryan," Clint broke in.

"'Sup?" Ryan answered without thinking.

There was a very brief pause. "Just ask her, bro. Details aren't as important as asking her. You're good for her, and we're all for this. Austin would be, too."

Ryan's throat tightened at that, his affection for Talia's son a tender subject, though he had never met him. In marrying Talia, Ryan would still consider himself as becoming Austin's stepfather, angel or not.

He loved the little guy, just as he would have if he'd lived.

"Yeah," Grizz agreed, his voice rough. "Yeah, he would." He clamped a firm hand on Ryan's shoulder. "You're good, Ryan. Just ask her."

Ryan nodded, managing a smile for both brothers, though only one would see it. "I will. No matter how I decide to, I can promise you that I will ask."

"Then we're good," Clint said simply. "Okay, headed out to warm up. See ya."

"Good luck," Ryan and Grizz said together before Grizz hung up.

Grizz looked at his watch, then grinned. "I don't have to be back for a while. Want to watch the game?"

"Sure," Ryan replied with a nod. "Gotta make a few calls first. That cool?"

"Yep, I'll be here." He turned to talk the bartender into changing the channel.

Ryan hopped down from his stool and headed outside, pulling his phone out and scrolling through his contacts. He pushed the call button, and grinned at nothing as it rang.

"Hi," Talia's voice greeted after one ring, sounding a little out of breath. "You're late."

"Sorry, I got tied up." He looked up at the sky, reveling in his feeling of ease at the moment, especially after days of anxiety. "How was class?"

"Blech," Talia replied. "I can't wait to get out of generals and into the good stuff. Why do I need math for hospitality, event planning, and marketing?"

Ryan chuckled at the question. "Maybe just to make sure you know two plus two is five? I dunno."

Talia laughed lightly, clearly not minding his terrible attempt at a joke. "I miss you, babe. When are you coming up again?"

"I miss you, too, Princess," he told her softly. "And I was thinking . . . What if you come down here for the weekend? Little bit of a getaway, and I spoil you for a bit?"

"Oh, that sounds amazing," she moaned. "I have no plans, can we really? Are you free?"

Tightening his hand into a fist of victory, Ryan restrained the urge to pump it into the air. "For you, my love, I'll clear my schedule completely."

"You're the best. I love you so much." The sounds of other people filtered through the phone, and he heard her grunt in annoyance. "Ugh. Gotta go. Love you."

He smiled at hearing it. "You said that already."

"So I mean it twice as much," she retorted. "So what?"

"I love you, too. A lot."

She laughed again. "I know, babe. I'll see you soon."

"Can't wait. Bye."

He'd barely hung up with her before he made another call, butterflies roaring through him like a rodeo crowd. "Kells? Hey, it's me. I think I've got a plan."

He was suddenly jostled, almost losing his balance.

"Excuse me," a soft voice apologized quickly.

Ryan turned toward it, smiling. "No problem." His jaw dropped when he saw the grinning face of his soon-to-be fiancée there, amber eyes alight with mischief.

"Ryan?" Kellie's voice chirped through the phone. "Dying here, what plan?"

"I'll call you back," Ryan told her, hanging up before she could ask any more questions. He shook his head, staring at Talia in wonder. "What in the world are you doing here? How are you here?"

"Nice to see you, too, cowboy," she laughed, adjusting the strap of the bag on her shoulder and tossing her gorgeous hair. "I thought I'd surprise my boyfriend, and my cousin was coming into town on a private jet, so he picked me up."

Ryan looked toward the entrance of Roosters with a scowl. "He did, huh? Figures."

Talia cleared her throat softly. "So do I get a hug, or . . .?"

He was to her in one stride, hands sliding along her cheeks and into her hair, tilting her face up for a hot kiss, the butterflies and nerves of the day roaring into a furious bonfire within him. Talia gripped him hard as she kissed him back, her fervency matching his and slowly dismantling him piece by piece.

It was terrifying how much he loved this woman.

No, not terrifying.

Exhilarating.

Like the greatest eight seconds riding a bull before an energized crowd. The most perfect ride known to any cowboy in the world.

Only it went on and on and on, always new and bright, always surprising him, and always giving him more than he deserved.

What in the world was he waiting for?

He parted from her a bit too quickly, cutting the kiss short with a jerk that caught them both off guard and sent Talia reeling into his chest.

"Um, wow, okay," she laughed, pushing back a little and running a hand through her hair with an awkward smile. "Change your mind or something?"

"No," he said instantly, moving one hand to slide around her waist and keep her close. "You know better than that, don't you? Please tell me you know that."

Her brows rose, and her smile turned tender. "Oh, babe, I know that. I was teasing. I know we're a lock, okay? You and me, all the way."

He couldn't have said it better himself.

He exhaled shortly and kissed her again, carefully this time, so he didn't start something. "Great. Okay. Then I have a question for you."

Talia nodded like an obedient student. "Shoot."

Kellie would kill him for doing this when she wasn't around, but he'd risk it. There would be no better moment than this.

He held his breath, searching her eyes for an answer before he asked the question. "Will you marry me?"

Amber eyes blinked once. "What?"

Oh, right. Kneeling.

Ryan dropped to a knee, his hands sliding to hers. "Talia James, will you marry me?"

Her lips parted, her eyes going round. An exhale.

His heart skipped. *She was going to say no.*

"Yes."

His stomach clenched tightly, and he gripped her hands. "Yes?"

Talia nodded repeatedly. "Yes. Good heavens, yes. Ry . . ." She laughed, the sound more watery than he'd expected. "Please, yes. Thank you, yes. How many ways can I say yes?"

"A thousand and three," he told her, his emotions shooting off into fireworks as he reached into the pocket of his jeans for the talisman he'd carried around for two-and-a-half weeks to give him courage. "And I want to hear each one of them until this doesn't feel like a dream."

He held up the ring for her to see, wordlessly asking once more.

"Oh, babe . . ." She clamped down on her lips hard, holding a shaking hand out for him. "Yes again. Yes always."

Sliding the ring onto her finger, he rose with a grin, pulling her close again. "Yeah? Just checking."

"I believe the woman said yes, Ryan," a deep voice rumbled from nearby. "Pay attention."

"Mind your own business, Grizz," Ryan called without looking at him, filling his vision with Talia, and only Talia. "You're in trouble."

"You're welcome. I'm still watching the game inside. Talia, come say bye before you head out."

Talia linked her arms around Ryan's neck. "Okay."

Neither of them actually noticed if Grizz went back inside, the moment too precious for intruders.

"I love you, Princess," Ryan murmured, thinking those words too small for what he was feeling.

Talia sighed in his arms, her smile luminous. "I love you, too. And I can't wait for our forever to start."

He nodded, swallowing hard. "I'm never letting you go. Ever."

"Good," she replied, arching up until her lips brushed his. "Neither am I. Got a problem with that, remember?"

"That doesn't sound like a problem to me. Not a problem at all." He grinned against her lips, then kissed her again.

Mariah's Easy Wheat Bread

In a large mixing bowl:
Mix with a fork or whisk-
1 1/3 cups warm water
1 Tbsp. Yeast
2 1/2 Tbsp. Sugar
Let sit for about 10 minutes.

Add to the yeast mixture:
5 Tbsp Butter (room temperature)
2 tsp. Salt
5 Tbsp. Powdered Milk
Mix these together

Add:
2 cups white flour
2 cups whole wheat flour

Mix with dough hook for 10 minutes.
Take out of pan and divide in half. Shape into loaves and put in greased bread pans.
Let rise for 20 minutes.
Bake at 350 degrees for 20 minutes.

Kellie's Mixed Berry Jam

3 cups strawberries
2 ½ cups blueberries
2 ½ cups blackberries
7 cups granulated sugar divided
1 (1.75-ounce) package fruit pectin
1 tablespoon freshly squeezed lemon juice

Meanwhile, prepare a boiling water canner. Heat the jars and lids in simmering water until ready to use. Do not boil. Set lid rings aside.

In a 8-quart saucepan, cook the strawberries, blueberries and blackberries over medium heat until soft. Lightly mash the fruit with a potato masher. In a large measuring cup, combine 2 cups sugar with the pectin.

Add the lemon juice and sugar-pectin mixture to the berries. Over high heat, bring the mixture to a full boil, stirring frequently with a wooden spoon. Boil for 1 minute. Add the remaining 5 cups of sugar immediately, and bring back to a boil for 1 minute, stirring constantly. Turn the heat on low to medium. Skim foam if necessary.

Ladle hot jam into the hot jars, leaving ½ inch space from the top of the jar. Clean the rim of the jar with a damp paper towel. Center the lid on the jar. Apply the lid ring until the fit is fingertip tight. Process jars in a boiling water canner for 10 minutes. Remove the jars and allow to cool completely.

Check the lids for seal after 24 hours. The lid should

not "pop" when the center is pressed. Store jars in a cool, dry place. Put the jars in a boiling-water bath for 10 minutes. Make sure the jars are covered in water. The sealed jars can be stored in a cool, dark place for up to 1 year. If a seal has failed, store the jar in the refrigerator for up to 1 month.

Rebecca Connolly writes romances, both period and contemporary, because she absolutely loves a good love story. She has been creating stories since childhood, and there are home videos to prove it! She started writing them down in elementary school and has never looked back. She currently lives in Indiana, spends every spare moment away from her day job absorbed in her writing, and is a hot cocoa addict.

Visit her online: RebeccaConnolly.com

www.ingramcontent.com/pod-product-compliance
Lightning Source LLC
LaVergne TN
LVHW021810060526
838201LV00058B/3307